A REAL SHOT IN THE ARM

A *REAL SHOT* IN *THE ARM*

ANNETTE ROOME

Crown Publishers, Inc.

New York

Copyright © 1989 by Annette Roome

All rights reserved. No part of this book may be reproduced or transmitted in any form or by any means, electronic or mechanical, including photocopying, recording, or by any information storage and retrieval system, without permission in writing from the publisher. Published by Crown Publishers, Inc., 201 East 50th Street, New York, New York 10022. A Member of the Crown Publishing Group. Originally published in Great Britain by Hodder and Stoughton Ltd. in 1989.

CROWN is a trademark of Crown Publishers, Inc.
Manufactured in the United States of America.
Library of Congress Cataloging-in-Publication Data
Roome, Annette.
  A real shot in the arm / by Annette Roome.
    p.   cm.
  I. Title
PR6068.054R4   1991   90-2233
823'.914—dc20   CIP

ISBN 0-517-57828-X
10 9 8 7 6 5 4 3 2 1
First American Edition

For Jennifer Friend,

with gratitude and affection

1

The years had crept up on me while I wasn't looking, and there I was, *forty*, standing in an untidy kitchen, having done very little since I was born but stand in kitchens in varying stages of untidiness and wonder what I was going to do next. It was just after Christmas, and the light filtering in from outside was as grey and as bored with what it touched as I was. I looked in the mirror. There was my face, looking like a weather map just before a particularly windy day: masses of lines running together into converging depressions. My hair, once auburn, was dull as a winter pond, and my eyes, which Keith in youthful passion (and with wild inaccuracy) had described as "traffic-light green for go", were now sunk into dark recesses. It was a bad moment. I looked around the kitchen, festooned with the unappetising debris of family festivities, and was overcome with a raging desire to destroy everything in sight. I didn't do it, of course; I'd have had to clear up the mess.

Instead, I did what I always did to drive away what people call the blues: I got a black plastic sack and started methodically disposing of the rubbish. Then I would set to with a variety of cleaning liquids and powders and several cloths, and after that there would be the rest of the house, Hoovering, washing, etc. By the time Julie, Richard and Keith came home I'd be feeling a lot better, and anyway I'd be so busy tidying up after them I wouldn't have time to think about it much. So, with a full programme ahead of me it's surprising I stopped to read the paper as I spread it on the floor but I did, and that momentary lapse changed my life. What I read was an advertisement in our local Tipping Herald for a junior reporter. Years ago, before babies and sterilising routines took their toll, I had wanted very much to be a newspaper reporter. Now, as I looked at the advertisement, the years closed up like a telescope, and a young girl's pulse brought colour to my cheeks. Later I told the family about it enthusiastically. My son Richard, age twenty, encouraged me to have a go; Julie, my sixteen-year-old, was thrilled – would we be able to jump queues for the cinema and pop concerts on my Press card? she wanted to know. Keith took a different attitude.

"You're nuts, Chris!" he said. "That's a full-time job! If you want to work, fine – get a part-time job in Marks and Spencer if you're so anti-office work – you'll even get a staff discount. I absolutely forbid you to be so stupid about this newspaper nonsense."

I went for my interview early in January, the day of the first snowfall. Mr Heslop, the editor, and I, established an immediate rapport. He had also recently suffered a severe trauma by courtesy of his mirror – that of waking up on his fiftieth birthday to be confronted by a bald man with bad skin and a pronounced paunch. He said he detected a kindred spirit in me: I was mature, sensitive, and yet youthful in approach. I don't know which of us he was trying to flatter. He gave me the job.

Keith was right of course: I couldn't cope with the house and Julie's emotional problems and getting the stains out of Keith's sports gear as well as the job. Worse, reporting on Council meetings and the appearance of brides at weddings was almost as dull as waiting for another day's dust to accumulate on the television screen, or daisies to open in the lawn. I only kept on with it because it made Keith angry, and we were entering one of our bad patches. I never knew what brought these on, but they were characterised by arguments he started with the words "you never", or "if only you would". If I didn't want to spend my time apologising for nebulous faults, then my only defence was to work out new ways of making him angry, and I was getting quite good at this. Anyway, one Monday morning in early July, Mr Heslop came to see me. He'd just had another row with Pete Schiavo, his senior reporter, who had a quick wit and a sharp tongue and always upset him.

"That's it," said Mr Heslop, breathing heavily. "I'm not sending him, and I think you're ready for it anyway." He beamed at me magnanimously. "The Conference on Drugs and Alcohol Abuse at the Clocktower Hotel. It's going to be quite a big deal, sponsored jointly by Leisching Pharmaceuticals and local businesses. *You* can cover it. That idiot would've just sat there knocking back vodka and embarrassed us. Let's see what you're made of. I know I can rely on you. It's nice to know I can rely on someone." He went off to his office, muttering, to have another ginseng tablet. A few moments later, Pete sauntered down the corridor, whistling. He was carrying a small off-licence bag crammed with the empties from the bottom drawer of his desk.

"Goodbye, Wonderwoman," he said. "I've got the rest of the week off. I'll bring you back a stick of rock. Don't do anything I wouldn't do – in fact if you can think of anything I wouldn't do let me know – I might like to reconsider."

I learned later that what had actually happened was that Pete had told Mr Heslop he wanted a week's holiday now, and that if there were any objections, bearing in mind that he hadn't had any holiday for two years, he would take the full four weeks to which he was entitled, starting 1st September. He knew quite well that Mr Heslop had an Apex ticket to New York booked for 1st September, which he would have had to cancel if Pete were absent. As I watched him disappear out into the sunshine I wondered which of the temporary typists would coincidentally go missing during Pete's absence.

The Clocktower Hotel, where the Conference was to be held, was a converted Victorian mansion on a hilltop overlooking the town. From my kitchen window I could just make out the white blur of the clock faces above the trees. The hotel had been bought in a somewhat run-down condition three years ago by the well-known London restaurateur Mr Eric De Broux. He'd spent a fortune, so it was said, on refurbishing the place, and had had built a superb Conference Hall with state of the art facilities. There'd been a champagne opening attended by everybody who was

9

anybody in the County. Mr Heslop had covered this himself. He had also been invited to become a member of Mr De Broux's new Gourmet Club, though he had chosen for financial reasons, no doubt, not to join. The Gourmet Club met on the first Saturday of every month at the Clocktower Restaurant, and members were treated (for an astronomical annual subscription) to a gourmet dinner, fine wines, and as much vintage port and brandy as they could hold. I thought there was a nice irony in this, bearing in mind the nature of the Conference, but Mr Heslop told me sternly not to "make waves"; the Clocktower had a regular half page advertisement in our paper and he'd no intention of losing it.

On the Tuesday evening before the Conference was due to start, a non-alcoholic cocktail hour was being held for delegates. Mr Heslop told me to go, smile nicely, and get a few quotes. Keith was furious. He had two martinis with ice and pointed out that it was *Tuesday* and the Sunday papers were still littering the living room.

"I thought you were still reading them," I said.

"Don't be silly! When do I get time to read? Somebody has to keep up with the weeding and you should see the blackfly on the broad beans!"

I felt guilty. I had sown the broad beans. "Please leave it," I said. "I'll come home early tomorrow and give them a really thorough spraying."

I shared my Mini with Richard, who normally used it in the evenings, but he was away that week with the vicar's daughter (about whom he did not permit us to make jokes), and so one family conflict was avoided. Once away from the house, I felt quite excited about the evening ahead. I wound down the window and the car was soon filled with the heady scent of nettle sap and cow-parsley, bruised by the passage of traffic. The road out to the Clocktower was little more than a narrow, winding lane barely wide enough for two cars to pass. The warm evening air was vibrant with the song of young birds and frantic swarms of insects, and I became so carried away by the sensual delight of it I almost forgot to hoot before the sharp bend round Rampton's Hollow.

Mr De Broux himself welcomed me to the Clocktower. I

10

wondered how he could consume so much rich food and maintain his svelte appearance. His dark hair was parted on one side and handsomely sculptured in a way that seemed to accentuate his strong, rather aquiline, nose. The overall effect was of an attractive, but cold, man.

"If you haven't been here before, do take a look round," he urged me. "Will there be anyone else coming from the Herald?" I shook my head, and he looked disappointed. It was his first big Conference, and I think he had rather hoped for a battalion of reporters and photographers. He directed me towards the bar, in front of which stood a sign, written in elegant blue and gold lettering. It announced "1987 Conference on Drugs and Alcohol Abuse, jointly sponsored by Leisching Pharmaceuticals and—" The list continued in smaller print. Perhaps Leisching were getting a conscience about the profits they made from the tranquillisers so many of my friends took.

The bar was plush in an understated, tasteful sort of way. It smelled of cigar smoke and toasted cheese canapés. I helped myself to a thick orange drink sporting a sunshade, and wished there was just a small shot of gin in it. I didn't drink much, and a small shot would have been enough to make me feel competent to talk to all these important people immersed in deep, meaningful conversations. Sitting quietly in a corner taking notes of what people said was one thing; confronting them and asking penetrating questions was another. I'd been sent out with Pete a few times to see how it was done, but had learned little. Pete would chat people up as though he were their long lost brother, then go away and write whatever he thought made a good story. I didn't think I could do that. Swallowing a large gulp of orange cocktail (and hoping I wasn't left with an orange moustache), I approached a couple I vaguely recognised. They were the Goodburns, Dr Rachel and Dr John, a husband-and-wife team; for some odd reason – I've been cut off short in my careful description of symptoms often enough – I thought I would be shown a little extra sympathy by the medical profession.

". . . always forgets to put the teaspoons in the right

11

compartment," Dr Rachel was saying.

"I told you we should have gone for the Bosch," Dr John replied. So much for deep, meaningful conversations!

"Er, excuse me," I began. "I'm Chris Martin from the Herald and I'm just trying to – you know – get some reactions from people on what they think might come out of this Conference."

They both stared at me blankly. Dr John was well over six foot, white-haired, and distinguished-looking. He was probably fifteen years older than his wife, who had a harassed, nervous air about her. He held his glass up to the light.

"Damn stuff's revolting! Typical De Broux – he ought to be forced to drink a couple of pints of it!" He spoke venomously, as though he would have liked to add, ". . . laced with several milligrams of arsenic." Perhaps he, too, would have preferred a real drink.

Rachel said nothing. She glanced at her watch.

"Would you say the drug problem in this town is increasing?" I asked bravely, smiling at Dr Rachel.

"Why should she say that?" demanded Dr John, belligerently.

"Well –"

"I'm certainly not going to say anything like that!" snapped Rachel. "You won't trap me that easily!"

"My wife is very tired," said Dr John, testily. "I'd appreciate it if you wouldn't badger her. She was up all last night, totally unnecessarily, with a woman in labour –"

"I don't desert my ladies, John, as you well know," she said, sharply. The veins in her neck were distended, her voice strained. I thought, not for the first time, that only women were able to commit themselves to others to the point of total exhaustion, and that I ought to make allowances for her unnecessary outburst. I smiled.

"But you must have a pretty good idea from what you do see, particularly of young people –"

"And why should I know anything more than anybody else about what you call *the drug problem*? A nice, tidy phrase, that, isn't it? So much suffering written off in three words – and no wonder, because people don't want to know about the suffering, do they? They just want scapegoats – Pillorying doctors has become a national sport! Take child-birth –" Here, Dr John tried to interrupt, but was ignored. "Childbirth was designed as one of nature's greatest joys – a reward for the female sex –" Baffled as I was at the turn the conversation had taken, I couldn't help thinking that nature's idea of rewards did not coincide with mine. She looked at her watch again, almost tipping her drink over my right foot. I jumped back.

"Sorry, sorry," she muttered. "This is an absolute pain, this whole thing. It has nothing whatsoever to do with medi-cine. It's not what I trained for. I don't know why we're wasting our time here. I told you, John, there's a patient I've simply got to see."

"I don't want to hear it!" said Dr John, irritably. "I've told you before, patients belong in the surgery – or better still, in their own damn homes. Don't drag them out with us in the evenings. Or on to the golf course, or to Tenerife, if we ever damn well get there –"

I recognised an argument beginning to fall into a well-worn rut, excused myself, and moved on. If ever there was an example of an interview being allowed to fall completely apart, that was it. If I'd been Pete Schiavo I would have asked her quickly, "Are you concerned at the crisis within the NHS?" To which she would have been bound to reply "yes", and then I would have written a nice little piece about a well-known local doctor being on the verge of crack-up over the underfunding of the NHS. At least I would have had something. In fact, I should have had something any-way; I remembered now that Pete had worked on a story about one of Dr Rachel's patients dying of a heroin overdose – if only I'd done some homework on the Herald's archives this evening instead of arguing with my butcher about the fat on his lamb chops!

I spotted the Reverend Harlow entering the bar and quickly turned my back. He was the father of Carolyn, with whom Richard was probably at this very moment enjoying none too spiritual pleasures. It was just my luck that he had come along to represent the Church. I gripped my notebook purposefully and walked towards two men leaning on the bar over a tray of assorted cheese biscuits. As I approached the younger man placed his arm in front of the tray defensively, as though it was the only food he'd seen all day and he'd no intention of sharing it. In his late forties, he wore a neatly-pressed shirt and tie over which he'd defiantly thrown a badly scuffed leather jacket. He could have done with shaving and combing his hair, too; no doubt his poor wife despaired of him. The other man I knew by sight as Major Duncton, Chairman of the Planning Committee, and "elder statesman" of local politics. The Herald sometimes referred to him reverentially as the "Father of Tipping's Town Plan". I didn't like him. He'd turned down our application to build a carport with the comment that it would be a "visual aberration on an otherwise well-ordered street". Well, maybe, but it was my Mini that was rusting. Not only that, but some streets in Tipping fairly bristled with carports – when was a visual aberration not a visual aberration? Perhaps when you have a relative on the planning committee, I had suggested, but Keith had told me not to be cynical.

"Excuse me," I said, "I wonder if you could spare me a moment?"

They stopped talking and gave me the vacant, slightly indulgent smile men reserve for women over forty who have let their appearance go, then saw my Press badge.

"Inspector Franks," said the younger man, adding with an air of disbelief. "You from the Herald?"

I smiled and nodded.

"Blimey!" He laughed. "You live and learn! You know Major Duncton here? Right – get your notebook out, love." I produced it obediently, no longer smiling. He took an exaggerated breath, and began, "I am here today representing the local police-force. We in the police intend to work in the community and with the community to combat the menace of drugs in our society. Got that? Not too fast for you?"

"No. Not too fast for me. Are you representing the Council, Major?"

The Major looked at me over his glasses. They reflected

the lights of the bar, as did the brass buttons on his blazer. "Got my own views on drugs, as on other things. People have to look out for themselves. Self-discipline is the answer, and plenty of it. You got children?"

"Yes."

"You should look out for them then. Nobody else will. It's the parents' responsibility. Put down good groundwork and you won't go far wrong." He leaned forward, and there seemed to be whisky on his breath. "Ladies like you would be better employed maintaining home rule rather than interfering in the machinations of authority."

The words "supercilious bastard" came unbidden to my mind – I was beginning to tire of negative reactions. I smiled with difficulty and made a few careful notes. The Inspector handed me the tray of biscuits.

"Take some of these, love, and then perhaps you'd toddle off. We're trying to have a serious business discussion here."

I refused the proffered biscuits and turned hastily away, almost bumping into a tall man in his mid-twenties carrying a full glass of tomato juice. He was quite stunningly good-looking. He had blue eyes, dark hair, and a slim, muscular build. In fact he looked a lot like Keith when I first met him, and I experienced the sort of odd little twinge midway between pain and pleasure one gets when confronted unexpectedly by an old photograph. He apologised unnecessarily, smiled automatically, and walked away without registering my presence. I felt another little twinge, because this was exactly the way Keith reacted to me nowadays.

Someone else was watching Keith's look-alike, too: a dark, intense girl with glasses. She seemed to be expecting him to speak to her, but he didn't. She slumped visibly at this rejection and clumsily topped up her orange juice with mineral water before gulping it compulsively.

None of the delegates I approached had anything very startling to say on the subject of drugs and alcohol abuse, and I was beginning to think I could have made up most of their quotes myself in the comfort of my own living room. Then there was a sudden ripple of interest in the bar at the arrival of Mr Sylvester Munroe. He was the editor of a gay

15

magazine based in Hudderston, and knew how to make a theatrical entrance. He doffed his wide-brimmed black hat, threw down his suitcase, and swallowed with audible gulps a tall glass of a striped fruit and egg concoction.

"Exquisite! Exquisite!" He gasped. "Oh, such a hot night!"

Everyone smiled politely and then turned away to make amused and derogatory remarks. I took the opportunity and approached him.

"Mr Munroe? I'm from the Tipping Herald. Do you think you could tell me what you hope to see being achieved by this Conference?"

"Call me Syl, dear," he said. "Just look at this room! What do you think of it? My friend Bernie did the décor. It's not to my taste, you know – more yours, is it? Well, we're not all the same. Bernie always says, get to know the customer, and you'll know what he wants. It's very important, putting the right person in the right setting."

"And the Conference? Your views on that?"

"Ah. Yes. Understanding, I hope. The more we talk the more we understand – provided we listen too, of course."

He broke off suddenly, appearing to concentrate his attention on someone behind me, but when I half turned to look he began to speak again. "And why are you doing a job like this? You look such a kind sort of person."

"Oh! Well – I'm quite new to it actually – I just wanted to give it a try."

Sylvester shook his head at the cocktail waitress and placed his empty glass on her tray.

"Well! Don't leave it too late to find out you're doing the wrong thing. I'm going to unpack. I'm booked into the Clocktower Room. Couldn't miss the opportunity to watch the sun come up over the Downs." He lifted his suitcase, taking another long look which I interpreted as yearning, at the person behind me. "When did you last watch the sun come up? Bet it was a long time ago. I'd do it every day if I could – it's a sort of daily renewal process. 'Bye now, dear."

When he'd gone I turned and saw that it was the tall, handsome young man with the blue eyes who was standing behind me. It gave me a rather odd feeling; I'd led a very sheltered life.

I didn't think I'd done at all well with the interviews and decided it was time to go home. I almost collided in the doorway with the Goodburns, who were also leaving. Rachel was fanning herself with a piece of paper, despite the air-conditioning, and John looked angry.

"Just leave it, darling," said Rachel. "It simply isn't worth it."

"I think I'm the best judge of that," replied John, scowling, but he followed her out of Reception.

It was on my way back from the Ladies' Room, as I passed the message board, that I spotted the note. It was written on turquoise notepaper and said, "M. Hi! After all this time! Hickory Dickory Dock, little mouse!" I stood and stared at it. Of course, it was none of my business, but it seemed the most interesting thing that had turned up all evening.

When I got home to my surprise the garage doors were open and Keith's car was missing. In the living room, Julie sat alone watching a French film with sub-titles which she hastily switched off as I entered. I thought, oh, it was that good, was it?

"Where's your father?" I asked.

"He went out, just after you did."

"Where to?"

"He didn't say. He was a bit cross. How were the non-alcoholic cocktails?"

"Awful. If you're not watching that I think you ought to go to bed."

We both took glasses of water and went up to bed. I experienced a sort of sinking feeling. Even when Keith and I had really bad rows we always went to bed together and slept with our backs touching. We'd had a row this evening and now he wasn't here. I lay awake for a while, listening for his car. I pushed back the covers, enjoying the slight cool breeze on the skin of my thigh, where my nightdress stopped. Oddly, despite Keith's absence – perhaps even because of it – I felt the slight stirrings of sexual desire. I pushed his pillow to the far side of the bed and waited for the feeling to go away. Some time later, I drifted off to sleep.

Over night the air turned humid and by the time I arrived back at the Clocktower Hotel the following morning, I was already perspiring. The hotel reception area was deserted except for the red-haired receptionist, who was fanning herself with a copy of the Daily Express.

"Would you believe it? The air-conditioning's broken down," she said, as I passed. "Mr De Broux is doing his nut!"

I slipped into the Conference Hall at the back. This was going to be easy. Just make a few notes of the salient points of the speeches, then pad out the story with observations on the packed and attentive audience, bursts of appreciative applause, etc. Mr Heslop said I was a good "bread-and-butter" reporter; I was always careful to spell people's names correctly and I got verbs in my sentences – well, most of them. What he was really saying was that I'd never uncover Watergate, but I'd do for the Tipping Herald. Looking around the softly-lit Conference Hall, alive with gently flapping agenda papers, and remembering last evening's débâcle, I thought perhaps I'd better be satisfied with that.

"And now," announced a new speaker, "we're pleased to be able to show you a film from America. It shows how a community in a very poor area of Chicago –"

A pall of cigar smoke had descended on the back row of seats. I got up. There was to be a discussion of the film after the coffee break so I'd soon pick up what it had been about, and now I was too hot and uncomfortable to concentrate. On my way out I passed the message board, and noticed that the turquoise note had disappeared – had it meant anything to "M"? I wanted fresh air, but the main doorway was blocked by men in overalls unloading dusty boxes and pieces of piping.

"You can't leave them there!" called the redhead, frantically, looking around as though she feared the wrath of Mr De Broux.

"We're not leaving 'em, love!" called one of the men reassuringly, and promptly left, accompanied by his mates.

The redhead looked despairingly heavenwards. I gave her a sympathetic smile and considered hitching up my skirt and climbing over the obstruction. I decided against it. At the rear of Reception were double doors marked "Fire Exit", which ought to lead out into the open. I had to put quite a bit of muscle into opening them. They gave with a crash on to the yard at the back of the hotel. A strong odour of decaying vegetable matter filled the air, emanating from an enormous overfilled dustbin, and I suddenly remembered that I'd forgotten to empty the bin in my kitchen. Oh damn, I thought, why can't anyone ever do anything around the house except me? And that's when I saw him, hanging around on the fire escape. Literally, I mean. By his neck. His feet dangled almost directly above my head, one floor up. He was wearing new black stick-on soles on brown soled shoes, and that's what stopped me screaming. You don't scream when you look at a pair of stick-on soles. He was swaying a bit in an air current, his dead fingers stiff and white at his sides.

"Oh God," I said aloud, but very quietly. "Oh God!" I'd have to go up and have a look. I wasn't a housewife now, but a reporter, and I'd have to go up there. The metal of the fire escape was warm and flaky, in need of a coat of paint. My legs carried me leadenly upwards, each wooden crump of my sandals carrying me closer. He was hanging from the landing beneath the Clocktower and I stopped opposite him, my hand to my mouth. It was the attractive young man in whom both Sylvester Munroe and the dark-haired girl had been interested. He looked very different now. Blue eyes wide-open, fixed, expressionless – mouth crookedly open too, a trickle of dried froth, like a slug's trail, running down the chin. His face was an odd greyish-yellow suffused with purple from the neck up, where the rope held him. Instinctively I waved a fly away from his cheek. Beginning to feel decidedly queasy, I forced myself to read his name badge – Michael Stoddart, Teacher. A voice inside my head declared in sombre tones, like those of a railway announcer: "You are looking at the work of a murderer".

19

2

"Don't be ridiculous! How can it possibly be murder? A hanging means suicide," said Mr Heslop. Over the 'phone, I could hear him stirring the artificial sweetener into his coffee.

"But – I've got a sort of gut feeling about it. I'm sure it's murder." "Gut feeling" sounded quite reporter-like – mention of voices in the head would have been most unwise.

"No, you haven't. Junior reporters don't get gut feelings. They get stupid ideas which give editors gut feelings known as indigestion." He bit into something that sounded hard and dry and crunchy, like a lump of smokeless coal, so it was probably a muesli biscuit. "Do you need to go home and change your dress?"

"Sorry?"

"I thought you might have puked all over yourself. I did when I saw my first corpse. Mind, it was spread all over a railway line and I'd just had Steak Tartare for lunch –" Another spasm of crunching. "Look, calm down. You sound as if you've got stuck in your spin-cycle. Keep on to it and see me about it later. I'll have this guy checked out and let you know."

The hotel yard was full of people standing around with their hands in their pockets. The body had been taken down now, and a man with a camera was taking more photographs of it, his flash and the slowly-revolving blue lamp on the police-car illuminating a dull, heavy morning. Occasionally the car radio would crackle into life, and the uniformed sergeant on guard at the foot of the fire escape had regular sneezing attacks, but there was none of the excitement and drama the phrase "scene of crime" invokes. Dr John Goodburn came slowly down the fire escape, wiping his hands on a tissue. I hurried over to him with my notebook.

"Excuse me – could you give me any information as to cause and time of death?"

He frowned, with displeasure rather than thoughtfulness.

"He's been dead some hours. He was hanging by his neck, as you see – I'm not a pathologist."

"No, but I wonder if you'd care to say whether there were signs of a struggle. I mean, did he put up a fight?"

His expression was wary, evasive, the way doctors usually are when you ask them questions like "Will this treatment work better than the last one?" or "Are you sure there won't be any side effects?"

"Look, Mrs, er, Martin, there'll be a pathologist's report in due course. I suggest you wait for that. Now if you'll excuse me, I'm missing the Conference, which is what I really came here for." He looked tired and very much older in the morning light. I thanked him and he returned to the hotel, limping slightly as though his back hurt. When I'd reported the discovery of the body to Inspector Franks, Dr Goodburn had had to be paged, because he was at that moment telephoning his wife at their home. Apparently she too was feeling unwell. Perhaps they had cheered themselves up with too many gin and tonics after leaving the hotel last night.

The body was being transferred to a stretcher and discreetly covered with a sheet. Eric De Broux advanced a few steps up the fire escape and caught Inspector Franks by the arm.

"You will be discreet about this, won't you?" he implored. "No sirens or anything? I've got to consider my guests."

"Not a lot of point to sirens, would there be, sir?" remarked the Inspector. "He's as dead as they come. I'll have to close off this area till the boys from forensics have had a look at it, but I don't think you'll be troubled further. Get that rubbish cleared, would you? It doesn't half pen and ink."

"Thank you, thank you," muttered Mr De Broux, stepping aside to let the entourage pass.

The sergeant sneezed noisily and I handed him a tissue.

"Thanks, love. Quite a to-do, eh? If only these bloody idiots would think of the trouble they're going to cause before they jump off buildings, stick their heads on railway lines – God, you should see the paperwork this'll generate!"

Yes, I thought, that's about it. You live your life the best way you can – probably the only way you can – and in the end you finish up filed away on pieces of paper in dusty filing cabinets no one ever looks at. The more spectacular the death, the more pieces of paper, probably – Michael Stoddart would get his name into the Herald archives as well as Tipping Police Station's, the DHSS, the Inland Revenue – and whatever.

As I re-entered the pleasantly cool atmosphere of the hotel (the air-conditioning had now been restored) I was stopped by the dark-haired girl with glasses who'd been interested in Mike Stoddart yesterday. She caught my sleeve, her eye on my Press badge.

"Please tell me! I've only just heard – is it true? Was it really Mike Stoddart they found hanging from the fire escape?"

"Yes, I'm afraid so. Did you know him?"

She stood rigid, staring at me as if electrified. Her name badge said Lynn Cazalet, Social Worker.

"Did you know him?" I repeated, getting out my notebook hopefully.

Lynn Cazalet gave a gulp as though about to be sick and dashed off in the direction of the Ladies' Room. Had I been Pete Schiavo I would have followed her in there and stood with my foot in the toilet door until she'd answered my questions. But I wasn't, and I didn't even have any questions ready.

I went instead to the Coffee Shop and ordered coffee and a sandwich. Everything in the hotel was going on as normal. Diana, the red-haired receptionist, smiled her glossy official smile, footsteps dissolved into the carpet pile, soft music drifted on the artificial breeze like anaesthetic, and in the restaurant luncheon was being served. In the bar I could see Inspector Franks in his shirt sleeves drinking a pint of beer. He was talking to Sylvester Munroe, who waved his arms

22

about a lot and kept shaking his head. I imagined the Inspector was asking him if he'd heard any strange noises in the night, as the body had been found just beneath his window. The two men didn't look as if they liked each other very much.

"Excuse me. May I join you for a moment?" A tall woman with blonde hair permed to the texture of a Brillo pad peered at me through thick-lensed glasses. I could tell she was about my age because, like me, she was dressed in colours you don't remember and wore pink lipstick in the mistaken belief that a hint of rosebuds would make her look younger.

"Dreadful business, isn't it?" she said. "Out there. I didn't go to look. I'm not morbid. I don't know how people can. A suicide, wasn't it? Dreadful! Do you know if it was one of the delegates?"

"Yes. A young man called Michael Stoddart. A teacher, I believe."

"Oh!" It came out as a girlish shriek.

"Did you know him?"

"Oh! No – no, I didn't." She started to get up, then sat down again. She had turned a dark shade of crimson. I looked at her name badge – Elaine Randall, Parent-Governor.

"Did he teach at your school?" I asked quickly.

"No. No, I'm with Northdales School, where my daughter goes. He taught at Shepherds Hill, I believe – I'd heard the name," she added hastily. Her colour was returning to normal. This time I felt the shock: my daughter went to Shepherds Hill. "It's dreadful, isn't it, when it's someone you know vaguely? Oh well!" She took a deep breath and shrugged it off. "What I wanted to talk to you about was the merger."

"The merger? Oh, the merger between Shepherds Hill and Northdales you mean." I'd received a fair amount of paperwork at home about this but hadn't really had time to study it. I was of the opinion that the Council would do what they chose whether I liked it or not, and anyway, as far as one could tell Shepherds Hill wasn't going to be much affected.

"Yes. It's absolutely awful, isn't it? Northdales is such a nice, happy, little school with a *wonderful* reputation for results. How they can even *consider* merging it with Shepherds Hill is beyond me! You *know* what their reputation is like – drugs and hooliganism – quite awful! I mean, what about parental choice?"

I could have said that as the mother of one of the drug-taking hooligans at Shepherds Hill I rather resented her attitude, but I let her carry on.

"So I would appreciate anything you could put in your paper that would represent our views. There's a tremendous amount of local opposition."

"Yes. I see. I will mention it to the Editor."

She smiled and rose to her feet.

"Thank you. Nice to talk to you," she said. "Was it – it was suicide, wasn't it?"

The suddenness of the question took me by surprise. I was just about to confide my own suspicions when my attention was caught by a commotion from Reception. Both Elaine Randall and I walked out of the Coffee Shop to see what was going on.

"You'd better get Mr De Broux out here! Now! There'll be hell to pay and I want him to know this has got nothing to do with me!" The speaker was the head waiter. He slammed a heavy object down on the reception desk and stood back, his arms outstretched in a dramatic gesture.

"I can't disturb him. You know what a morning he's had. He's having lunch in his office. Where did that come from?"

On the desk was a marble cheeseboard. Displayed upon it were an oozing wad of Camembert, several cheeses I couldn't immediately identify and a slab of Stilton. Protruding from the Stilton was a disposable plastic syringe, of the type I have sometimes seen discarded in public toilets.

"From – my – restaurant!" exclaimed the head waiter, almost apoplectic. "I've got a room full of customers!"

"Leave it with me," said Diana. "I'll tell him about it when he's had time to calm down."

The head waiter strode back to the restaurant, muttering,

24

and Diana, Elaine Randall and I stared at the syringe. Syringes must surely provoke fairly negative feelings in most people, but embedded in good quality cheese they look particularly obnoxious. Diana was obviously thinking much the same thing because she raised her delicate red tipped fingers from the desk and I realised she was going to take hold of the syringe.

"Don't!" I yelped, gripping her by the wrist. "Aids!"

"Oh God!" She jumped back. "What shall I do?"

"Best get rid of it. Got any thick envelopes?" She produced a handful. "You'll have to throw the cheese away anyway. Put the whole thing inside two envelopes and drop it in the bin. That way you won't have to expose the needle."

"I watched while she did it.

"Absolutely first-class advice, if you ask me," said Elaine Randall, approvingly. "You can't be too careful these days."

The rest of the afternoon passed off without incident. I tried to concentrate on a debate about the laws on solvent abuse, but my mind kept returning to the corpse swinging gently in the still morning air. Perhaps this was because there was an empty chair next to me where Michael Stoddart might have sat. I was so *sure* he'd been murdered. It was silly, of course, suicide was the logical answer, but the voice inside my head was seldom wrong. Twenty-five years ago when I'd first set eyes on Keith across the table of a coffee bar, it had said "you'll never forget this boy's face", and it had been right; a few years later, every time we made love in Keith's sleeping-bag in the woods behind the station, it had said, "this is not a wise thing to do", and it wasn't (well, I love Richard and wouldn't be without him, but you get the point). I thought of the handsome young face I'd seen at the Cocktail Hour last evening and the death mask of the morning; what had driven him to it? Why put stick-on soles on your shoes if you were not going to wear them out, why dress smartly, why come to the Conference at all, if life was so unbearable you planned to end it? It made no sense to me.

Eventually I decided to leave a few minutes early and pop into Tesco's on the way to the office, because there's nothing

like a stroll behind a supermarket trolley to bring you back
to reality. Mr De Broux was standing next to my car. He had
his hands on his hips and his raven hair was flopping
uncharacteristically over his face. The perspiration on his
brow made his sallow skin look like molten wax.

"I'm sorry, Mario," he said, "but the decision is made.
You used to use the stuff and I can't take risks in the
kitchen."

"But Mr Broux!" whined Mario, wriggling on the seat of
his scooter and passionately shaking his helmet as though to
knock some sense into it. "I'm clean now! You know that! I
not do this dirty thing!"

Mr De Broux shook his head and ran his hand through his
hair. "There it is. I did my best for you."

He turned on his heel and walked off without a glance at
me. I guessed I had just witnessed the closing scene of the
syringe incident. Poor Mario. He muttered off down the hill
on his scooter, still protesting his innocence.

Mr Heslop handed me a sheet of paper.

"This is the teacher's address. Get round there first thing
in the morning and interview the next of kin. It might look
insensitive if you go tonight." As though twelve hours would
make it look any better! I was still inexperienced enough to
be horrified.

"But – what about the Conference?"

"It's not so riveting you can't miss an hour – it's the wind-
up session that matters. Come on, there might be some
human interest here. You know, a messy divorce, something
like that. It's bloody difficult filling a newspaper in summer.
And – look – I hope you're being discreet up at the Clocktower."

"Discreet?"

"Yes. I've just had De Broux on the 'phone panicking
about coverage. He's even invited me to a Gourmet night!
You're not tramping around looking for potential suicides
on window-ledges, are you?"

"No. I did come across a syringe in the cheeseboard,
though." I told him about it.

26

He laughed. Other people's misfortunes always seemed to relieve his tensions. "No wonder! What with corpses on the Clocktower and syringes in the Stilton he must think God's got it in for him. It's surprising how many people think God can be influenced by newspaper coverage, isn't it?"

"Yes," I replied. "And most of them are newspapermen."

I shut the door quickly, half hoping he hadn't heard.

It was still hot and humid when I returned home that evening, but the house had been shut up all day and felt strangely cool. The odour of yesterday's kippers greeted me as I opened the front door. I rushed round, trying to repair last night's damage before tonight's onslaught began. Keith's breakfast cornflakes were welded to the bowl, and a wasp was pickled in the martini and tonic he'd left unfinished in the bathroom. I opened every window and made Julie's bed. It seemed she'd been home this afternoon, microwaved a pizza and finished off a carton of raspberry ripple ice-cream. No wonder she had spots. Now she was out with a friend, and probably wouldn't be back until bedtime. She'd spent a lot of time recently at the home of a girl called Angie, whose mother was more sympathetic than me, she said. I'd agonised over this a good deal, and come to the conclusion that it was all part of the rebellion phase, though there were things about Angie's mother I didn't quite like. Keith said I ought to put my foot down if I didn't want Julie to be influenced by her, but I'd never been much good at putting my foot down, and had decided to let things run their course. My only real objection to Angie's mother, whom I had never met, was that she was divorced and seemed to enjoy life to the full. I had several other friends who were divorced, and they appeared to be no happier than I was, a circumstance I found a lot more reassuring.

Keith came home late, hot and with a headache. I gave him a cold lager and a kiss, and then realised I hadn't spoken to him since early the previous evening. I was eager to tell him about what had happened that day, but instead tried to be diplomatic.

"How was your day?"

"Bloody awful! I hate this weather."

"I hope you enjoyed yourself yesterday evening?"

"Yes, I did, thank you."

"Where did you go?"

"What do you mean, where did I go? I went out with some of the lads from the Club. Where did you think I went?"

"Oh, I don't know. You didn't say, that's all."

"Well, I don't have to always say, do I? You can't expect me just to sit at home while you're off gallivanting!"

"No. But really, it wasn't gallivanting, it was incredibly boring –"

I started lining up chops in the grill pan. Keith picked up a tea-towel and began putting away last night's washing-up, which was a gesture of reconciliation.

"Keith, you'll just never believe what happened today – I found a dead body hanging from the fire escape at the Clocktower Hotel!"

He looked at me. He didn't look in the least surprised or excited.

"A dead body. I don't suppose by a remote stroke of good fortune it belonged to that bloody Heslop or Schiavo or any of the rest of them you're always going on about, did it?"

"Oh Keith! Come on – aren't you interested? When have you ever gone into work and found a dead body?"

"Never, I'm glad to say! I do a proper job, I work hard, I earn good money, and all I ask from life is a wife who'll keep the house halfway decent and provide me with a bit of companionship in the evenings. Companionship, I say – we won't go into the other services you're so reluctant to provide! And what do I get? Bloody bodies hanging from hotels and a wife whose idea of sodding companionship is to bugger off in the evenings with a notebook in pursuit of some schoolgirl fantasy about being a reporter!"

We had been through this one before, so I didn't answer. We both felt better now that it was said, in the way that a distant clap of thunder on a hot night makes you feel you have missed the eye of the storm.

Richard came home about nine. He sneaked in with a hold-all full of dirty washing and his Walkman and went straight to his room. He looked tired.

"Nobody's speaking to me in this house," I said. "Did you have a nice time?"

He nodded and kissed me. I noticed he hadn't shaved that morning.

"You do look tired. Are you all right?"

"Of course I am! Don't fuss, Mum." He spoke cheerfully, showing the boyish grin and twinkling blue eyes Keith had once had. "How about you? You're all flushed."

I told him about Michael Stoddart being strung up on the Clocktower. We sat on his bed and shared a lukewarm Coke he'd found in his bag, and he listened open-mouthed.

"Really? You found him? My own Mum found a dead body? Fancy that! The minute my back's turned something exciting happens. Must've been awful, too – eyes bulging out, tongue black and everything – poor old you!"

"No, it wasn't that bad. He just looked – asleep, I suppose."

I pulled open his bag and was going to help him unpack, but he hastily snatched it from me and put it on the floor behind his desk.

"He can't have hanged himself then," he said. "Must have died of something else and been hanged later."

"What on earth do you mean?"

"Well, don't you remember that book I had, the one you didn't like me reading. You said it was gruesome. 'The Wild West – True Facts' it was called, something like that. It had all about lynching in it, and there were photos, too. It described people hanging – how long it took them to die and so forth. Apparently the eyes bulge out and the tongue –"

"Have you still got it?" I was suddenly excited. "Where is it?"

"You're joking! You gave it to a Church jumble-sale, which I thought was pretty vindictive."

"Richard, are you *sure* about this?"

"Mum, I'm studying to be an accountant, not a doctor! But that's what it said in the book. Let's work it out." He gripped his own throat and started jerking his head about,

29

half choking and poking out his tongue.

"Don't do that – it's awful! You know you could be right. But why didn't anyone else notice it, Inspector Franks or the doctor?"

Richard shrugged. "Maybe they haven't seen people who hanged themselves before. It's not an everyday occurrence, is it? Maybe their mothers wouldn't let them read 'True Facts about the Wild West' either!"

I stood up and straightened Richard's bed covers again. He was opening drawers and tucking things into them, and some of the drawers were so crammed they wouldn't shut properly.

"What you need is a good night's sleep," I said. "Several in fact. And at least one evening spent at home tidying up this room!"

Richard gave me a mischievous wink.

"Now that's more like the Mum I know and love!"

3

Michael Stoddart's address was 23a Edgeborough Avenue.
This had once been an attractive street, lined with trees and
ornate gas lamps, with the Sports Ground on one side and a
row of substantial Victorian houses on the other. The houses
had long gardens ending at the railway embankment, which
was discreetly shrouded in woods. It was the sort of street
doctors and bankers moved their families into. But all that
had changed when the by-pass was opened, and Edgeborough Avenue became a "rat-run" for heavy lorries seeking a quick back-entrance to the town. I suppose the houses
were rather large for modern families anyway, and soon fell
prey to partition walls and multiple doorbells. I knew the
history of Edgeborough Avenue, because ten years ago,
when the area was just beginning to go downhill, Keith and I
had planned to buy a house there. The semi-wild garden
would have been a paradise for the children, and our intention was to use the top floor of the house as living-quarters,
and the ground floor as offices for the civil engineering
partnership Keith and two colleagues were hoping to set up.
We were told, though, that there was *no way* we would get
planning permission to use the house for commercial pur-
poses: Edgeborough Avenue was residential, and would
remain so, because of the outstanding architectural value of
the buildings. Now, as I drove along it, I spotted signs for
Video Rentals and Emergency Plumbing. Abandoned cars
rusted on the pavement and a skip outside an empty property had weeds growing in it. It was probably just as well we
hadn't moved in here; residents, many of whom were squat-
ters, were reputed to spend a good deal of their time robbing
one another.

Stepping over discarded plastic bags of glue, I approached

number twenty-three. It was one of the best kept houses in the street, though that wasn't saying much. The flat of the deceased (as I respectfully thought of him) was on the ground floor, to the left of the imposing front door. The label on the bell just said Michael Stoddart. The front door was ajar so I went hesitantly inside. The bare hallway smelled strongly of cats and curry. I wished I hadn't come. Whatever do you say to grief-stricken relatives? I knocked on the finger-marked door. No one answered. Suddenly a voice came from behind me.

"You from the social? You got the wrong flat. It's her upstairs you want."

The door to the other ground-floor flat was half-open. A pale face, framed by thinning grey hair and slashed with scarlet lipstick peered out.

"Sorry?"

"She took the kids up the doctor's. You got the wrong flat." She'd plucked her eyebrows completely and pencilled them in shakily with a ginger crayon. Her face looked like a badly drawn skull.

"I'm looking for Mrs Stoddart."

"There ain't no Mrs Stoddart. It's Mrs Norris you people come to see. Upstairs. Only I told you. She's gone out."

I took a deep breath. "I think we'd better start again. I'm Chris Martin from the Tipping Herald and I'm following up the story of Michael Stoddart's unfortunate death. Can you tell me if he lived alone?"

Her face brightened up.

"Oh, the papers! I 'aven't spoken to any reporters since my Harold was took off nine years ago! How exciting! Stop struggling, Gladstone!" This last remark was addressed to a large ginger cat I now saw she had tucked under her arm. "You know you can't go out. They'll try to poison you again."

Harold? Gladstone? Poison? It was like inadvertently changing channels on your remote control unit in the middle of a film. I was about to have another go at the question when the front door spilled light into the hallway and Lynn Cazalet entered.

32

"Oh, it's you!" exclaimed Gladstone's owner accusingly. "Now here's another one, I never know who she's come to see!" She retreated into her flat. The door slammed and there was a protesting wail from a cat.

"She doesn't like me, poor old soul," said Lynn. "She's got fifteen cats in there and it's unhygienic. *What* can you do?" She stared at Michael Stoddart's door. Her eyes were pink-rimmed and small, underlined with the grey of misery.

"I don't know if you remember me," I said. "I'm Chris Martin from the Herald. I found Mr Stoddart's body and now I'm trying to get some information about him. Were you a personal friend?"

"I was once," she replied enigmatically. "We weren't friends any more – his idea, not mine. I saw him yesterday, for the first and last time for a month." She produced a key. "I know I shouldn't do this, but there's something in there I wanted to get. You can come with me – in fact I'd be rather glad if you would."

The flat smelled musty, but less strongly of cats than the hall and there was a subtle, seductive hint of aftershave. Michael Stoddart's presence hovered in the stillness. His books and papers littered the table, and the bed was un- made. Next to a coffee mug, still stained from his last drink, lay an exercise-book in Council grey. He had stopped in the middle of marking someone's homework. Looking around, I saw that the walls were lined with photographs, mostly in black and white, their subjects ranging from street scenes to close-ups of lips round cigarette butts – the sort of photo- graphs regarded as artistic by people who see great merit in distorted images.

"Did he take these?" I asked.

"Yes. It was his hobby. He won prizes sometimes. He said you could do a lot with a camera." She looked round the room and said sadly. "It's gone."

"What?"

"A photograph of me. He took it. It just made me look nice, that's all." Her hair was lank and greasy, and she had two red spots on her chin. I expect he'd taken it in soft focus, using some sort of filter. "He must have thrown it away –

33

probably about the same time he threw me away," she added bitterly. "I always knew he was out of my league really."

I felt sorry for her. I'd thought Keith was out of my league, too, but I'd hung on and hung on and persistence had triumphed.

I said, "Look, I know this seems awful, but I'd appreciate any background information you could give me on Michael Stoddart. Who is his next of kin?"

"He hasn't got a next of kin. He was abandoned at four weeks old in a shoe box outside Woolworth's in Putney High Street. He told me all about it. He got shunted from one children's home to another. Why he wasn't adopted I can't imagine, but there we are. I think the system let him down rather badly. It does sometimes, you know."

"I see. And he wasn't married?"

"He wasn't married." She thought about this for a moment, then added. "He never even said he loved me, so I suppose I've only myself to blame."

"What exactly did he do? You seem very bitter."

"What did he do? Just what men always do. Took what he wanted and then discarded me like an old sock."

I thought, that's not what men always do; sometimes they take what they want and carry on arguing with you about it for years.

Lynn said, "He was a bit strange really. I never could quite understand him. Still, I should have known someone so good-looking would never really fall for me."

She was about to succumb to self-pity. I said, "Why do you think he killed himself?"

This provoked a sharp reaction. "Mike? Kill himself? I don't believe that. He used people, he didn't get used by them. He didn't strike me as a potential suicide – and I do have some knowledge of these things. I just wish I hadn't been such an idiot about him –" She had started to walk around the room as she spoke, studying the photographs on the wall and her ex-lover's shirts hanging limp and un-ironed from the picture rail. Now she stopped suddenly at the chest of drawers.

34

"That's odd. Look at the state of this."

All the drawers were pulled out, and the bottom one lay half on the floor. Its contents – mainly boxes of film, packets of lens cleaning paper and photographic magazines – were in a jumble. It looked just like Richard's bedroom and not very remarkable.

"Mike always kept his things tidy," said Lynn. "Especially this drawer. He used to let me clean the place for him and press his clothes, but he never let me touch this drawer. He kept a lot of his equipment here. Look – there's a lens there, rolled under the bed."

"Is anything missing?" I asked, suddenly interested.

She picked things up delicately, almost fearfully, as though he might walk in any minute and shout at her.

"I can't see the negatives. He kept them in a box with dividers, everything numbered and listed. I only saw it once when he was looking something up. And his camera's not here. "Bastards!" she shouted suddenly, making me jump. "This area's terrible. The number of break-ins – you tell the police and they just don't want to know. Just so long as all the rich people with their two-car garages and swimming pools and little red box burglar alarms are kept happy, to hell with everyone else! I really hate this town!"

On top of the chest of drawers was a little stack of one pound coins and a five pound note. I said, "It's a bit odd, someone breaking in and stealing a camera and negatives and leaving cash behind. Shall we have a look round and see if they've taken anything else?"

It didn't take us long to search the small flat. I checked the window and the door locks, but neither appeared to have been forced. There was no sign of either the camera or the negatives. Lynn said the camera was a Pentax, and expensive, but it seemed odd to me that whoever had taken it had left behind the lenses that went with it. In the kitchen, next to Mike Stoddart's unfinished last meal (which had been a frozen chicken curry, by the look of it), was a notepad on which were listed the odd numbers between seventeen and thirty-one, against some of which were written names. "Greyfield Properties" appeared twice, as did the name

Harlow; I wondered if it could have anything to do with the Reverend Harlow, father of Richard's Carolyn.

"Have these numbers got any connection with the negatives?" I asked Lynn.

She shook her head. "I don't really know. I told you, he never let me touch any of his photographic things. Actually, I've just thought of something."

"What?"

"The camera might be in his car. He had a blue "V" registration Cortina. It must still be in the hotel car park."

"Yes, I suppose it must." So much for that mystery! "The negatives are probably there too."

"Oh no. I'd be very surprised. That box of negatives never left the drawer. You'd think they were gold dust – if only I'd meant half as much to him as those bits of celluloid –" She sighed deeply, and with finality. Perhaps now he was gone she was released from the burden of yearning for him.

"I must be off," she said. "I should be at the Conference."

"Me, too."

We left the flat, locking the door behind us. Lynn pocketed the key, said goodbye, and left. I hesitated in the hallway. The idea of negatives and possibly a camera being stolen from the flat intrigued me. Perhaps it was only wishful thinking, but I was becoming convinced that there was far more to Mike Stoddart's death than suicide while the balance of his mind was disturbed. I was about to knock on the door of Gladstone's owner, when it opened slightly and I glimpsed a pale face hiding behind it.

"Hallo again," I said, smiling.

"Hallo," came the timorous reply. Pete Schiavo's advice, "Be friendly, make them think you're on their side," came into my head, and to my surprise I heard myself say, "I've got a cat just like that one." The door opened wider. I haven't got a cat at all. I felt awful.

"Is it true cats become very attached to their homes and will tend to wander back if you move?" I asked, writhing inwardly against stabs of conscience.

"That's right, dear. I never let mine out at all. It's the best way. Give them chicken and liver and love – it's a cruel world out there."

"You didn't tell me your name."

"I'm Edie Clough, pleased to meet you."

"Tell me, Edie, did you notice if Mike Stoddart had any visitors yesterday? Maybe someone let themselves in with a key?"

"Oh! We get a lot of visitors to this house. It's her upstairs, you know. All them social workers and people. I got a lot to do with the cats and trying to keep up with my reading, I can't watch everyone!" She gazed at me thoughtfully, anxious to please. "Yesterday was the day the gasman come, and that lady doctor, and the health visitor with the squint – no, she was the day before. And a young police-lady come in the afternoon and banged on his door."

"Did the policewoman actually go into his flat – or the gasman?"

"No. The gas meters are out here, see, and the police lady didn't have no key. She was only a youngster. You'd think they'd've sent a man round, wouldn't you, to force the door, like on the telly?"

"You mentioned the health visitor and the lady doctor – would that be Dr Rachel Goodburn? Funny, I thought she was at home ill yesterday morning."

"Oh no, she's ever so good – she come out to me in the middle of the night once when I had me gastric trouble. There's not many will do that. They're coming and going from this house at all hours, I can tell you. Like her." She jerked her thumb in the direction of the front door, and the departed Lynn Cazalet. "Mrs Norris's battery's got wore out twice."

"Her battery?"

"Yes. For the doorbell."

I smiled and put my notebook away. Edie was obviously a less than reliable witness. I had said goodbye when she called me back.

"If you're worried about your cat when you move, I'd look after him for you. They need a lot of love and time and I've got both."

Stung by guilt, I thanked her for the kind offer and left.

37

The sun had come out and turned the inside of the Mini into an oven. I wound down the windows and tried to convince myself that the resultant air circulation would have a cooling effect. Poor Edie. Was that what happened to you if you had no husband or children, or was she in her own way happy in her solitude? Perhaps it's just as well you can't get inside other people's heads.

By the time I passed the end of my street on the way to the Clocktower, trickles of sweat were running down behind my knees and my hands were sticky on the steering-wheel. On impulse I turned left towards our house. The van driver behind me hooted angrily at this sudden manoeuvre, but I ignored him. Keith would have raised two defiant fingers and sworn blind to anyone willing to listen, that he had signalled his intentions beforehand and the bastard couldn't have been looking, but I know I'm not the world's best driver and would prefer to keep quiet about it.

As I opened the front door there was a flurry of move-ment upstairs. I gasped and dropped my keys noisily to the floor.

"Who's there?" My voice sounded shrill and imperious.

"It's me, Mum." Julie appeared at the top of the stairs, wearing only a towel and looking sheepish.

"What on earth are you doing here?" All sorts of dreadful possibilities ran through my mind.

She hugged the towel tightly round her and sat down at the top of the stairs.

"I've got a free period this morning."

"Well, why aren't you dressed?"

Tears filled her eyes. I ran up the stairs, two at a time, fearing the worst.

"I'm so fat, Mum. I keep weighing myself and I just don't get any thinner. I've only had a yogurt today – that's just liquid – but I'm a pound heavier than I was last night! What am I going to do?"

I restrained the desire to laugh, putting my arm round her.

"You're not fat at all, Julie. Who says you are?"

"Heather said I looked lumpy in my yellow sun-dress."

"Who's Heather?"

38

"Angie's mum."

"Oh yes." I leaned her fair head on my shoulder and tickled her neck, as I used to when she was a toddler. "Well, you're not fat at all, though I don't think that dress fits you very well. Would you like me to see if I can do something with it?"

"Could you?"

I nodded. "I'll try. But actually, you don't eat very sensibly, you know. Shall we sit down tonight and try and work out a proper diet? I don't mean cottage cheese and carrots and stuff. I know you don't like that."

"Heather says –"

"Never mind about her. Now listen, I'm supposed to be at work. I only came in to get changed. Let's both go and put something on, shall we?"

My room looked like the aftermath of a jumble-sale. I changed into a white cotton dress that shows rather too much neckline, especially when that neckline is pale from lack of exposure, but the washing-basket was erupting alarmingly in the corner, and at least white would be cool. Julie came in, already dressed, and sprayed us both with perfume.

"Was it really you who found Mr Stoddart's dead body?" she asked.

"Yes. Oh dear, are you very upset about it? I didn't think."

"No. I didn't like him all that much. Some of the girls did though. Two of them went home crying after lunch yesterday. They said they were all going to wear black this morning. I couldn't borrow your black tee-shirt, could I?"

"I thought you didn't like him?"

"Well, I don't want to be left out." She started rummaging through my drawers. "I can think of one stupid, stuck-up little cow who'll be eating her heart out!"

I ignored the language. "Who?"

"That Sari Randall from Northdales. She said she was having it off with him twice a week in the back of his car."

This time I was shocked. "That's no way to talk! You shouldn't repeat that sort of gossip."

"It's not gossip. It's what she said!"

"Wait – did you say *Randall*?" I remembered Elaine Randall, the parent-governor.

"Yes." She'd found the tee shirt and was wrenching it this way and that. She liked her clothes baggy – I didn't and I snatched it from her angrily.

"If you're going to borrow my things at least look after them properly. Look, this Sari Randall, do you think she was really – er – having a relationship with Mr Stoddart?"

"I don't know. She said so, and Angie and I saw his car outside her house once. Well, why not? Heather says age is all in the mind. She's the same age as you, Mum, but she buys her clothes from the same shops as Angie and me. We all go together. *And* she goes to the Ace of Spades disco with Angie."

I decided to put my intuition to the test.

"Heather wouldn't by any chance have a dishy boyfriend about ten years younger than herself, would she?"

Julie looked surprised. "I didn't know you knew her. Don't tell anyone, will you, because Ken is *still married*." She spoke the last sentence in a slightly awed whisper.

I thought, oh God, this is worse than I imagined. I said, "Look – about Mr Stoddart. This nonsense about him having relationships with pupils, is that serious?"

"Well, I never heard of anyone except Sari. *I* thought he was a bit strange. He had funny eyes, sort of cold. Angie said – Angie said his eyes went right through your clothes." She giggled. "We had him once when Old King Cole was away – all the girls started doing their hair and the boys made stupid remarks." She shrugged, losing interest, and sighed. "I don't think I'll ever have a boyfriend."

On the way to the Clocktower Hotel I had two things to think about. One was that I really must take Julie in hand before Heather convinced her that extra-marital affairs and being able to wear size ten trousers (I was sure Heather would have size ten hips) were the most important things in life. Julie had to be brought up to appreciate real and lasting values. The other thing that was exercising my mind was

Mike Stoddart. I had been instructed to write a human-interest story about a suicide; what I had found was something a good deal more sinister.

4

The Reverend Harlow was standing on the steps of the Clocktower Hotel, enjoying Eric De Broux's best filter-coffee and God's warm July sunshine. I couldn't avoid him.

"Ah, Mrs Martin!" he greeted me. "Just got here? And how are things in the exciting world of the media today?"

"All right, thank you. Have I missed much this morning?"

"I shouldn't think so. It's all rather above my head, I'm afraid. One is aware more of the human tragedies than underlying social trends, economic factors, etc. One leaves that to the experts! A very distressing occurrence yesterday – I do hope you have recovered from it?"

"Oh yes." My thoughts turned to the hotel yard, where a strand of black and yellow police-tape would be all that remained of the drama.

"Tell me," said the Reverend Harlow. "Has old Bill decided about my 'Thought for the Week' yet? A dissertation on what might happen if *God* were to take a holiday – most timely, I thought."

"Yes, I'm sure, but Mr Heslop doesn't take me into his confidence, I'm afraid. Would you excuse me? I must get a coffee." I wanted to make my escape before he brought up the subject of Richard and Carolyn.

"Certainly. Excellent it is, too."

The Conference was just about to resume and the girl in the Coffee Shop gave me a black look when I ordered coffee. I think in her eyes I wasn't a Real Delegate, but a Real Person, like herself, and therefore ought not to expect service. On my way through Reception I briefly inspected the sponsors' stands, and helped myself to a few leaflets. This is what it's really all about, I thought – "you came to our Conference, now buy our products –". On the Leisching

Pharmaceutical stand there was a placard advertising what they called a "simple, external remedy for that personal, private discomfort all women suffer from time to time". Who could walk past such a message without feeling a twinge of – well, something or other? I picked up a leaflet. A young man in a dark suit smiled at me politely, and I hoped he wasn't thinking what I thought he was thinking. Anyway, I nearly lost coffee, leaflets, notebook and dignity in the doorway of the Conference Hall as Major Duncton pushed past me on his way to the telephone. There was someone who didn't even think of me as a Real Person.

It was the closing speech of the afternoon that provided the big surprise. A tall, thin man, whose bald head glowed in the lights with an almost ethereal radiance, took the floor to make a speech on behalf of Leisching Pharmaceuticals. We all sat to attention when we got through the polite applause, as befitted the man whose Company had paid for the lion's share of the proceedings. The tall, thin man waited for complete silence, and then launched into the expected blurb on Leisching's contribution to research and concern on the subject of drug abuse. He congratulated everybody concerned with the Conference for all the work they'd put into it – and then came the crunch, the reason for Leisching's heavy involvement:

"What my Company is proposing is the setting-up, in this town, of a Dependency Unit. This unit will provide care, rehabilitation and above all support for Dependency victims. It will not cost the NHS or local ratepayers a penny. My Company will match, pound for pound, every contribution made by local businesses. What we are trying to do is stimulate local means to fight a local problem – and by local in this case of course I mean countywide."

A ripple of surprise ran through the Hall, and the speaker gave a satisfied smile.

"Now, you are probably asking yourselves – yes, I can see a few cynical expressions over there – why should Leisching Pharmaceuticals be prepared to enter into such an arrangement? Well, I will tell you. We are an expanding company with, as you may know, offices throughout the country and Europe. What we are now proposing to do is to centralise our operations. We have looked around this area and we like it; we *hope* to become part of it." He paused dramatically. "In the very near future we are hoping that a suitable site can be found in Tipping for our new head office complex. This project will, of course, provide hundreds of new jobs. We shall be part of the Tipping Community. Ladies and Gentlemen, your problems will be our problems. Let us set out to solve them together."

I was on my feet the moment he'd finished speaking, collecting up handbag and notebook. This was news! I ran to the 'phones in the hall with applause drumming in my ears and dialled the Herald's number with frantic fingers.

"Mr Heslop's only just gone to lunch," said his secretary's voice. "Can you call back in half an hour?"

This probably meant he'd been squatting on the floor of his office for the last few hours, meditating, and trying to put off eating the organic vegetable salad lunch which was to be his only sustenance until dinner time. However, I didn't want to be the one to suggest this.

"Not to worry," I said. "I'm coming in."

On my way out of Reception I caught up with Sylvester Munroe, leaving with his suitcase. He was pale and perspiring in his leather coat.

"Don't be in such a hurry, dear," he said. "Life is short. You'll get to the end soon enough."

"Yes, of course," I said, stopping for a moment. "Somebody ended his life just beneath your window the other night, didn't he?"

Sylvester closed his eyes and shook his head, as though he didn't want to be reminded of it.

"Come and see me when you're in Hudderston. We of the media must stick together."

I had another quick look round the car park for Mike Stoddart's blue Cortina, but couldn't see one with a "V" registration. Perhaps the police had already taken it away. Two hard news stories in as many days! I felt like a real reporter at last. I drove down the narrow road with the wind

44

playing wildly through my hair and my tyres screaming as I rounded the bend at Rampton's Hollow too fast. I suppose I should have known that this good feeling wouldn't last for ever; I've seen those films where the hero walks down a sunny street whistling, only to have a tree fall on him. Still, the trees stayed upright for the time being.

When I got to the office Mr Heslop's door was open and he was studying the lay-out for the front page. This was a Thursday afternoon, and the Herald flops through people's letter-boxes on Friday morning, so he'd need quite a few indigestion tablets and probably a surreptitious shot of whisky to get him through the next few hours. I told him about Leisching Pharmaceuticals' sensational announcement, and he rubbed his hands.

"Oh, that's good! That's much better than the dead-bird-in-the-milk scandal. Get it written up and *check* it and *double* check it." This was his rather meaningless catch-phrase repeated ad infinitum to junior reporters. "And how's your suicide coming along?"

For a moment I thought this a callous reference to my own mental state.

"Well, actually, I'm really convinced it wasn't suicide."

"Facts, Chris!"

"Well, I wasn't able to track down a next-of-kin. He lived alone. You see, as far as I can gather –"

"Right! Bottom of page two. Don't just stand there! I want that Conference story."

I gave him my most beguiling smile. "Can I have my name on it?"

He was reaching for the 'phone with one hand and a peppermint with the other.

"Yes, yes! Go on, scoot. I've got to get this page re-done." He swallowed down a belch. Heaven knows what his stomach would be like if he worked on a daily paper.

By the end of the day and several hundred words later I was still feeling pleased with myself. I decided to take my courage in my hands and call at the police-station for the post-mortem results on Mike Stoddart. Bravely I parked on a single yellow line close to the station, combed my hair, and set off. Inspector Franks passed me on the pavement without a second glance, not even at the car. My fragile new-found self-esteem took a knock. After all, if someone doesn't remember you when you've just pointed them towards a dead body, there really must be very little about you that is worth remembering. Shoulders slightly slumped, I continued slowly towards the entrance, from which emerged a large familiar figure with his nose buried in a handkerchief. It was the sergeant who had stood guard at the foot of the fire-escape.

"Oh hello, love!" he said, surprised. "I remember you. You work in the kitchens at the Clocktower, don't you?"

I opened my mouth, but words failed me.

"Here, this'll interest you," he went on. "That bloke they found hanging from the fire escape – apparently he didn't hang himself at all. He was killed by a massive heroin overdose! Bit of a turn up for the books that, eh? Inspector Franks is doing his pieces, he's had to set up an Incident Room. He was hoping to take a long-weekend after the Conference finished. Him and that Major Duncton have got a boat down at Chichester Harbour. Should stick to playing with boats in their baths if you ask me."

"Look, are you telling me it wasn't suicide?"

"No, love, that's right. It only just came through. Be detectives all over your place in the morning – hope you've got an alibi!" He laughed uproariously. "Biggest joke of all is that the bloody Inspector was in the bar there till around 11.30 that night with the Major, and this bloke died around that time – they were bloody nearly witnesses! Serve him right, him and his fancy friends – poncing about at Conferences – bloody yachts!"

Sometimes it helps to look like a kitchen-maid; he wouldn't have said that to a reporter.

"You don't like the Inspector much then?"

"You like your boss, do you?"

"Well – is there a 'phone round here?"

"Yes, love, just round the corner – if the vandals haven't

been at it."

I thanked him and told him I hoped his cold would soon get better, then raced round the corner to the 'phone box. It had no door and was full of empty bottles and fish and chip wrappers, but it worked. Mr Heslop congratulated me on my initiative, and said he'd see to it. The story that eventually appeared on page two bore the headline "Bizarre Death at Local Hotel". You had to read it right through to discover that the hotel in question was the Clocktower, the promise of a free gourmet-dinner having worked its magic on Mr Heslop. Also, the word "murder" did not come into it – the police were apparently only treating the matter as a suspicious death. Still, I felt things were progressing.

It was on my way back to the car laden with shopping that I noticed Pete Schiavo sitting on a bench in the little garden which was normally the province of old ladies with shopping-trolleys and old men with cider bottles. My first reaction was a feeling of gratification, because it looked as if the latest recipient of his amorous attentions had had second thoughts about going on holiday with him. I'd spent half an hour on my very first morning at the Herald in the Ladies' comforting a temporary typist who'd hoped in vain to become a permanent fixture in his life, so I was pleased to see he'd failed to get his own way on this occasion. Then I saw that he was talking to two boys of about eleven, who were identical to each other, and identical to him – dark and good looking with perfect oval faces. The difference was that their curls were not streaked with the grey of his forty-three years, nor were their eyes underlined with deep semi-circles. He'd seen me, so I struggled over with the shopping.

"Get up, lads," said Pete. "This is Chris. Andy and Dave."

The boys smiled politely but did not speak. There was something touching about looking at the three of them together, as though, in seeing the boys' faces, I was seeing Pete as he was when young and untouched by life.

"What are you doing here?" I asked. "I thought you were on holiday."

"We were. You wouldn't believe it, but it rained solidly for three days in Torquay, so we came back." He glanced at the boys, who were out of earshot. "Do you want to know something? I'd've given anything for a little time with those two but now I've got it, and it's bloody hard going."

"Don't worry. I live with my children and I often feel like that." Pete's battles for access rights to his three children were, in his own words, the stuff of which legends were born.

"So – how did the Conference go?" asked Pete. He looked at my spotless white dress and added with a half-smile. "Have they done a conversion job on you?"

"No. I never did drink much anyway."

"Really? What do you use for anaesthetic then? That looks like a pack of lager you've got there. I'll love you for ever if you let me have one."

I gave him a can and he took a long drink with exaggerated relief. Then I said, "You'll never believe what happened. On the first morning of the Conference I found a man's dead body hanging from the Clocktower fire escape!"

He smiled vaguely and placed the can on the seat next to him. He stared at it. "Jesus!" he said. "This must be potent stuff! Or maybe it's time I gave up drinking for a while. I could have sworn you said you found a dead body on the Clocktower."

I laughed. "No, really! That is what I said!" He gave a sigh of relief, and grinned. "You know, you look quite attractive when you laugh like that, darling. I wish you'd do it more often. You usually walk round the place looking like a wet Monday in Scunthorpe."

"Do I?"

"Yes. Now what's this about a dead body?"

I was thinking about the wet Monday in Scunthorpe. A compliment and an insult almost in one breath; that was typical of Pete.

"Well, there he was, hanging by his neck from the fire escape. I'd seen him the night before, too, and he looked all right then. The police treated it as suicide by hanging to begin with, but I just came from the police station and

48

apparently he died of a heroin overdose. *Heroin*, not hanging, so how –" Suddenly something clicked into place. Heroin overdose – hypodermic syringes – the syringe in the cheeseboard – "Oh my God!"

"What's the matter?"

"Oh God!" I said. "I think I've done something awful!"

5

The sun was getting uncomfortably hot on the back of my neck. I had explained to Pete about the syringe and accepted the offer of a sip of lager from the can. It didn't make me feel any better.

"Well, if it were me," said Pete, "I'd put on a pair of handcuffs and go down to the police-station and give myself up. The police have some pretty inventive ways of extracting confessions, so I'm told."

"Oh God!"

"That's the third time you've said that. You're worrying about nothing, darling – you weren't to know. They won't exactly give you a Citizen of the Year award but at least you'll save them looking in all the wrong places. Volunteer to help with enquiries."

"Everybody knows that means getting slapped round in a police-cell all night."

"What papers do you read, for Christ's sake?"

"Dad," said Andy. "Can we go now? We're starving!"

"I'll have to go anyway," I said. "My fish-fingers are melting."

"All right, lads, say goodbye to Chris. You may not see her for a couple of years – unless she gets remission for good behaviour."

The boys stared at me. They took a few steps backwards.

"Come on, Andy, what's up with you? I was only joking about her being a criminal. Shake hands and say goodbye properly."

Two pairs of brown eyes regarded me reluctantly. I felt uncomfortable.

"Dad –" Andy seemed to be spokesman. "Dad – Mum said if we met any of your lady friends we weren't to talk to them. She says they're – not nice."

Pete's face registered shock as if he had been slapped. He stared at his sons in disbelief. Then he sighed.

"All right," he said. "Wait here for me. I'll help Chris to the car park with her shopping."

He picked up my carrier bags and started towards the car park.

"I'm sorry," he said. "I'm really sorry about that."

"It's all right. It doesn't matter. It's not your fault."

"When they're a couple of years older they'll see my side of things. They'll be more objective." He didn't sound convinced by his own words.

"They're nice boys. You must be very proud of them."

"I can't really claim credit for them. I've had very little to do with their upbringing since they were five."

When we got to my car, he said, "Look, this dead body of yours, are you really interested in it?"

"Yes. It's the only one I've ever found."

"Did Heslop let you follow it up at all?"

"He's not very interested."

"He'll hand the story to me, you know, if there looks like being anything in it. I tell you what, we'll work on it together. I'll send the boys to the pictures tomorrow and we'll meet in the Star about two and see what we've got. What do you say?"

"O.K." Why not? It might get me away from planning disputes and flower-shows for a while.

"And if it turns out to be the story of the year, and I get a job on a decent newspaper as a result of it, I'll buy you anything your little heart desires – an electric yogurt maker, a set of Janet Reger underwear, anything. Shake on it."

We shook hands. As he walked away, for the first time I felt some sympathy towards him.

To my amazement, Keith was in the kitchen wearing an apron and a slightly bemused expression.

"I put the washing in the machine," he said, "but it doesn't seem to be doing anything."

"It's just heating the water." We exchanged a chaste kiss

51

of greeting.

"I'm really sorry about last night," said Keith. "I'd had an absolute bastard day. I'm sorry. I bought you something – it's out on the patio."

I went out to look. He'd bought me a new pink fuschia to replace the one which had died after I forgot to water it. I thought guiltily that I would rather have had half-a-dozen red roses as a peace-offering, but I thanked him with another kiss and told him not to worry about anything in the kitchen.

After dinner Keith and I sat on the patio enjoying the whine of other people's hover mowers, the scent of grass and a sunset sky streaked with the purple promise of a glorious day tomorrow. I told him about finding the body, and the Conference, and confessed to being rather nervous at the prospect of visiting the police station tomorrow. He reacted quickly to this.

"You shouldn't let yourself get involved in this sort of thing. Writing nice little stories about the Council's problems with dustbin-liners is one thing, but coming up against the police is another."

"I didn't do it on purpose. Pete says they'll be understanding about it anyway. And from now on, I'm going to be investigating it with him, so I won't make any more mistakes."

"Who is this Pete?"

"Pete Schiavo. You met him once in the pub."

"Oh, him. Yes, well, if he's such a great reporter what's he doing working for a paper like the Herald?"

"I think he's had a lot of personal problems."

"Personal problems! You mean drink and women and driving sports cars into ditches – I recognise the type. He is just exactly the sort of person you ought to avoid like the plague – no sense of responsibility!"

The conversation turned to other acquaintances of ours who had got themselves into sorry circumstances through lack of responsibility, a favourite topic of Keith's. When young, he had sown his wild oats, and owned a motorbike, and done all the things young men usually do, but, on passing his thirtieth birthday he'd cut his hair, subscribed to a private pension, and started buying the Financial Times. His idea of pleasure these days was anything that didn't cost a lot of money, i.e. supermarket own-brand alcohol, cricket (if that can be described as a pleasure), and anything with balls in it on television. I sometimes wondered if you could overwork your sense of responsibility. What if a jumbo-jet fell on the house tomorrow and killed us all, I'd once asked. "Don't be silly," Keith had replied quite seriously, "I wouldn't have bought this house if it were in an airport flight-path."

The evening ended with Keith telling me he'd run into an old friend of ours that day, whose wife had just started a nice little business making wholemeal quiches. She was getting an enterprise allowance and a bank loan and all sorts of other inducements, and would no doubt need an assistant. A vision of wholemeal pastry cases riding off in solemn procession into the sunset flashed before my eyes, and Keith said he'd written her 'phone number down in my book for me. I thanked him, and promised to bear it in mind.

Friday morning dawned clear and hot, with everybody in the neighbourhood except me wearing the cheerful, self-satisfied expressions people always adopt on sunny Fridays that look like turning into fine weekends. I put on what I considered to be my most efficient looking outfit – navy linen skirt and crisp white blouse – added some colour to my cheeks, then stood back to examine the effect. Immediately the police-sergeant's remark about my working in the hotel kitchens came to mind, but it was too late to do anything about it. I met Julie at breakfast, tousle-haired over a yogurt, and I said, "Do I look awful?" She said "No", in a questioning tone, having scarcely glanced at me.

"Will you do me a favour?" I asked, on the spur of the moment. "Come shopping with me tomorrow. Help me choose some new things, and some make-up. I'm tired of looking like a middle-aged waitress!"

Somewhere in the police-station someone was whistling

"Love is a many splendoured thing", to shouts of "piss off"
and "give it a rest", and the young officer on the desk was
delicately picking bits of undissolved milk powder out of his
tea.

"Good morning, madam, what can we do for you?" he
asked cheerfully.

"I'd like to see Inspector Franks, please."

"He's very busy this morning, madam, couldn't I help?"

"Well –" I forced my brightest smile. "I've got some
information on the Michael Stoddart murder case."

"Have you now!" He picked up his 'phone and stabbed a
button. "Sorry, sir, but I've got a lady here with some
information on Michael Stoddart. Yes. Right away, and two
sugars, sir." He put the 'phone down and smiled at me.
"This way, madam, second door on your left."

I started to walk along the bare corridor, my footsteps
echoing erratically and my heart beating fast. Just as I
reached Inspector Franks' door it opened and he emerged.
He leaned in the doorway, one hand in his pocket, the other
gingerly fingering a shaving-wound on his cheek, and he
looked me up and down.

"Oh yes, you're the lady from the Herald, the one who
found the body," he said after a while. He didn't smile, nor
did he look as if he ever would. "What have you come *here*
for – we always keep the Press informed – ask your colleague, what's-his-name. Now, if you don't mind, we're
trying to get on with some work." He gestured along the
corridor with an expression of mock politeness.

"No, look, I think I've got some information for you. I
believe you're looking for a hypodermic syringe in connection with Michael Stoddart's death?" He nodded, slightly
surprised. "Well, I think I may have seen it. It turned up in
the restaurant and I thought it might be a health hazard, so I
helped the receptionist to – er – dispose of it."

"What?"

"She wrapped it in an envelope. I think she put it straight
in her wastepaper-basket."

Inspector Franks clenched his fist and scowled at me.

"I've got half-a-dozen men and a dog on their way up to

54

the hotel right this minute to search the grounds – why didn't you come forward earlier?"

I could feel my cheeks flushing, but I still kept trying to smile.

"Sorry, but I only thought of it last night – I thought this morning would be soon enough."

He swore softly to himself and called over his shoulder to someone in his office.

"Get on to the Clocktower. Tell them to switch their attention to the dustbins and wastepaper-baskets. Christ, it was the day before yesterday! Better get on to the Council as well – we may end up having to search the tip. God, on a day like this!" He wiped perspiration from his brow. I was sweating, too.

"I'm sorry," I said. "But honestly –"

"Yes, all right, missus." He seemed to be letting me off the hook, but he spoke with an unpleasant snarl. "And just while we're thinking of it I don't suppose you tripped over any machine-guns or machetes in the Ladies' Powder Room, did you? Didn't tidy them away into your shopping-bag by any chance, did you?"

I shifted my gaze nervously. The walls of the police station were painted a light turquoise, and it was probably this that triggered off a memory.

"Well, no, but there was a note –"

Inspector Franks' expression changed instantly. He took me by the arm and snapped his fingers to a passing constable.

"Interview Room 1. Get me a WPC."

He led me into a small windowless room lit only by a fluorescent strip light. It was completely bare apart from a formica topped table and three wooden chairs. The table-top was pocked with cigarette burns, and on the green, tiled floor there was a large, sticky, brown stain that looked like spilt coffee.

"Sit down," he said abruptly. I sat down. Inspector Franks sat opposite me, leaning forward on his elbows with an expression of deeply-held malice. A shiver of fear ran down my spine.

"I must caution you that tampering with evidence is a very serious matter. If you think that just because you carry a Press card you can walk on and off the scene of a suspected crime, helping yourself to anything that looks like it might make a nice juicy little news item –"

"No, no!" I interrupted. "I haven't got the note. I didn't touch it. I saw it the night before the murder. It was on the hotel message board."

The door opened to admit a solemn-faced young policewoman. She took up a position just inside the room, hands clasped behind her back, gazing intently at a spot on the wall.

"So, we're not talking about a note you removed from the body?" asked Inspector Franks.

"No. I told you, I saw it on the hotel message board. It said, "To M. After all this time! Hickory Dickory Dock. Don't forget, little Mouse", or something like that. It was on turquoise notepaper."

The Inspector sighed and waved the policewoman out of the room.

"What happened to this note?"

"I don't know. It was gone in the morning."

"This has got absolutely nothing to do with the investigation, has it?"

"Well, it was addressed to *M* –"

"A lover's note, in a hotel. I *would* say you've been reading too many detective stories, but it sounds more like Mills and Boon to me." He stood up, a sarcastic smile lifting the corners of his lips. "I think that's all for now, Mrs – er – Go back to your paper and tell them to let you stick to reporting flower-shows and bouncing-baby competitions."

We got up and he ushered me along the corridor. The glow of embarrassment had spread from my cheeks up to my hairline and down my neck. The young policeman from the desk was approaching us with a cup of tea.

"Inspector. Here's your tea, sir. Sir – that car that was found at Rampton's Hollow, we just heard; apparently it was registered to Michael Stoddart."

I glanced round sharply at the Inspector, and was about to

56

enquire about the camera and the box of negatives, but I thought better of it.

It was dark and cool inside the Star. The barman was polishing glasses and two men sat at tables by themselves, frowning over crossword puzzles. From the public bar came ripples of female laughter and the thud of darts into a board. I had never felt entirely at home in pubs – I'd spent too much time shivering outside them with crisps, and orange squash, and children squabbling over swings.

Pete said, "You look as if you need a large gin. That is what you drink, isn't it?"

"Yes, but a single is fine, otherwise I won't be able to think clearly."

"Aren't you lucky! How did you get on at the station?"

"It could have been worse."

He ordered the drinks, then said:

"I rang my contact at the police-station last night. He gave me the post-mortem results. Have you had lunch? In that case I'll skip the anatomical details." He produced his notebook. "Right – the big news is that Mike Stoddart was probably an ex-heroin user. He had scar tissue on his forearms indicating prior use of injectable drugs."

"What – you mean he was an ex-junkie?" He hadn't looked anything like my idea of an addict.

"Seems so, though it was some years ago. I shall be interested to hear what the Education Authority have to say about that! Anyway, he died of a heroin overdose, as you said, and he'd been dead for up to an hour when he was hanged from the Clocktower by person, or persons, unknown."

"Any signs of a struggle?"

"There was some bruising on his upper arm, but nothing major. Actually, whoever killed him must have really struck lucky, jabbing straight into the vein of someone presumably not co-operating. With that amount of heroin he would have gone into a coma within a minute."

I didn't care to speculate on the details. "Anything else?"

"Let's see. Time of death estimated at between eleven

p.m. and one a.m. Oh, and analysis of the stomach contents showed recent ingestion of a moderate quantity of alcohol."

"Well, he didn't drink that at the non-alcoholic cocktail do!"

"He didn't drink it in the hotel bar afterwards, either. The police seem quite positive about that."

"Oh, they would! Inspector Franks was in there till eleven-thirty with Major Duncton."

"You seem remarkably well-informed. Anyway, if it wasn't for the fact that he got himself hanged from the Clocktower, it would appear to be a clear case of accidental overdosing by an ex-addict returning to the habit."

"So – it looks as if someone used heroin to murder him and then for some strange reason hanged the body – like a sort of dreadful warning perhaps? Sounds almost medieval!"

Pete shrugged.

"The police are assuming a link with the local drugs scene. In fact, this weekend they'll be putting the screws on every known pusher and user in the area, so I wouldn't think of topping up your supplies of pot or coke or whatever it is you get off on. They expect to make an early arrest."

"Really?"

"No. They always say that."

"Did you know they found his car in Rampton's Hollow?"

"No, I didn't." He looked blank. Even though he hadn't been brought up in Tipping, and would have no memories of Rampton's Hollow as a courting spot, I'd have thought he would have remembered it. It had been the subject of a bitter local battle earlier that year, when the County Council proposed to route the new Hudderston link road through it. This would have destroyed the little pool and ancient oaks for ever, but, at the eleventh hour, a colony of rare tree-frogs had been discovered and the course of the road diverted. The conservationists had been delighted, and so, I imagined, was Mr De Broux. The new road would cut a swathe over the hilltop, right in front of his hotel, putting it squarely on the map.

"Rampton's Hollow," said Pete. "Yes, I remember. The dramatic discovery of the tree-frogs. Thames TV sent a crew down and there was this little blonde make-up girl – well, well. Rampton's Hollow's only a couple of minutes' drive from the Clocktower. So he was either murdered there, and put in another car and taken up to the Clocktower, or he was killed at the Clocktower and somebody made off with his car. Weird. But then this sort of thing usually is."

"Well – shall I tell you what *I* found out about Mike Stoddart now?"

"Go ahead."

"Well, for a start, he seems to have been very much a loner, single, no known relatives. I spoke to his ex-girl-friend, who incidentally was very bitter about the way their relationship ended. She let me into his flat. She seemed to think his camera and all his negatives had been stolen."

He raised his eyebrows. "That sounds interesting. Perhaps he had some photos someone didn't want him to have."

"*And*, according to my daughter, there's a possibility he may have had a relationship with a schoolgirl from North-dales."

Pete gave a broad, delighted grin.

"This is great stuff! We'll have another drink on that. Drugs and sex with teenagers – this is News of the World material! You can start measuring yourself up for that silk underwear. You wouldn't happen to know the girl's name, would you?"

I hesitated. "As a matter of fact, I do, but what's the point? The man is dead and the girl's probably suffered enough. I mean, she's hardly a murder suspect, is she? You're not seriously intending to make something of this?"

He smiled and reached into his inside pocket for his wallet. He pushed it towards me. Inside the plastic window was a picture of a very pretty girl with honey-blonde hair and dark-brown eyes. Behind it, half-hidden, was a black and white photo of a strikingly attractive blonde in sixties' make-up, who bore some resemblance to the girl.

"*Pour encourager les autres*," said Pete. "That's my daughter, Catherine, and for all I know her school may be full of men like Mike Stoddart. God knows I never get near enough to find out. Every time someone like Stoddart is

59

exposed, alive or dead, it scares the shit out of the others. That's what the point is."

I had a sneaking feeling he'd gone through the wallet routine before. I sighed. I didn't feel qualified to argue. The barmaid refilled our glasses and Pete said "Cheers!" very cheerfully. I pointed to the black and white photo.

"Is that your ex-wife? She's very pretty."

"Yes, that's Helen," he said, snapping the wallet shut. "The face that launched a thousand Exocets." He looked at his watch. "Are you doing anything this afternoon that can't wait?"

"No, I don't think so."

"Then come to the school with me."

"What – to see this girl – now?"

"Yes. I've got a feeling about this. I think it's going to turn into something big. Don't you ever get feelings?"

I shrugged. Again, I didn't mention the voice in my head.

6

Pete drove a dark green MGB which was immaculate on the outside, but whose seats were always littered with an assortment of abandoned rubbish – crisp packets, torn maps, a length of Christmas tinsel. I sat down, disentangled my seat-belt, and gripped the seat-edge tensely in preparation for the journey. Pete did not seem to be aware of the existence of any speed below fifty miles per hour.

"Have you ever driven a sports car into a ditch?" I asked after a particularly close call with an oncoming petrol tanker, and remembering what Keith had said.

"No. Up a tree once, but I'm careful these days." He didn't seem surprised by the question. "By the way, I didn't congratulate you on your Conference piece. Quite a couple of days for you, eh? A murder and this Leisching project. Of course, it's bad news for us, this development thing. It means we're in for months of argument about office-blocks and environment and Tipping losing its bloody character – Christ, I hate it!"

"I suppose *you'd* prefer stories about sex and drugs and violence and bits of bodies all over the road."

He glanced at me and sighed. "What I'd prefer, darling, what I'd prefer is not to have to do this crap at all. I'd like not to have to support solicitors and off-licences and bloody motor-insurance companies – I'd like to be driving a Porsche across Europe and writing brilliant best-selling novels that would support literary agents and all kinds of expensive habits."

"You don't want much, do you?" I said, and thinking about the wet Monday in Scunthorpe, smiled.

"No. Actually I'd settle for vodka on an intravenous drip feed." He brought the car to a sharp halt outside the entrance to Northdales School.

We sat gazing in silence at the chestnut-tree-lined approach, with its neatly weeded verges innocent of sweet papers. It seemed a shame that the County planned to close such a well-kept school, though frankly, as the parent of a child at the reviled Shepherds Hill, I couldn't help but feel a twinge of malicious pleasure. Pete pressed a switch and the growling guitars of Dire Straits filled the car and spilled out in the summer air. He felt around under his seat and produced a Polaroid camera, to take photos of Sari Randall, he said. Almost immediately a rising babble of high-pitched and enthusiastic voices signalled the approach of school-children. The younger ones came first, schoolbags carelessly thrown over their shoulders or dragged viciously through the dust. They inhabited their own world, oblivious to anyone over the age of twenty, their only concessions to the beauty of the afternoon being loosened shirt-collars and the frantic fanning of dog-eared exercise books. They walked in carefully sexually-segregated groups. Then came the older ones, more self-conscious, some with adult minds in awkward, immature bodies, others with adult bodies that responded to the impulses of juvenile minds.

"Come on, we'll start with these," Pete said, indicating a group of girls aged about sixteen. He got out of the car and approached them slowly, smiling pleasantly behind dark glasses.

"Hello, ladies, you all from Northdales?"

"That's why we're wearing this stupid uniform," replied a tall blonde girl, running her hand down from her breast to her very brief skirt hem indicatively. Pete pulled his Press card from his shirt pocket and flashed it at the group.

"Did you know Mike Stoddart?"

"He didn't teach here – he was at Shepherds Hill!" replied the blonde indignantly, and the others giggled.

"Is that your car?" asked a short girl with a pretty, impish face. "*My* boyfriend drives a Porsche!"

"He doesn't – she's making that up!" said the blonde. "Her boyfriend drives a bread van!" There was a lot of laughter and some scuffling amongst the girls at this. The blonde advanced on Pete. "If you want to know something about that teacher Stoddart, give me a ride in your car and I'll tell you." At this, all the girls hooted and whistled and a number of boys stopped to look.

"I don't think so, darling," said Pete.

She gave a sulky shrug. "My *Dad* likes Dire Straits. *I* think they're rubbish!"

Pete held up the camera.

"Come on, girls, let's take a few photos. You all look like Page Three girls to me."

They started giggling and playing with their hair and the boys walked away in disgust. Then the blonde girl began unbuttoning her blue and red striped uniform dress and thrusting herself forward provocatively. The boys stopped again, and a tall, broad-shouldered youth took off his glasses and approached Pete uncertainly. I could see a very nasty situation developing.

"Does anybody here know Sari Randall?" I asked desperately.

"Yes," said one of the girls. "Old Stoddart was knocking her off."

"Shut up, he wasn't! She just made that up!" exclaimed someone else. "She's a silly little cow. No one'd look at her."

"Well, who'd look at you?" asked the blonde, raising a long leg and caressing it. Pete obligingly took her picture, and she made a Brigitte Bardot pout and jumped up and down joyfully. "Anyway, here she comes, look. *She'll* never make it to Page Three."

A tall girl with short, mousey-brown hair emerged from the gate. Unlike the others, who were all dressed in some version of the school uniform, she was wearing a long sleeved black jumper and black wool skirt. Her face and neck glistened with beads of sweat. When she saw that she was the focus of attention she hesitated and fumbled with her schoolbag, as though she had forgotten something. I stepped between her and the others.

"Are you Sari Randall?" I asked.

"Yes." Her voice was soft and childlike.

63

"I'm doing a story about Mike Stoddart, who taught at Shepherds Hill, and I think you may have known him."

"Yes, I did a bit," she replied, her lower lip trembling.

I nodded. "Did you know him outside school?"

"Yes." She was keeping an eye on the other girls. "I did know him outside school!" she exclaimed suddenly, in a loud voice, so that they all looked at her. "Why shouldn't I? He came round to my house and he took me out in his car. Lots of times! Ask anybody you like!"

She stared back at the others defiantly, tears rolling down her cheeks. She hadn't been talking to me at all, it had been for their benefit. Then another tall girl with red hair ran up and grabbed her by the arm. Someone shouted, "There goes the gruesome twosome," and the two girls were swallowed up in the jostling crowd that had gathered around us. I tried to follow but Pete tapped me on the shoulder.

"Leave it. There's a couple of teachers coming out." He gave the blonde girl a broad smile and added suggestively, to shrieks of delight, "You've got it all ahead of you, darling."

We jumped into the car and he drove quickly down the road, over the hill, and out of sight of the school. He parked on the grass verge.

"Jesus, it only takes one," he said, removing the glasses and rubbing his eyes. He looked disappointed.

"Sorry. I didn't do very well," I said.

"Yes, you did. You did fine and I got a couple of good pictures of the girl." He studied them. "The point is, I think we're out of luck. I think she made the whole thing up."

"Why?"

"Oh, come on, surely you remember being that age? When I was fifteen I was almost suicidal because I thought I was the only boy in the class who hadn't been in the stationery cupboard with Mary Speck – it was ages before I realised most of the others were making it up. I was a good little Catholic boy in those days," he added, with a smile.

"Yes. I see. So shall we just forget about all this?"

"No, of course not. There can't be smoke without at least a spark, can there? But I wish we had a photo of Stoddart."

"You know – there might be one on file. Shepherds Hill

did a production of 'Oliver' and there were a couple of group photos he might be in. It's worth checking."

"Now, why didn't bloody Heslop think of that? 'Local Teacher Murdered' and a photo. The trouble with him is, there's no part of him above the stomach that works – or below it probably, for all I know."

A straggle of Northdales pupils appeared. Safely out of sight of the school, boys and girls were entwined in one another's arms, lips seeking lips, faces flushed with sun and newly-awakened sensitivity. We watched them in silence for a few moments.

"Yes. Well," said Pete, sighing. "All good things must come to an end." He handed me the photos of Sari. "If I give you these and you can get the one of Stoddart, will you show them round the shopping centre tomorrow? See if you can find anyone who's seen them together."

"Me?"

"Yes, you, darling. I've got to take the twins back to Maidstone. Try anywhere young people hang out – use charm and initiative, of which I'm sure you have plenty."

I accepted the photos reluctantly.

"By the way," I said. "Did I tell you about the note?"

"What note?"

"The note at the hotel." I told him about it. He smiled and to my surprise slowly placed his index finger on the end of my nose.

"You know what? I think the best thing I can do with you is take you home, lie you down on the couch and hypnotise you. We'll probably find you witnessed the entire murder."

For a moment I had a disturbing vision of myself lying on a couch with Pete. I blushed. I pushed his hand away and he laughed and turned on the ignition. As we accelerated down the hill I thought, God, he's very attractive – it's the eyes or the smile, or something – no wonder he has such an effect on vulnerable females. Then I thought, if I've got the sex hormone deficiency Keith says I have, how is it I can still recognise the charms of other men?

"You look hot," remarked Pete.

"Yes," I said. "I think the sun's getting to me."

I had already arranged to go on a shopping trip with Julie, so the easiest thing seemed to be to combine this with the task Pete had given me. Having Julie along would add to my credibility in approaching teenagers, I reasoned with some cynicism.

"You don't have to do it if you don't want to," I told her apologetically.

"You're joking! This is fantastic!" exclaimed Julie, turning up her shirt collar and donning dark glasses. "This is the most exciting thing I've done all summer!"

Oh dear, I thought, whatever happened to youthful idealism; I go into this thinking it's immoral and my daughter thinks it's fantastic.

We showed the photos to a group of Northdales girls in a boutique, and they recognised Sari but not Mike. In Woolworth's, a delighted shop-assistant said she knew Mike from television and declared herself free any weekend for filming in front of a studio audience. Apparently she had mistaken Mike for Leslie Crowther and thought I was a TV talent scout. It took us about half an hour to talk our way out of this. Later, we stopped at a café full of teenage smokers, and coughed over coffee and Danish pastries while we displayed the photographs. It seemed to be a lost cause. What surprised me was that of the fifty or so people we approached that morning, not one questioned our right to be prying into Mike and Sari's private lives, and most seemed quite eager to help. Perhaps Crimewatch has a lot to answer for. I didn't think Pete would be pleased.

When we got home, Julie helped me apply the new make-up she'd chosen, though she seemed a little impatient with the result.

"It's your hair really," she said.

"I'm having it permed next week."

"Dad won't notice, whatever you do."

"I bet he does."

"Go on – I'll give you fifty pence if he notices when he

comes in! What an easy way to make money – he never notices you. Heather says the day people stop looking at each other is the day they stop caring."

"And I'll bet she also says you're only as old as you feel." I didn't choose to argue the wider implications of Julie's remark.

"No, Mum, *you* said that. *She* says you're only as old as you let yourself look."

I bit back an acid comment about what I considered to be Heather's excessive reliance on cosmetics, and switched the subject to Julie's diet. We were discussing the various uses to which lemon juice might be put when Keith came in.

"My cricket shirt's not still in the wash, is it?" he asked, with an air of menace.

I raised my unusually heavy lashes and treated him to a wide-eyed gaze. "I've put everything away in your sports bag, dear."

"Oh. Good. Right, I'll be off then. Will you be popping down to watch this afternoon?"

My heart was sinking slowly. "I think I ought to mow the lawn if it doesn't rain."

Keith gave a cheery, slightly absent-minded wave and was gone. I gave Julie her fifty pence.

Later, in the kitchen, I reflected on the fact that I might not be a *femme fatale* but I was a passable mother. *My* children didn't have affairs with their teachers or unbutton their shirts for newspaper reporters. From time to time they both formed unsuitable friendships, it was true, but I always kept my cool and handled these situations with tact and understanding. I'd won Julie back today, and Richard had turned out well. Richard had never really given us any problems – apart from when he was at Nursery School and had come home every afternoon with his pockets crammed full of Council Lego. Anyway, in the long run being a successful parent was more important than looking like a cover girl. Looks, in many cases (and almost certainly in Heather's) weren't even skin deep.

Despite these feelings of saintliness, I slept badly that

night. It was hot and thundery and Keith was snoring exceptionally loudly. I became aware of noises downstairs, followed by heavy footsteps on the landing. Wondering which of the children was raiding the refrigerator, I pulled on my dressing gown and went out to investigate. The glowing red numerals on the alarm clock proclaimed that it was four twenty-seven.

"Richard!"

He was standing in the corridor, fully clothed, his face so ashen, his fair stubble looked dark and thick. He stared at me, frozen rigid.

"Have you only just got in? Oh my God, it's not the car, is it?"

He was still staring at me, but he glanced downwards for a moment and I saw that he had something clasped in his hand. The other hand was attached to the door of the loo.

"Whatever's happened? For God's sake tell me!" My voice had risen from a whisper to a yelp and Richard shushed me. He turned towards his room and beckoned me to follow. He sank down on his bed, head down, and gave a great sigh.

"We were busted, Mum. I'm sorry to wake you. Please don't get Dad."

"Busted?" I felt wide awake but my brain didn't seem to be functioning. "What do you mean?"

He hesitated. "Busted. You know – busted! Drugs and all that!"

"Busted? Drugs? No, I don't know! Tell me what you're talking about."

"Only pot, Mum. Just pot. And I didn't have anything on me."

There followed a long pause while I tried to take it in.

"Are you trying to tell me," I began, in a voice that sounded hard. "Are you trying to tell me that you and your friends smoke *pot*?"

Richard didn't answer. He studied his thumbnail and chewed it.

"Oh God, you silly boy! Have you got Carolyn involved in this?" My son and the vicar's daughter done for possession of marijuana.

"No. Carolyn and I had a bit of a barney. She wasn't –"

"Well, thank God for that at any rate! How could you do it? Have you gone mad? And what's that you're hiding from me?"

He held out his hand, palm upwards, displaying a small tinfoil packet.

"I'd got this at home. Emergency supplies," he added, ruefully.

"And where did you get it from?"

"Oh, Julie got it for me. It's easier to get at school –"

"Julie? I don't believe this!"

"It's all right, Mum. She doesn't use it. She says it gives her spots."

I sat down on the bed next to him, pulling my dressing gown round me and feeling suddenly very cold. I took a deep breath and tried counting to five. It didn't really help.

"All right. Tell me what happened."

"Well –" He hesitated, sighing. "We were in this pub –"

"What pub?"

"The Earl of Derby. And suddenly it was full of police. I mean one minute we're having a quiet drink and listening to Paul Simon, and the next the music's shut off, it's "up against the wall, hands behind your backs". Some people tried to get out but there were more police outside."

"Did they search you?"

"Yes. One of the guys I was with had some stuff on him, so they pushed us all out into a van – one of those ones without any windows. Then we got to the station and it was like the railways when there's a strike on – you know, everybody shouting and pushing and nobody knowing what's going on." He gave his head a shake, as though to wake himself from a nightmare. "I was stripped and searched, which wasn't very nice." I clasped his hand sympathetically, but it crossed my mind that if he'd been born female he would have found examinations of this sort went with the territory in a multiplicity of circumstances.

"Then they put us in a cell and we were there *hours*, Mum, not knowing what was happening. There was

69

somebody down there singing 'She'll be coming round the mountain' at the top of his voice. He just went on and on getting shriller and hoarser and every so often he'd have these kind of fits of hysterical laughter." Richard kicked off his shoes savagely and lay down on his bed, eyes closed.

I said, "Was that it then? They just let you go?"

"Well, yes, after this detective questioned me. I was taken up to the Interview Room, and it's name and address all over again, what had I been doing in the pub, did I know this guy or that guy, where did I usually get the stuff –"

"You didn't tell them about Julie?"

"No, of course not! They kept on and on, over and over again, asking the same stupid questions. Did I know I could be charged with a very serious offence? Did I wish to make a voluntary statement?" I imagined my son, confused, frightened, sitting in that windowless interview room with the turquoise walls and the coffee stains. "Oh, and they had a picture of that Mike Stoddart, the guy you found. They kept asking me if I'd ever seen him in the Earl of Derby or if he'd tried to sell me drugs."

"And had you seen him? Had he ever approached you?" I asked sharply. Richard opened his eyes and gave me a long, hurt stare.

"Mum, I don't know. They got me so confused in the end I'd almost have told them anything just to get out."

I pulled him up into a sitting position and started unbuttoning his shirt. I was amazed at how calm I remained.

"You've been very stupid – you know that, don't you? I just hope Carolyn will be understanding about it –"

He laughed. "*Carolyn*? *She* was the one who –"

I thought, oh, was she? Well, well, Reverend Harlow! I said, "We'll discuss this later. Go and have a wash, and you'd better flush that stuff down the loo. Isn't that what you were going to do?"

"Yes. Somebody said they might come round to our houses."

"Oh God!"

"Will you tell Dad?"

"Well, I'll have to! But listen, I'll make a deal with you.

You promise not to touch this stuff any more, and not to bring it to the house and, even more important, *never* involve your sister again – and I won't tell him about that part of it."

He gave a sigh of relief. "Thanks, Mum."

"And Richard – *don't* flush the tinfoil down the loo. You might block it up."

I staggered back to bed. I felt as if I'd been hit over the head with a sledge-hammer. I had half a mind to ring up the Reverend Harlow that very moment and ask him if he knew his daughter was encouraging other people's sons to take drugs – but only half a mind; he was still a Vicar and I hadn't been inside a church since Julie's christening. He might point out my guilt if I pointed out his. What I couldn't understand was *why* – it was children from problem families who took drugs, surely? In the case of Carolyn, there was probably an element of rebellion, rejection of her sheltered upbringing. But *Richard* – we had neither over-protected him nor subjected him to the traumas of a broken home, etc – there was just no accounting for it. Keith kept on snoring, his great roars ending in little blips, the way they always did when he was sleeping off a large quantity of lager. For Richard's sake, I hoped he wouldn't have a hangover in the morning.

I didn't sleep again. Just after six a thought occurred to me: Mike Stoddart – had the police arrested his killer? Last night, was it possible that in a cell adjacent to Richard's the killer of Mike Stoddart had sat, quietly listening to the repeated chorus of "She'll be coming round the mountain"?

7

I jerked out of a technicolour doze just after seven o'clock, and as always averted my gaze from the badly-positioned mirror at the end of the bed. In the room next door my potentially junkie son lay sleeping, beyond that my daughter the pusher was plugging in her heated rollers, and beside me lay the husband who didn't understand me. This was another bad moment of epic proportions. However, a chink of light appeared amid the gloom: Keith and I had always suffered together, in harmony, through the children's little crises (tonsillectomies, bed-wetting, etc.); perhaps this would draw us closer. His face was turned away from me and I watched the gentle movements of his throat. When we were first married I used to wake him every Sunday morning with a kiss on the neck, and he'd wake up and kiss me back and I wouldn't complain that his mouth tasted musty. Then, usually, we'd make love. My head throbbing, I got up and went downstairs to make tea.

"Keith," I said, shaking him gently. "Keith, wake up."

He opened his eyes and stared at the steam rising from the mugs.

"Keith, something happened last night with Richard."

"Oh God! What's he done to the car?"

"It's not the car. Have some tea."

I told him most of what had happened.

"The bloody idiot!" he said. "Bloody idiot! I'll wring his bloody neck!" He had gone very red in the face and he clutched at his head as though it hurt. I found some aspirin on the dressing-table.

"I wouldn't be surprised if he's learnt his lesson already," I said. "He's really shaken up."

"I don't care! He's not getting away with this."

"It's only pot –"

"Only pot! Only pot!" He looked as if he might burst a blood vessel. "Why are you so bloody stupid? I give that boy a bloody generous allowance – he could lose his job! This isn't your precious 'sixties when jobs grew on trees."

"*My* precious sixties?"

"I'll beat it out of him!"

"Wait, let's talk it over. Let him sleep –"

"Let him sleep! I've had to work hard for every penny I've got. Him – he's had everything – you think I'm just going to pat his head and tell him not to be naughty again? You leave this to me."

He stormed out of our room and there was a lot of shouting from the room next door, all of it from Keith. After a short pause, and a dramatic, thunderous flushing of the loo Keith returned, looking murderous but triumphant.

"Right – you won't hear any more about this," he said. "I've told him that if I ever just so much as suspect him of this kind of thing again, he's out on his ear. And don't look like that. He won't give up his nice cushy life here for half an hour of pleasure."

I thought, not everyone is as fond of their home comforts as you are. "Well, if you want my opinion, you're being rather hypocritical. I know it's not an exact comparison, but I distinctly remember your being carried out of the Young Conservatives' New Year's Eve Dance in 1968 –"

"Not an exact comparison? I should say it's not! This is our son we're talking about – *our* son, on the verge of becoming a junkie."

"Oh, surely that's going a bit –"

"Yes, and what's more I blame you for it! Yes, you, and your left-wing 'Legalise Marijuana' and 'Say No to Capital Punishment' ideas! Thank God I stopped you joining the SDP, or –"

"The SDP? Come on. That's got nothing to do with anything and I never did sign that "Legalise marijuana" petition."

"And another thing. Ever since you took this ridiculous job, gallivanting out at all hours, neglecting the house – *You*

73

should have known what he was up to. You're his mother. That boy could end up with a criminal record and it'll be your fault."

Downstairs, the newspaper flopped heavily through the letterbox. Keith gave an angry snort and, quitting while he was ahead, stamped off downstairs to collect it. I sat on the bed, stunned. Normally I was only too ready to accept the blame for anything, on the grounds that I'd failed the children by not breastfeeding them or stopping Richard from keeping a hamster, or for omitting to teach Julie to swim until she was eight because I was embarrassed about the bulges at the top of my thighs – but I didn't feel obliged to accept the blame for this.

"Now look here, Keith," I said, trying to keep calm. "I'm sorry you don't like my working for the Herald, but there it is. I've spent my whole adult life looking after you and the children and I don't begrudge a minute of it, *but* – and you'd better believe this! – I am not going to give up my job just because you don't like it!"

As usual, when challenged, he drew back from accepting the gauntlet. He sat down hard on the bed and dealt the Sunday Telegraph a savage blow to flatten it. I suppose I had won a point, but I had a feeling that I was losing the game.

Keith, Richard and I were eating breakfast in stony silence when Julie came down, still in her nightdress and with an enormous roller attached to her fringe.

"Dad, there's something wrong with the loo. I can't flush it."

Richard and I exchanged horrified looks.

"Is it blocked again?" asked Keith.

"No. It's the handle thingey. It won't do anything."

Keith got up with bad grace and went to investigate. While he was out of the room I gave Julie a strong admonition to stay away from Shepherds Hill's drug pushers, and she went red and said that she would. I also couldn't resist asking her, as the police had asked Richard, if Mike Stoddart had ever offered her drugs. She looked incredulous.

"He was a *teacher*, Mummy!" she said.

Keith spent the rest of the morning going through Yellow Pages for a plumber who would come at short notice and not charge the earth. Eventually he found someone who would come in his lunch hour on Monday provided he was paid in cash. There then followed another argument about who should take time off work to let him in. I lost. Keith then retired to the garage, which had become the repository for a considerable amount of equipment which had fallen off the backs of lorries, and spent the rest of the day hiding things rather ineffectually under dust sheets, in case of a visit from the police.

Pete hadn't suggested it, but I used my initiative and called at the late Mike Stoddart's house on my way to work on Monday morning. The front door was closed, and several bottles of milk stood in the morning sun, mustering the energy to turn sour. I rang Edie Clough's bell, and after a few minutes a curtain moved. Slow footsteps crossed the hall.

"Good morning!" I didn't feel anything like as cheerful as I sounded. "I don't know if you remember me. I'm Chris Martin from the Herald."

"I don't want to answer no more questions," she said. "It gives me a headache."

"Yes, I know, it must be most distressing. You've had the police round here, have you?"

"Yes, but I don't know nothing. I said to them, like I told you, he didn't have visitors, that Mr Stoddart, and I've got my cats to see to. And it wasn't a row neither, just them talking. I said that."

"Sorry?"

"With him. Next door." She inclined her head towards number twenty-five. "I said they just talked. I mean I can't go watching people all day. Neighbours talk to one another, don't they? I can't be expected to know what they say."

"No. No, of course not." I'd almost forgotten what I'd come for. "Look, if I show you a photo, can you tell me if

75

you recognise the person?" I produced Sari Randall's photo and showed it to her. She shook her head.

"No. I don't know her. But my telly's on the blink. I only get BBC2."

I counted three, quietly.

"You've never seen this girl come to this house?"

"No, miss, I haven't. She's from 'Grange Hill', isn't she?"

I put the photo away quickly.

"Actually she's from a school round here. Tell me, who else lives in the house? A Mrs Norris, and who else?"

"She's a one-parent family!" exclaimed Edie, seeming proud of knowing the correct term. "And there's that Paki who works on the railways, and his brother sometimes. I call them Sing-Sing. How's your cat?"

"She's fine, thank you."

Edie collected her milk. There was a lot of screaming and wailing coming from upstairs and I decided against ringing Mrs Norris's bell. I pressed the bell marked "Singh" several times, but no one answered. I thanked Edie for all her help, said goodbye, and stared across at the mural on the house next door. Number twenty-five was definitely worth a visit.

I ascended the front steps and found myself nose to nose with a sleepy looking polar bear painted on the front door. There was no bell, so I gave the door a push between two igloos and entered a dark, gloomy hall just like the one at number twenty-seven, the difference being that this one smelt strongly of damp and the staircase leading up from it had half its treads missing. To my right was a door on which was spray painted, over the top of a delicate flower design, "Ian keep out". This seemed a trifle ambiguous. I knocked gently at the door and after a pause a young male voice called out suspiciously, "What do you want?"

"Er – I'm from the local newspaper. I wondered if you could spare the time to answer a few questions?"

"Oh, did you?" replied the voice, in a tone of consummate lack of interest. There was a long silence followed by the sound of several large bolts being drawn back. The door opened and a pale face stared at me intently. I stared back. The face was framed by long, slightly greasy, dark curls and there were deep violet circles beneath the eyes.

"Want to come in?" he asked, standing back from the door. The room was not quite as I had expected. We'd had friends in Notting Hill, years ago, who had squatted in a flat, and they'd hung it with oriental drapery and artistic, if slightly obscene, posters. This was quite different. The wall-paper, where it still existed, had been painted with water-colour scenes of animals and naked children, but over the top was an angry assortment of four letter words and explicit sexual instructions in heavy black spray paint. Most of the furniture was broken, and there was a slight odour of urine. It reminded me of the waiting-room at Tipping Station.

"I'm sorry to disturb you but I've got a couple of photos I'd like you to look at. Would you mind?"

He shrugged. "Got a cigarette?"

"Sorry, no."

He shrugged again and produced one from behind his ear. "Got a light?"

"Sorry."

"Not got much then, have you? Where's the pictures?"

I showed him the photos of Sari Randall and Mike Stoddart. He studied them both carefully.

"Got a fiver?" he asked, his eyes narrowing.

This was actually the first time I had been faced with such a question. After a moment's hesitation I produced a note from my handbag and gave it to him.

"I've seen him. Not her."

I watched my five-pound note disappear into his trouser pocket.

"Well, he lived next door to you, didn't he? So you would have seen him. In fact I believe you didn't get on with him particularly well?"

"Believe that, do you? Well, you can sod off out of it then because I've answered questions from pigs all weekend and that's all you're getting."

I wanted value for money.

"What, questions about Mike Stoddart?"

"I gave you what you asked for. Shit, I go for a drink and get hassled and now you're here with more crap. Can't you read what it says on the door?"

I thought carefully. "Go drinking in the Earl of Derby, do you? Have anything on you when they picked you up?"

He laughed unpleasantly. "Not me. I'm careful. I don't get caught easy."

"Well, you see, I'm trying to put together a story on Mike Stoddart, and if you know anything about him, anything that might help, I daresay my editor would consider some sort of payment. Not me, though," I added, holding up a warning hand. "I'm not authorised."

"Oh, sweet sixteen and never been authorised, eh? Well I don't give a toss, see, because I didn't know that shithead. Once I spoke to him, that's all, and that was enough. He told me to get off his car."

"Would that have been early last week?"

"What's it got to do with you? Maybe it was, I don't know. You think I keep a calendar in here? I never touched his car. What do I want with cars? They're all rust and shit! Aren't you going to sod off yet?"

I began to appreciate what the term "hostile witness" meant. On an impulse I tore a page from my notebook and wrote my name and the Herald 'phone number on it.

"Here," I said. "Keep this. If you can think of anything that might be helpful, give me a ring." On the way out I pointed to the flower design on the door. "You didn't do that, did you?"

"Course I didn't. That was Clare."

"Does she still live here?"

He raised his eyes to the ceiling in an exaggerated expression of disbelief.

"Don't you read your own crappy newspaper? She's dead. She O.D.'d. Back in the spring."

Yes, of course, I did remember. It was the story Pete had covered, involving Dr Rachel Goodburn. It seemed more than a coincidence that this girl, Clare, had lived (and died) next door to Mike Stoddart, who had also died of an overdose. The police were obviously right; there was a drugs connection.

My desk was covered with badly written notes. I deciphered
them all, and two of them were bad news. The first was from
Mr Heslop; it said: "Shepherds Hill/Northdales merger
meeting. Seven p.m. Wednesday. This one is all yours."
Wonderful! Keith would be thrilled. The second was signed
P.S., which after a moment's puzzlement I realised was
Pete. It said: "See you in the Star, twelve-fifteen. Don't be
late." I thought about the plumber, about Keith, and about
the loo. A tension headache started at the back of my neck.

At ten to twelve I went slowly downstairs, still undecided
which appointment to keep, nervously jangling my car keys.
In the foyer, a woman of about fifty was pleading with our
elegant but stony-faced receptionist.

"Oh I know," she said, "I understand all about deadlines,
but my husband will be *so angry* if he finds out I was late –"
Her face was sad, pale, underlined by thirty-odd years of
striving not to make her husband angry. I didn't hear any
more.

"To hell with the loo!" I remarked to the surprised messenger, who happened to be passing. I put the car keys back
in my bag.

Pete had topped up the alcohol level in his blood and was
looking generally pleased with himself.

"I just scared the shit out of the headmaster of Shepherd's
Hill," he said. "I asked him for a comment on the fact that
he was employing ex-junkies to teach the young people
entrusted to his care."

The word "junkie" struck a raw nerve, and I said sharply,
"So what did he say?"

"Oh, he was ready with his little speech about the County
not having a laid-down policy at present on the employment
of ex-addicts – but it was a nice moment. I had him really
rattled."

"You just love it, don't you? Upsetting people."

"Of course. That's the fun part of the job."

"Oh, is it? So what's the bad part?"

He thought about it briefly. "Going through people's
dustbins for torn up love letters and other things, waiting in

79

the rain at railway-stations for people who have gone by car, getting kicked, punched in the face, and sworn at – having buckets of emulsion paint, potato peelings and much worse thrown over you – shall I go on?"

He looked amused, as if he were enjoying alarming me. I said, "Well, if people did all those things to you, I've no doubt you deserved it."

"Jesus! What have I done to offend you?"

I took a large sip of the gin and tonic I'd planned not to drink and tried to massage the pain away from the back of my neck.

"Actually, it isn't you. I've had an upsetting weekend. My son got involved in a drugs raid on a local pub. It seems he's been smoking pot with the Vicar's daughter."

He laughed. "Oh dear. Any charges?"

"No, but my husband seems to think it's all my fault because I work for the Herald instead of staying at home and washing the floors!" I instantly regretted saying this, because Pete shot me a sharp, inquisitive glance. People who have been unhappily married are always on the lookout for signs of marital discord in others.

"Kids are pretty good at getting themselves into trouble, whether their floors are washed or not," he said. "How did you get on with the photos?"

I shook my head. "No one's seen the two of them together. It was a waste of time."

He didn't look convinced. "Maybe."

"Do you know if the police arrested anybody?"

"No, they haven't. They haven't found the syringe yet, either – it's nose clips and spades down at the local tip even as we speak. They did make one interesting discovery though. They searched the hotel on Friday and found a camera and a set of keys to Stoddart's flat wrapped up in a Boots carrier bag in the wastepaper bin in the Conference Room."

"Oh. And what about the negatives?"

"No negatives."

I thought it over. "Mike Stoddart was killed on Tuesday night, the syringe turns up in the cheese on *Wednesday*, and on *Friday* the camera and keys are found in the Conference Room. What does that mean?"

"It doesn't mean anything to me, darling."

"Well, I think it's rather odd. I mean, it sounds as if the murderer keeps going back to the hotel and disposing of pieces of evidence. It has to mean that, doesn't it? They must empty the hotel wastepaper-baskets daily."

He thought about it and smiled indulgently. "For what it's worth, you could be right. Tell you what, Heslop's sending me up to the Clocktower to do a real hype-job on the place – you know, 'Tipping's Gourmet Crap Spot', that sort of thing. While I'm there I'll see if anybody can shed light on when the camera might have been dumped."

We drank in silence for a few moments.

"Have the police got any other leads?" I asked.

"Well, they're not so smitten now with the idea of a drugs connection, having hauled in everyone whoever came within inhalation distance of pot-smoke and drawn a blank. But on the other hand, no one's come up with a better suggestion."

"My son says they were asking if Mike Stoddart ever tried to push drugs to anyone, and my daughter tells me that he didn't."

"Your kids are full of tricks, aren't they? What does your husband do – read palms?"

I smiled. "Are they following up the note?"

"What note?"

"The one I saw on the message board."

"I don't think so. At the moment they're trying to track down where he went between leaving the hotel 'do' and snuffing it."

I moved suddenly and knocked over my empty tonic bottle. "The note! To M – 'Hickory Dickory Dock, the mouse ran up the clock –' Sylvester Munroe was staying in the Clocktower Room. I bet it was some kind of cryptic invitation for Stoddart to come up to his room! You should have seen the way he was looking at him –"

"What – are you suggesting Stoddart was *gay*? A gay killing? Christ, I hope not. I hate going into those gay bars. You've no idea –"

81

"I'll go and see Sylvester Munroe," I interrupted. "I can say I'm doing a follow-up on the Conference. It's only in Hudderston, and he did invite me to look him up when I was in the area."

Pete sat back and looked at me for a long moment. He seemed surprised. "You know, you amaze me. When you joined the paper I had you down as a wholemeal leek quiche and 'Women Against Everything' person, but I've got a suspicion that if we took a blood sample we'd find you've got quite a few red blood cells floating amongst the polyunsaturates and sugar substitute."

I thought, you're not far wrong about the quiches.

"I must go," I said. "Shopping."

"Wait. We're not finished with this Randall girl yet. I think we'll approach the mother though, before we see her again."

"*What?*"

"Yes. It's worth a try. Let's think how to go about it."

"Well –" No wonder he got things thrown at him. "There is a meeting at Shepherds Hill on Wednesday night about the merger with Northdales. Mr Heslop's assigned me to cover it. I know Mrs Randall is very strongly anti-merger, so she's bound to be there."

"Great! We'll catch her off guard. We can chat up a few teachers, too. *And* upset the headmaster," he added, with a wink. I got up to leave.

"Chris," said Pete. "When are we going to have this hypnotising session? I'm quite looking forward to it."

I was feeling cheerful for the first time since Saturday afternoon. I smiled and ignored the question.

8

I found an emergency plumbing firm located in Edgeborough Avenue, with the aid of a pin and Yellow Pages.
The advert said "No job too small – your service is our
pleasure", and the bored telephonist warned me that a call-
out after six would be very expensive. Fortunately the man
arrived before Keith, but he blocked our drive with his van,
and this was not a good start.

"What the hell happened to the other man?" demanded
Keith. "How much is this going to cost me?"

"Don't worry about it," I said frostily. "I'm quite prepared to pay for the privilege of not coming home in my
lunch-hour."

He took it fairly well, but then Monday night was cricket
practice night (or sitting around in the Club House drinking
warm lager and discussing absent team members night, more
likely), so he was in a fairly buoyant mood. The plumber
fixed the new cistern with the minimum number of black
finger-marks and chips to surrounding paintwork, and
sipped a cup of tea while I fainted over my cheque book.

"Give you my card, shall I, missus, though I don't know if
there's much point in it."

"Why not?"

"Oh I dunno. We're having our lease terminated, or
something. They're going to redevelop the site. Put up an
office-block, I reckon. I don't think the boss'll want to start
up again somewhere else. He's going on sixty."

I was surprised. "Edgeborough Avenue is mostly residential. I don't think they'd get permission for an office-block. I
was rather surprised to see firms like yours being allowed to
operate from there."

"Missus," he said, with a meaningful frown. "There's

ways and ways. I could tell you a thing or two!"

"Could you?"

He tapped his nose significantly. "Where there's a will, there's a way, and there's some with bigger wills than others, if you get my meaning." I didn't, but I tried not to let it show. "Anyway, it don't make no difference to the likes of me. I'll just be on the dole with the rest of the four million that aren't supposed to exist! Ta-ra, missus, thanks for the tea."

When he'd gone, I scooped a handful of hair and scum from the bath waste. It was too late because he'd probably already seen it, but I wanted to get it off my conscience.

The editorial offices of Shout About It, Sylvester Munroe's magazine, were located over a second-hand furniture showroom and in the shadow of a multi-storey car park. Now, I must admit to having led a fairly sheltered life, and it was with some trepidation that I ascended the dark staircase, and pushed open the door to Reception. I was debating with myself whether it would be best to avert my eyes from photographs on the walls, or study them brazenly with an attitude of mild disinterest or professional critique. In the event I was to be disappointed. The only pictures on the walls were of parrots, and the receptionist shared her area with a large rubber plant, a *monstera deliciosa*, and several ferns, all of them as sparkling fresh and green as they would have been in their natural habitat. The receptionist looked about Julie's age and was engaged in a giggly telephone conversation. (Actually, she was wearing a flying suit and had short, highlighted hair, and I looked at her twice to be one hundred per cent sure of her gender). She pressed a button on her intercom and mouthed something unintelligible at me. I heard the distant hum of a buzzer and presently the door marked "Editor" opened. Sylvester Munroe, clad in turquoise and black leather, and wearing an enormous diamond stud in his lapel, appeared.

"Ah, dear Mrs Martin," he exclaimed. "Such a delight to see you again so soon! Do come in."

He led me into his office, which contained another rubber

84

plant and an enormous desk. There *were* photographs here, but they were just ordinary pictures of ordinary-looking people smiling self-consciously at a camera. Most of them were signed. I recognised one extremely well-known comedian, who had scrawled "Good luck, Syl, dear," across his own forehead.

"Coffee, my dear?" enquired Sylvester, puffing water from a sprayer at the rubber plant.

"Yes, please. Do they like that?" I asked, indicating the plant.

"Love it! Wouldn't you, on a hot day? Two coffees, Terry," he added, into the intercom. "Say, before we start on the chat, do you know what's happened about that *dreadful* business? Have the police made an arrest?"

I hesitated. "They're following up several lines of enquiry, I believe. Have they been to see you since the Conference ended?"

Sylvester stopped puffing the sprayer and looked at me sharply.

"What makes you think they would, dear?"

"Well –" At that moment the door opened and to my surprise an extremely attractive girl entered. She was dressed in a brief white dress and thigh high boots of soft white leather adorned with swinging thongs. She put the tray of coffee down on Sylvester's desk, smiled a glossy smile at us both and left. I realised that he was watching me and that there was a look of glee on his face.

"My dear, your expression!" he exclaimed. "You were expecting a lovely little *fellow* in tasselled boots weren't you, dear? Well, that would be lovely, but most of them can't type and besides, we have to keep the advertisers happy!" This was obviously a long-standing joke, but I wasn't quite convinced of the logic behind it; Keith said everybody in advertising was bent. Anyway, I'd lost my temporary advantage. I decided to regain it.

"I gather you knew the late Michael Stoddart quite well."

His expression froze. He studied me through narrowed eyes, wondering if he could bluff his way out of it.

"Yes, I did know Mikey," he said at last, picking up a gold

85

pen and tapping it against his chin. "How did your people get on to that?"

"As a matter of fact I happened to read the note you left on the message board in the hotel. Why, is it supposed to be a secret?"

He leaned forward suddenly in the chair and dropped the pen heavily. His face, beaded with sweat, was close to mine. "Have you told the police about this?"

For a moment I felt hemmed in by the jungle plants and by the large figure of Sylvester Munroe. I couldn't make up my mind what would be the best answer, so I fell back on what always seemed a safe response: "No."

He got up and walked round the rubber plant, flicking imaginary dust off the leaves.

"Look," he said. "A man in my position has to be very careful. Even in these enlightened times, don't you think I've suffered my share of harassment? My God, you're a woman, you know what it's like to be always on the bottom of the heap. Forget about the note, dear, it's best forgotten about."

I nodded. "You don't want the police to know that you knew Mike and invited him to your room. All right, I can understand that, in the circumstances," I said, with a smile intended to be sympathetic. "So perhaps you could fill in some background – did you know him before he came to Tipping?"

"Yes, yes, that's right, dear." He seemed eager to please. "When I had my flat in Notting Hill. He moved in next door with some – well, undesirables. A nice lad, he was then, such a shame. He'd been brought up in a Children's Home, you know – several in fact. They chuck them out when they're of age, and sometimes the poor boys can't cope. He was about seventeen, I think, and I was in my music phase, so we're talking about – oh – ten years ago? Yes. Dear, dear."

"Was that when he started taking drugs?"

"Yes. My dear, I implored him not to! I mean, we all like a good time, don't we, but with heroin the pay-off's too great. He was such a bright boy too. I said to him, 'Get your life together, Mikey, work out what will *really* make you

86

happy! Take me, for instance, I'm a *communicator*. What I do best is *communicate* – so – Shout About It'! I mean, I could have gone down the same road as Mikey very easily, but I resisted it."

"Did he take your advice?"

Sylvester nodded proudly. "He was a bright boy – he knew I was right. He stayed at my place for a while and we had a little benefit 'do' for him – I used to be in a band, would you believe! Anyway, he went away to this clinic and got himself cured. He trusted me, you see, and with Mikey, that was something. Do you remember – yes, I'm sure you must – that saying about never trusting anyone over thirty? Well, with Mikey it was anyone over twenty. And I'm afraid he didn't care too much for the ladies. Probably something to do with his mother abandoning him. Very unforgiving, was Mikey."

I hesitated. "You mean he was –"

"No!" Sylvester looked hurt and angry. "Do you imagine I did what I did for him for carnal reward? My God, I expected better of you – you with your kind face!"

I blushed. "I'm sorry. It was a stupid remark." I tried to move the conversation on. "So then he went into teaching?"

"Well, to be honest, dear, we lost touch. You know how you do. Until last week. Of course teaching was the logical thing. Teaching or photography – that was his other love."

"Why do you say teaching was the logical thing?"

"Well, because he loved kids, simply adored them. I mean, he'd suffered so much at the hands of authority – doctors and social workers and so forth, all of them adult, of course. Everybody has to love something, dear."

"Of course. So he had a chip on his shoulder?"

"A big one."

I decided to cross more dangerous ground.

"And you ran into him at the Conference, just by chance. Why did you write him the note?"

He smiled. "You mean, why not just stroll up and chat to him? Well, my dear, I've had enough rebuffs in my life. He might not have wanted to know me. So I wrote the stupid note."

I picked up my coffee cup and drained it of its by now lukewarm contents.

"And did he meet you?"

Sylvester looked at his 'phone, probably willing it to ring and save him.

"I'm telling you the truth," he said, putting his hands on the desk, palms upward. "Because I don't want to hassle with the police. If I tell it to you as it really happened, will you keep mum about it?"

"Well –" Pete would say yes, of course, and look sincere. I said "Yes".

"Mikey came to my room just after ten. I had a hip flask of Scotch. We drank and we chatted – old times, new times. He was a good listener, you know. He'd got hard, mind, I could see that – upbringing will out, you know."

"And?"

"*And* he left, just after eleven. That was the last I saw of him until – well, you know when we all next saw him. I asked him to stay and have a sandwich or two – Scotch always makes me peckish – but he said he couldn't. He said he was meeting someone."

"Did he give you any idea who it might be?"

"Absolutely not. At that time of night I assumed it would be a lady, perhaps a married lady he didn't want to be seen with. Who knows? He was no great admirer of the fair sex, but there are urges that need to be satisfied, aren't there?" I opened my mouth to question him further, but he held up a hand. "Now, dear, it's no good asking me who or where because I just don't know. If I knew then I'd have to go to the police, but I don't. I don't really know anything. Now, if I hop along to the police-station and say, look boys, when you asked me did I hear anything funny under my window that night and I said no – which was true because I'd taken a sleeping-pill after the Scotch – what I should have told you was that Mikey was an old friend and came to my room for drinks – well, they're not going to believe me, are they? I mean, they're not kind and understanding, like you! They're going to start all their nasty tricks on me and it won't be fair because I don't know anything!" He stared down at his

88

fingernails as though they were in imminent danger of being ripped out.

"Mike left you just after eleven, and you didn't see him alive again?"

"No, dear. Oh God, you're not going to the police, are you?"

I stood up, adjusting the shoulder strap of my handbag.

"In your own interests, Mr Munroe, I think you should volunteer this information, but I have no plans to contact the police myself."

He put his head in his hands. "God, I'm drained!"

I was half way through the door when he called me back.

"What about your follow-up story on the Conference?"

"Thank you, Mr Munroe, you gave me what I came for."

Pete was not at his desk, but his 'phone rang and I answered it. A woman, who revealed herself through what sounded like clenched teeth to be his ex-wife, requested that he ring her. She was very sarcastic when I asked, out of habit, if he had her number, but she gave it to me anyway. I'd just finished writing it down when Pete appeared with a cup of coffee.

"I've just put the 'phone down on your wife," I said.

"Well done, I usually do that as well," he replied. "And she's my ex-wife, darling."

I handed him the note. He studied it absently, then said, "Will you do me a favour? Ring her back and say you're awfully sorry but I've been run over by the Council dustcart. Tell her they've got me in the operating theatre, trying to stitch my balls back on, using microsurgery. Helen would love that."

I tried not to laugh. "That isn't funny. It might be important. She was very insistent."

"She's always bloody insistent. She's married some other idiot now so she can go and insist to him, can't she?" He screwed up my note and tossed it accurately into the waste-paper-basket, adding aggressively. "What's it to you anyway?"

"Nothing. It's your life. I only wanted to tell you what

89

happened with Sylvester Munroe."

"Who's he?"

I gave an exasperated sigh, hitched my skirt up an inch or two and perched uncomfortably on the edge of a table.

"Sylvester Munroe is the editor of a gay magazine and I went to see him this morning – as we agreed – to find out if he was the author of the note I saw on the notice board the night Mike Stoddart – you do remember Mike Stoddart? – the night Mike Stoddart died. Well – he was." I paused for dramatic effect. "They were old friends apparently, on a purely platonic basis. They had a few drinks together in Sylvester's hotel room, and then Mike left. To meet someone, possibly a married lady."

Pete said, "You really have got very nice legs, Chris. Did you know that?"

"Oh, for Heaven's sake, you're not listening!" I pulled my skirt down angrily.

"Yes, I am. My eyes and ears work quite independently. You are saying that you have turned up new evidence in the Stoddart case, and I congratulate you, on both your initiative and your legs. I haven't been very fair to you and I'm sorry. I didn't take much more notice of you when you told me about the note than the police did. Am I forgiven?"

I was not used to being apologised to. "Yes. All right."

"The thing is," Pete said, "we're really obliged to inform the police about this. How do you feel about that?"

Another visit to Inspector Franks held little charm. I said, "Well, I promised Sylvester that I wouldn't go to the police, and suggested that he should go in voluntarily. I really don't like breaking my word."

"Oh dear. Conscience. All right, it's up to you. Let's stay one step ahead, shall we?" He leaned his chair dangerously far backwards, tempting gravity. "A lady, eh? I wonder. I was up at the Clocktower this morning. and I had a look at the fire escape. It would take a pretty strong woman – or man for that matter, to carry a dead body up there. Especially without making any noise. Do you think your friend Sylvester was telling the whole truth?"

"Yes, I do, actually." I thought over my interview with

90

Sylvester Munroe. "Yes, I'm sure he was."

"So – one possibility that presents itself is that Mike Stoddart was murdered by a very large woman, or I suppose, an average sized woman with the aid of a fairly large accomplice. Personally, *I* always avoid getting involved with very large women, or women with very large husbands, but I suppose there's no accounting for taste." At that moment he attempted to bring his chair back into its proper position, badly misjudged the manoeuvre and fell forward on to the desk, splitting open his lower lip.

I said, "Are you all right?"

"Yes, of course I am," he snapped, swallowing blood and checking his teeth for solidity. He obviously wasn't all right but would have died rather than say so. I know better than to trample on a man's macho image of himself, so I gave him a clean tissue and didn't laugh.

"Er – when you were at the Clocktower, did you ask them about rubbish collection?" I asked, tactfully changing the subject.

"No, darling, it hardly seemed the right moment. De Broux was like a cat on hot bricks, tiptoeing around after me, offering free drinks. There are times when it doesn't pay to upset people. But I did find out that he visits his London restaurant every Friday, so we could have a nose round then, while the cat's away."

He mopped blood from the desk top. Mr Heslop emerged from his office and gave Pete an astonished look: it was rare indeed to see a Herald reporter shedding blood over his work.

"Oh dear!" he exclaimed jauntily, glancing at me. "You two not getting on too well?"

Pete muttered something that sounded like "Get stuffed," into the tissue.

"We're going over the evidence in the Stoddart case," I said quickly.

"Really?" He turned to Pete. "You mean to say you've let yourself get taken in by her enthusiasm for that routine piece of unpleasantness? You do surprise me." He looked more amused than surprised. "Anyway, to more important things.

91

I've heard a little whisper."

"Get your hearing-aid checked, Bill," Pete said, rising from the desk. Mr Heslop's expression changed to a scowl as he watched his departing figure.

"He'll go too far with me one day, you know," he said. "He might not think much of this paper, but with his record I'd like to see him get a job anywhere else! I'll tell *you*, then, as you're involved. The Leisching development. Rumour has it that Edgeborough Avenue is going to go under the bulldozer."

"Edgeborough Avenue! But I thought that was zoned as residential."

"Where there's a will there's a way," remarked Mr Heslop, sounding off an echo in my memory. "See if you can get a quote from someone on the planning committee. There'll be months of wrangling about it. It'll run and run, Chris, wonderful stuff." He walked off, rubbing his hands.

It'll run and run, will it, I thought, looking down at my recently complimented legs. Like disputes over the closure of schools, statistics, advice columns, cheap non-drip gloss paint, cracks in a marriage that won't stay papered over. Back to normality with a bump.

9

There was a time when the designation "Councillor" in front of someone's name would have inspired in me a measure of awe, but over the past few months I had come to realise that they were, after all, only human. Perhaps even surgeons, queens, and company chairmen are, too; I haven't found out yet. Anyway, a few of Tipping's local Councillors were ordinary middle-aged women, like myself, who had decided that the best way they could keep their minds off their wrinkles (and their husbands') was to serve the community; most were people who would like to have made it in national, not to say international, politics, but were held back by being (in their words) "too nice", and all wished to leave their mark on the hearts and minds of Tipping's residents. Still, it was over-ambitious of me – inspired by my success with Sylvester Munroe – to approach Major Duncton that afternoon. I selected him because "everybody knew" that the Major was the only one on the Planning Committee who really mattered, but I knew it was a mistake as I drove between the banks of overgrown rhododendrons that brooded along the driveway to his house.

Major Duncton lived on a hilltop overlooking Tipping, so he could look down and admire its neatly planned streets (with or without carports), tasteful office-blocks harmonising with local architecture, and the green open spaces that had been thoughtfully provided for the use of residents on the closely-packed council estates. It did look good from up here; you couldn't see the vandalised wastepaper bins on the open spaces, or the bits of concrete fascia falling off the office blocks. On a clear day there was a view of the trees surrounding the Clocktower Hotel.

Parked outside the front door was Major Duncton's

Rover and his wife's Renault. I felt a twinge of alarm; there was no room for me to turn the car round and I'd have to reverse out down the long drive, something I wasn't good at. I tidied up my hair with my fingers and rang the doorbell. The woman who answered it was in her fifties, one of those women who hasn't had a waist for years and who wears a belt to remind her where it used to be. The passing years had drained her face of colour, and she wore heavy tortoiseshell spectacles studded with rhinestones which threw her pallor into relief. She confirmed that she was Mrs Duncton.

"The Major's out with the landscape gardener," she said, "but he'll be back in a moment. Won't you come in?"

She led me into what she called the drawing-room. It was cool, Persian-carpeted, and smelt of furniture polish and – oddly – mothballs. I only had time to examine the ivory carvings in the glass-fronted cabinet before Major Duncton appeared. He shook hands without smiling.

"We met at the Conference," I reminded him. He looked blank. "We've heard a rumour at the Herald that Edgeborough Avenue is being considered as a possible site for the Leisching complex."

"Have you indeed!"

"Is there any truth in it?"

He sighed. He reached into his pocket for a cigar and proceeded to light it. He didn't ask me if I minded.

"It's being considered along with other sites."

"But I thought Edgeborough Avenue was supposed to be strictly residential?"

"So it was, but the position is now under review."

"But –" My personal knowledge of Edgeborough Avenue emboldened me. "But I thought the houses there were considered to be of outstanding architectural merit?"

He sighed again. "You'll get your chance to object at the proper time Mrs, er –"

"Martin. And I don't want to *object*. I simply want to confirm the story with a few facts. I'm a reporter from the Herald," I reminded him.

He chuckled and seemed to be enjoying the cigar. "A reporter – yes, of course, you did say. Just that I'm used to

94

reporters being rather differently constructed. What happened – couldn't you get on the TOPS course you wanted?"

I took my breath in sharply.

"No need to be offended, Mrs Martin! If you were a little more experienced you'd know I never talk to the Press. An unnecessary waste of time. Things run along quite smoothly without being reported by the media. A lot more smoothly, as a matter of fact. Proper announcements will be made at the correct time and those concerned can have their say then." He might have added "For all the good it'll do them".

"I see – but this is a big development and concerns the whole community really – I mean –" I was defeated.

"Yes, of course, it does," he replied soothingly, releasing a great cloud of fragrant cigar smoke. "And I – we, in the Planning Committee, will look at all aspects and come to the decision which is best for the whole community. Now that's all I have to say on the matter." He sank into a large leather armchair and looked disapprovingly at the highly polished small table next to him. "Ruth!" he roared. "Ashtray!"

Ruth came at a run and I left. As I crossed the driveway to my car, she called after me fearfully, "Will you be able to get out all right? The Major's only just had that little ornamental wall built over there –"

I looked at the little ornamental wall with horror. It curved beautifully round the corner of the drive and had built-in niches for plants. I kept my eye on it all the time as I reversed. It was only when I'd completed the turn and looked back at the still intact wall with triumph, that I realised I'd completely flattened a small bed of begonias and lobelia on the other side of the drive. I didn't have the courage to go back and apologise.

I thought about the Edgeborough Avenue affair as I drove back to the Herald. Why was it all right for Leisching Pharmaceuticals to put up a giant office block on Edgeborough Avenue when it had not been all right for Keith and me to convert one floor of one house into an office? How could buildings possess outstanding architectural merit one year, and not possess it a few years later? I wondered if Keith

95

would take it personally when I told him; probably not; he hadn't had to endure the character derogation that went with Major Duncton's pronouncement. I didn't feel sorry about the begonias.

Predictably, Keith was more upset about my Wednesday evening assignment than about office-blocks being built on Edgeborough Avenue. I shouldn't have used the word "assignment", of course; a stint of baby-sitting or a Tupperware party would have been O.K.

"We never do anything together these days," he complained. "You used to walk round the garden with me in the evenings, spraying the greenfly."

"Well, that was because I'd been in the house all day and it was a relief to have someone to talk to. You never answered anyway."

"I did!"

"Yes. Sort of ums and ahs."

"Well, I'm tired in the evenings."

"Not too tired for cricket practice at least once a week."

"I need the exercise. Do you want me to have a coronary or something?"

He went off up the garden to stab the compost heap with a fork before I could answer. In any case, I'd lost the battle over his devotion to cricket years ago.

I arrived at Shepherds Hill early, I thought, but the car park was already full and cars were encroaching menacingly on the playing field. People advanced on the auditorium in noisy, animated groups, some carrying sheafs of the papers we'd all been sent by various interested parties in the dispute over the merger plans. Of course, it goes without saying that everyone present that evening was against the scheme; no one gives up a pleasant couple of hours in the garden to go out and congratulate the County Council on the excellent job it is doing, and there's nothing like a good protest meeting to convince the population of a small town that democracy works. I saw Ernst, our photographer, strolling in sullenly, with his equipment. He didn't say anything to me, but then I didn't expect him to. A man of few words, was Ernst, and none of them wasted on lady reporters.

It was standing-room only inside, and I shouldered my way to the front, remarking "Press" with a confident smile to anyone who looked like arguing. The County Education Officer opened the meeting with the very unwise statement that we shouldn't be thinking of the merger as a cutback; it was nothing more than a light pruning, a reshaping of the framework through which flowed the sap of – I didn't get the rest of this, because I couldn't remember the shorthand outline for "framework" in time. Anyway, it didn't matter, because the assembled protesters were all consumers who knew only too well that when a washing-machine manufacturer announces "will not tangle your clothes", what he actually means is "for God's sake don't ever put tights, bras and pyjama cords in the same wash". People leapt to their feet, shouting "Rubbish!", and a woman in St. John's Ambulance uniform told everybody repeatedly that her father hadn't fought and died in the Netherlands so that his grandchildren should receive an inferior education. I got down a fair amount of this, but all the while I kept one eye on Elaine Randall, who was in the front row amongst the most vociferous protesters.

The meeting broke up in noisy disarray, and I somehow managed to push my way out with the teachers and officials, arriving at the front of the building out of breath and slightly dishevelled.

"What the hell's going on?" demanded Pete. "I had to park a mile away."

Mr Patience was talking to the County Education Officer. He saw Pete and hastily turned his back. I had been thinking of asking for his reaction to the meeting but decided I'd already got so much material it wasn't worth the effort in the circumstances. Pete spotted a group of teachers emerging from the school and we approached them.

"Seems like a fun way to spend your evening," he remarked in a friendly way.

"Certainly is." The teacher who answered was in his late thirties, dressed in an out-of-fashion corduroy jacket with leather patches on the elbows.

"We're from the Herald," said Pete, "doing a story on a colleague of yours. Mike Stoddart."

"Yes? Didn't really know him. Kept himself to himself. Sorry."

"Surely there must have been talk in the staffroom?" The three of us walked along together, slowly.

"There's always talk in the staffroom, not much of it about teaching!"

Pete said, "Well, you must have all been pretty shocked by what happened?"

"That's fair comment." The teacher turned as if casually to look back at Mr Patience, who was still in conversation with the official.

"Look," went on Pete. "If you tell us anything, it'll be in confidence. We're from the local paper, but if you get the boys from the nationals in here they won't be worried about reputations and confidentiality. And this could turn into a big story, as you'll appreciate – murder, drugs and so forth."

"Well –" The teacher hesitated. "Matter of fact, he wasn't particularly liked. Didn't mix socially. Kids loved him which, well, I suppose it meant he was a good teacher. Yes, I'll give him that. But he was a real loner. Whatever he did in his private life he kept it to himself." He hesitated again. "When he came here about a year ago, I knew someone who taught at the school in Brighton where he was before."

"And?"

"Well, it's only a rumour, of course, but the story is that he left suddenly because he was having an affair with a school-governor's wife."

Pete raised his eyebrows and nodded appreciatively.

"Any more?"

"Well, I could give you the 'phone number of this chap in Brighton, if you like."

"Thanks, that would be a big help."

I nudged Pete. "There's Elaine Randall."

"You go," he said. "I'll catch you up."

I hopped over a flower-bed, catching the stiletto heel of my sandal in soft earth, and ran after the matching figure of Elaine Randall. Her legs were a lot longer than mine, and so were her husband's. The Randalls were still talking high-spiritedly to another couple about the "next stage of the battle".

"Excuse me," I said, panting slightly. "I don't know if you remember me – we met at the Conference, Mrs Randall. I'm Chris Martin from the Herald."

"Oh yes, I do remember." She smiled behind the glasses. "I'm so glad you were at the meeting. It did go well. I don't see how they can go ahead with this frightful plan when there's so much opposition, do you?"

I got out my notebook and wrote down her views, making appropriately sympathetic noises. Pete joined us unobtrusively.

I said, "Mrs Randall, on a slightly different topic, we're doing a story about the Shepherds Hill teacher who died, and I believe your daughter Sari knew him?"

"Sarah?" She looked surprised. "Well, yes, I suppose she did know him. She seemed to quite like him."

I don't know what answer I'd expected, but it wasn't quite this one. I struggled to choose the right words.

"Would that have been – did she know him through some form of out-of-school activity?"

She looked even more puzzled. "I'm not quite sure what you mean. She knew him through me."

"Through you, Mrs Randall?" Pete put in quickly, with a deceptively pleasant smile.

"Yes." Suddenly her face changed. She flushed, looked from one to the other of us, and then across to her husband, who had walked on ahead. "I knew him because of my involvement in local conservation. He was a most helpful young man. I mean, I can't imagine how he can have got mixed up in such a terrible thing. Is it true what they're saying, that it was all something to do with drugs? Well, of course, I only knew him as a photographer, and I mean, not at all, really –"

Pete interrupted her by placing his hand on her arm.

"Mrs Randall, there are times when we all do things which are indiscreet. Sometimes we end up in trouble we never imagined. It's always best, if you can, to clear problems up

99

before they go from bad to worse."

Elaine Randall's face was by now bright scarlet. She stared at Pete as though transfixed.

"Elaine!" The voice of her husband broke the spell. "Come *on*! We're going to be hours getting out of this lot!"

"I'm sorry – we must go – we haven't eaten yet. My husband –"

She sprinted after her husband, like a hare escaping from a hound.

"What was all that about?" I asked Pete.

"Well, don't you see? It was Mrs Randall herself who was having an affair with Stoddart, not her daughter. He must have had a penchant for older women, not kids at all. Maybe it had something to do with his mother abandoning him – I don't know, I'm not into psychiatry –"

"Oh, you can't be serious! Mrs Randall is just an ordinary sort of woman, like – well, like me, I suppose."

He raised his eyebrows. "What do you expect, for Christ's sake? Are you saying you're completely immune to bronzed biceps?" I didn't answer, and he laughed. "This is looking good. She's a big woman, your Mrs Randall. I can just imagine her climbing up the fire escape with young Mike slung over her shoulder. He'd probably told her they were through, and –"

"Oh, this is really silly. I'm going home," I said. "I'll bet there's a perfectly reasonable explanation for her knowing him and not wanting to talk about it."

"Yes. Sex."

I rummaged angrily through my bag for my car keys.

"You've got a very low opinion of women," I said.

"I haven't! Men, women – it's all the same. The two commonest motives for doing anything are sex and money. Take your pick."

"I see. You're saying that nothing else matters except sex and money. Doesn't say much for you, does it? What's *your* motivation?"

For a moment, he seemed to be considering the question seriously. Then he grinned. "Why don't you offer me both, see which I accept?"

This probably had the desired effect. I blushed.

"Come for a drink," he said. "We'll discuss it further."

"No, thank you." Then, because I had sounded prim, I added, "I don't want to go home smelling of alcohol. It wouldn't be appreciated."

"All right. Come back to my flat instead, have a look at my unfinished novels."

There is a right way of dealing with this sort of suggestion, a casual, sophisticated way that leaves the suggester knowing that you are a woman of the world, haven't taken offence and didn't take it seriously anyway, but aren't to be trifled with. I didn't know what that way was. I got into the car.

"Goodbye, Chris, have sweet, innocent dreams," said Pete.

On the way home I thought a lot about Elaine Randall. When I'd first met her at the Clocktower I'd immediately empathised with her. I didn't quite share her concerns, but I did understand her motivation, and it wasn't sex. Sex wasn't my motivation either, and nor was money. Pete was making the mistake of judging others by his own standards. All the same, she was a large woman and she had looked very shaken. There had to be a reason for that.

10

I awoke on Friday morning to an unaccustomed feeling of well-being. Mr Heslop had complimented my piece on the merger meeting, and yesterday after coming out of the hairdresser's with my new natural-look perm, a van driver at a zebra crossing had smiled at me and looked at my legs. Why the hairstyle should have made him look at my legs, and why I was almost as pleased about it as I was about my success with the story, I can't say, but there it is. I peered at myself through the dust and finger-marks on my bedroom mirror and tried on eyeliner and a little blusher. The 'phone rang downstairs. Keith shouted, "Somebody answer that, I'm late," and the front door slammed. I stood up, noting that if I breathed in my stomach was almost flat, and went downstairs to answer it.

"I hope I didn't get you out of bed," said Pete.

"No, you didn't." Richard ran past, looking pale and tired and worried. His tie was undone. "Do your tie up!" I called.

"I'm not wearing one," said Pete. "As a matter of fact I'm not even wearing a shirt. I'm wearing an old tee-shirt and jeans. We're going down to Brighton, you and me, to see Mike Stoddart's ex-ladyfriend. Bring a bikini and bucket and spade, if you like."

"Oh! I thought we were going to the Clocktower today."

"We'll go there on the way. Look, I thought you'd be impressed I managed to get hold of the address *and* arrange for us to have a day out at the seaside in this weather."

"All right, I'm impressed. Shall I be ready in half an hour?"

"No. Twenty minutes," he said, and hung up.

I went back upstairs and threw open the bedroom window. Already the air was sharp with the scent of dehydrating foliage and the sun's heat was strong on my arm. Julie lent me a white cotton sun-top and I put on dark glasses. A day at the seaside. I looked about ten years younger – only because the glasses hid the wrinkles round my eyes, but an illusion is an illusion, and Heather may have had a point when she said you're only as old as you let yourself look.

Pete said, "I like your hair," and smiled appreciatively as if he meant it. I was surprised he'd noticed, because it had taken Keith most of the evening to comment. We drove to the Clocktower with brilliant sun and deep shadow deluge-ing alternately through the open sun-roof. There was no other traffic on the road, and the hotel car park was almost deserted. We parked under a tree, then followed a signpost for "Deliveries only". It led into the service yard at the rear of the hotel, from which the fire-escape climbed bleakly to the Clocktower Room. Suspended from the landing beneath the topmost window was a limp black shape. It was a frilly negligee, unmoving in the still hot air. Pete and I exchanged amused (and in my case slightly unnerved) glances. A young man in white overalls unbuttoned to the waist lounged on a box in the corner of the yard. He was eating a Mars bar, smoking a cigarette and listening to his Walkman. His eyes were closed. Pete deftly removed the Mars bar from his outstretched hand. He jumped as if awoken from a deep sleep.

"What's up? Where did you spring from?" he exclaimed, snatching back the Mars bar. "I'm on my break!"

"That's all right, we just want to ask you a couple of questions," said Pete.

He looked immediately suspicious. "I don't think I answer questions. You're from the Hotel Guide, aren't you? Oh God!" He threw down the half-smoked cigarette and stamped on it, then immediately regretted the action. "Hey, I'm on my break – Mr De Broux says we can smoke out here."

"No, we're not from the Hotel Guide. We're here about the little incident you had the other week," Pete said, nod-ding towards the fire-escape. "Were you here then?"

103

"Yes, but –" He looked from one to the other of us, but particularly at my sun-top. "Who are you anyway? You look more like the Hotel Guide than the police. I've never seen police going round dressed like that, except on the telly." He seemed pleased with his ability to distinguish real detectives from the fictional variety.

I said, "We're not the police either. I was here for the Conference, for the Tipping Herald. I'm the one who found the body."

"I *can't* talk to you then! Mr De Broux sent us a memo saying it's instant dismissal for anyone who talks to the press. I *need* this job. I was unemployed for –"

"O.K.," said Pete. "No names, nothing. Just a couple of routine questions, a tenner for you and we're gone. What d'you say? Deal?"

He looked doubtful. "What are the questions?"

Pete took out his notebook and looked at it.

"Do you know anything about the cleaning and rubbish disposal system here?" The boy nodded. "O.K., so tell me when do they normally clean the rooms and empty the wastepaper-baskets?"

"Oh, every morning between nine and twelve. The guests are usually out then – when we have any."

"And would that apply to the wastepaper-basket in the Conference Hall?"

"No. The bins in the reception areas and the downstairs loos and the Conference Hall are emptied at night and put out with the kitchen rubbish. Mr De Broux is very particular about that. He won't have the guests coming down for their fancy breakfasts and finding full ash-trays and bins." He lit another cigarette and inhaled gratefully, as though on a life-support machine.

"In that case," persisted Pete, "what time of night does the kitchen and reception area rubbish get put out?"

"About eleven-thirty, after the restaurant and the bar close."

I said, "So thinking back to last week, to the night of the, er, incident, anything put in the Conference Room bin after eleven-thirty that Tuesday night, or during Wednesday,

104

would be there until it got put out with the kitchen rubbish at about eleven-thirty p.m. on the Wednesday?"

"Yes, that's right."

"So how could something put in the bin in the early hours of Tuesday still be there on Friday morning?"

He shook his head. "It couldn't. Mr De Broux was fussing around like an old hen, both mornings before the Conference started, checking everything. I know, 'cos he dragged me round with him. The bin in the Conference Room was empty both mornings."

I frowned. "In that case the bin in the Conference Hall ought to have been empty when the police got there on Friday –"

"Ah. No." The boy shook his head. "There was a bit of a to-do here, after the Conference finished on Thursday. A guy was sacked –"

"Mario," I interrupted.

"Christ! How do you know these things?" he exclaimed, awestruck by the supernatural powers of the press. "Well, Mario was sacked and we were short-handed – and then there was a union meeting to discuss unfair dismissal. That was Thursday afternoon, right after the Conference. Mr De Broux was cursing something rotten and he just locked the door on the Conference Room and nobody touched it again. We'd've done it Friday morning, but the police came –"

Pete produced a ten-pound note from his wallet and put it in the hand that held the Mars bar. "Thanks. You've been a big help."

The boy eyed us both suspiciously. "I still say those are bloody funny questions for a newspaper. You sure you're not doing some sort of hygiene survey for the Hotel Guide?"

"Don't worry about it," said Pete. "Plug yourself back into your music, close your eyes, and when you open them again we'll be gone. Just like magic."

As we walked back to the car, I said, "It was almost certainly one of the delegates who put the camera and keys in the bin, and they did it during the Thursday session."

"Yes," agreed Pete. "And it was almost certainly Elaine Randall!"

* * * * *

Brighton shimmered under one of those hot white mists which severs a seaside town from the rest of the world, almost from reality. The heat had subdued even the naked brown children on the beach, and bubbled up the tarmacked pavement in black beads of sweat. Pete handed me a street map and an address, and we negotiated our way through wealthy suburbs where most roads were labelled "Private – no access except for residents", and anyone driving anything less expensive than a Ford Granada was viewed with suspicion. You could almost smell the money; it was a pity the residents couldn't smell the ozone they'd paid such a premium to be near, for fear that the opening of a window would set off an alarm in the police station. The address we'd been given belonged to a sprawling colonial-style bungalow guarded by two stone lions. There was a warning notice about guard dogs, but I didn't see any. Pete rang the doorbell.

"We've called to see Mrs Jordan-Booth," he said to the maid of indeterminate nationality who answered it.

"Not here," she said, keeping the chain on the door.

"We've come all the way down from London, darling. Is there any way of contacting her?"

"Sure." The maid consulted her watch. "Now she be at Duke's Head. O.K.?"

"Is that far?"

The maid gave us rather confused directions involving a level-crossing and two churches, and we set off. Pete drove too fast, as usual, and we never found the second church, but suddenly there was the Duke's Head. I said, "This can't be right." It was a large, modern pub on the edge of a Council estate, all glaring new brick and garish mock-traditional signboards. I've seen more tasteful public loos. In the car park were a mini-van, several motor-cycles and an old Ford Capri with enormous tyres and no glass in the back window.

Pete put the Krooklok on his car and we went inside. It was a spacious, characterless bar, with a salt and pepper pot on every table to make you feel you ought to order something to eat. The barman wore a bow tie and a bored expression.

"A gin and tonic, a vodka tonic, and whatever you're having," said Pete. "Would you happen to know a Mrs Jordan-Booth?"

The barman nodded and pointed over to a window table. A woman sat with her back to us, alone except for a cigarette and a whisky glass. Her hair was blonde, sloping neatly into the nape of her neck, and beneath it several rows of pearls glistened milkily. We collected our drinks and approached. She turned to look at us, and there followed one of those awful moments when you have to pretend not to be shocked. The face of the woman did not belong to the hair. She must once have been beautiful, but now her skin was taut over high cheekbones, giving her a perpetual smile, and the lips and eyes were painted in – with extreme skill – but still, painted in like those of a doll. I guessed she was the wrong side of fifty.

"Hi," said Pete. "Mind if we join you? We're just down for the day. Do you live round here?"

"I do, darling, but I don't wish to be reminded of it when I'm enjoying myself." Her voice was a low drawl, sexy, I suppose. She drew deeply on a pungent-smelling French cigarette, and her gaze poured over Pete like double cream on a strawberry. "Sit where I can see you. I just love a new face!" We sat down and she leaned back elegantly in her chair, the hand that held the cigarette chunky with diamonds.

"So, what goes on in these parts?" asked Pete, smiling his disarming smile.

Mrs Jordan-Booth sipped her whisky. "Absolutely nothing goes on around here, not for those who are still half-alive. That's the trouble, darling. Most of the people round here have been dead for years and no one's noticed!" She thought this a great joke, and we laughed as though it was. "Best pub in Brighton, this," she added, looking admiringly at the acres of plastic seating and twinkling arcade games.

Pete took out his notebook. "That's interesting. We're from a London newspaper, researching a piece on English

107

seaside resorts."

"Oh, are you really? How awfully exciting! Do you know, that's not what I'd've guessed you did for a living. Especially not you, darling," she added, touching Pete's hand. "You're so awfully photogenic I'd've said show business was more your line. Male model, perhaps."

"You haven't seen my passport photo," remarked Pete, slightly taken aback.

"Nobody understands what it means to be photogenic," mused Mrs Jordan-Booth. "I was a model you know, just after the war, when it was a real profession. My, those were the days –" She sighed, dreamy-eyed. "I could tell you a tale or two –"

And she did. She talked through three double whiskies without slurring a syllable. She told us about her suitors and the parties, and how she'd never known what it was like to go to bed before dawn. She'd appeared on cat-walks in London and Paris and New York, breakfasted at Tiffany's and dined at the Ritz – and now the high spot of her day was opening time at the Duke's Head. She didn't seem bitter, just bored; she'd replaced the fresh glow of youth with the timeless glitter of diamonds, and taut muscle with expensive plastic surgery, and maybe she no longer knew the difference. Maybe it didn't matter. Maybe all that mattered was having someone look at the result. After three gins, nothing much mattered to me. While Pete was at the bar, Mrs Jordan-Booth said, "I hope you appreciate your colleague. He's a *darling*, and such a good listener! They're not all like that, you know."

"No," I said, leaning forward conspiratorially. "Especially not when he's your husband!"

"Oh, and *that's* the truth!" she replied in delighted sisterhood.

Pete put the drinks on the table. Mrs Jordan-Booth downed hers with one flamboyant gesture, and announced that her taxi would be here in a few minutes. "And I haven't told you anything you wanted to know about Brighton," she added. "Still, lunch ready, you know, and Bernard will be expecting me. Hello Sid!" Sid clapped her on the shoulder chummily as he passed by with a bottle of Daddies' sauce. Several of Sid's friends, at a nearby table, called out, "Watcha, Val!"

"Do you know," said Pete, "I've just remembered. I used to know this guy who lived round here. Mike Stoddart's his name. He's a teacher. Wouldn't happen to know him, would you?"

For the first time since we'd met her, Mrs Jordan-Booth looked lost for words.

"Surely he wasn't a *friend* of yours?" she asked finally.

He shrugged. "Acquaintance."

She sat down again, picking up her empty glass and studying it with disappointment.

"Odd coincidence, actually," she said. "Bernard's governor of a school where he used to teach. I got to know him rather well." She glanced at me, and instinctively I gave her a smile of encouragement. "Yes, *rather* well. He was a good-looking young man, and I'm very fond of good-looking young men. Turned out to be a right bastard, though, if you'll excuse my French."

Pete raised his eyebrows. "What, Mike? Really?"

"Yes. Wanted money. Very nasty."

I leaned across the table more heavily than I intended, nodding sympathetically. The movement made me feel slightly dizzy. "You don't mean – he wanted money not to tell your husband?" I asked.

"Oh no! Goodness, Bernard doesn't give a hoot what I do! Not a hoot, as long as I'm discreet. We have a very understanding marriage. No, it wasn't that. It was the photographs."

Pete said sharply, "What photographs?"

"Taxi, Val, love!" shouted someone at the door.

"What photographs?" insisted Pete.

"Photographs of me, darling. In the nuddy. Kept my figure, don't you think? Young Michael took super photos, but it wouldn't do, would it, having copies all round the school. Bernard nearly had a heart attack –"

"Come on, love, meter's running!"

Both Pete and Mrs Jordan-Booth stood up at the same

109

time. He wasn't smiling now, and he put a detaining hand on her arm.

"Did your husband pay money to Stoddart to get those photos back? Was that why he left Brighton?"

For a moment she looked surprised, and I think she knew we'd been deceiving her, but she shut the knowledge away quickly behind the façade of gaiety.

"Yes, darling, and I popped them away in my album. Toodle – oo!"

We watched her go, in almost open-mouthed silence. Pete grabbed my hand and held it up in a boxer's victory gesture.

"We've done it! We've cracked it. He blackmailed Mrs Jordan-Booth and got away with it and he tried the same trick on Elaine. You and your social worker friend were right about there being negatives missing. Elaine was not only a jilted lover, she was a blackmail victim – I don't think you could have a clearer motive than that."

I closed my eyes for a moment. I'd had far too much gin. "So – what now?" I asked.

"Well, right now, I feel like giving you a big kiss, but I suppose you'd object to that." He studied me for a while, then finished his drink. "Anyway, what we do now is put it all together. We need a statement from the social worker about the negatives, we need to find out where the lovers met – my guess is Rampton's Hollow – and we need to find out where she got the heroin that killed him. I admit that's a bit of a puzzle. You wouldn't think she'd have that kind of contact. Still, a woman scorned and all that – she must have seen the old needle holes while they were writhing all over one another. It's open and shut, darling. And then it'll be a front page exclusive – hello Daily Mirror for me and hello weekend for two in Paris for you."

"Paris – for two – for me?"

"Yes. A romantic weekend in Paris with your husband. Isn't that what you'd like?" He put his glass down and looked at me, smiling exactly the same smile that had charmed Mrs Jordan-Booth, Elaine Randall, the girls outside the school and numerous others into saying more than they intended.

I smiled back. "Well, we're off to Portugal in October for our second honeymoon."

"Oh really? In my experience people go on second honeymoons in a last desperate attempt to stay out of the divorce courts."

I looked away, out of the window. I hoped this wasn't true but I didn't comment. Mrs Jordan-Booth's hand waved regally from the window of the departing taxi.

"There's one thing I don't understand," I said. "What on earth does Mrs Jordan-Booth see in this place?"

"Well." Pete looked out of the window. Sid and his friends were strolling across the car park giving the thumbs up sign in Mrs Jordan-Booth's direction. "I think it's because *here*, she's still somebody."

We bought fish and chips and pickled onions with a liberal dressing of salt, and ate them on the sea front. It was easy, under the seductive influence of sun and gin, not to worry about sodium and cholesterol levels, or anything else for that matter. My mind drifted pleasantly and effortlessly like the haze on the softly-lisping waves. I shouldn't have had the third and fourth gins. Pete suggested a walk on the beach to clear our heads, and we took off our shoes and strolled across the warm sand towards the sea.

"All right," he said, suddenly and firmly clasping my hand. "Confession time. Why does someone as attractive and intelligent as you take a job like this?"

"Oh God! Flattery!" I exclaimed, fearing a send-up, though I had been thinking how nice I must look with the new hairstyle and the start of a suntan.

"And it won't get me anywhere? I'd still like an answer."

"Why?"

"Well, perhaps because I think you're attractive and intelligent. Or is that sexist and offensive?"

I couldn't read his expression behind the dark glasses.

"I don't know. I don't know why you keep thinking of me as a feminist. I took this job because it was a childhood ambition of mine to be a reporter. Now laugh."

"I'm not laughing."

111

We'd reached the sea, and let it wash over our ankles.

"Someone told me you once had a novel published," I said. "Why did you give up writing?"

"You've obviously never read the novel! It was naive and irrelevant. Anyway, I didn't give up writing, I just stopped finishing things. Probably something to do with not believing in anything that isn't seventy per cent proof and bottled in Poland. I asked you over the other night to take a look at my unfinished novels and you wouldn't come!"

He was still holding my hand and I released it quickly.

"Of course I wouldn't come! I'm a respectable married woman and I can't be enticed to men's flats to read their unfinished novels!"

He laughed. "All right. I'll give you the finished one then and you can read it in the privacy of your own home. But I warn you, you won't like it."

"I don't know how you can be so sure."

"Actually, I can't be where you're concerned. I'm still trying to get to the real you." He reached out and pulled the strap down over my shoulder, and for a stunned moment I thought he was furthering this ambition. "You're burning, darling. Don't worry, I've got some sun-cream in the car."

When we got back to the car he opened the glove compartment and a lot of things fell out – maps, garage repair bills, an empty vodka bottle. He handed me a plastic tube of sun-cream. It had exceeded its "sell by" date by two years, and was the wrong stuff anyway, but I didn't say anything. I pulled down my shoulder straps and began smoothing in the cream. He watched me.

"Would you like me to do that?" he asked.

It was quiet in the car, just the distant murmur of waves and sleepy insects. My ankles still glowed from the cool embrace of the sea. I would have liked Pete to touch me; I would have liked to feel his fingers move slowly over my skin, trace down across the contours of my breast. I blushed and shook my head, and the tube fell through my slippery grip on to the floor. Pete leaned over and retrieved it. As he handed it back to me, he said, "I just want you to know how

112

sorry I am."

"What for?"

"For your being a respectable married woman. It really is an awful pity. On such a lovely day. And in Brighton."

I looked at him sharply, and he winked.

11

I felt very guilty about that moment on Brighton sea front. It had been the gin, of course, the gin and the heady atmosphere of success on the Stoddart story, but all the same it was just as well Pete and I wouldn't be working together much longer. There was nothing wrong in feeling mildly attracted to someone, and nothing wrong in allowing that person to flirt with you a little, but you had to know when to stop. Clearly that moment was now, before anyone started taking things seriously.

We had large steaks for dinner on Saturday evening, after which I went up to bed with a glass of Alka-Seltzer, and Keith poured himself a brandy and sat down to watch the late-night horror double bill. If there wasn't too much screaming he'd probably fall asleep on the sofa. I've never understood some people's passion for watching terrified women being devoured by bloodstained rats; time and tedium are well able to devour both men and women quite horrifically without the aid of rats, and one has to watch it every day.

Anyway, there was Pete's novel on the dressing-table. I opened it where somebody had opened it before, at the scene where Nick (one of the two central characters) had his first sexual experience with an au pair girl called Trudi on Shepherds Bush Green. I shut it again quickly. It was very explicit. Nick spent a lot of time having sexual experiences and agonising over them afterwards, usually to Marty, who'd had an incestuous relationship with his sister, over which he quite understandably agonised constantly. In the end Marty severed his head on a railway-line in Kent, and this was described in gruesome detail. I almost stopped reading at this point, but my eye was caught by the description of the girl who now entered Nick's life. She sounded very much like Pete's ex-wife Helen. From here on the story became a romance, poignantly told, of how Nick was saved from slow self-destruction by the love of this girl. It ended with a touching little scene where the young lovers threw their last few pound notes in frail, fluttering succession off Westminster Bridge, and vowed to love one another for ever or until separated by death. I closed the book and put it under my pillow. Poor Pete, I thought, if you really believed love wouldn't cost you anything.

I woke early, determined to do something about the front garden. Keith had mysteriously found his way into bed beside me some time after television close-down, and I eased out from under the covers without waking him. Clad in old jeans and stout gloves I prepared to grapple the bindweed from the roses. He'd be pleased – no amazed – when he saw the result. I'd reckoned without Mrs Taylor, though. She was best avoided unless you had half-an-hour to spare. I dodged optimistically behind a dwarf conifer.

"Hello!" she called cheerfully. "Lovely day again!"

"Yes, isn't it?" I replied, removing the gloves reluctantly and walking towards her.

"Did you have a nice day out on Friday with your friend?" she asked, eyes gleaming.

"Er – well, it was a working trip, actually."

"Oh, must be nice to have a job like that. Where were you off to?"

"Brighton." I could see her brain responding to the connotations of that and carried on quickly. "What about you – I hope you made the most of the nice weather."

"Oh, well –" To my dismay she put down her Mail on Sunday and leaned against the gate-post. "I was up at the doctor's again, I'm afraid." She then proceeded to give me a long account of her hot flushes and the hormone-replacement therapy she'd been receiving, ending with the cheering comment that I'd got it all to come.

"Oh yes. Oh dear," I said, which is about all you can say.

"Anyway, I'm going to have to change my doctor soon. I don't know what I'm going to do."

"Oh? Why's that?"

"Well, I only went over to their practice because I'd heard Dr Rachel was so good with these things, I mean it's not convenient for me unless I have the car. So if they're going there's no point in my travelling all that way, is there? Do you know I'll have changed doctors three times in the last five years? I suppose you're allowed."

"Sorry – did you say the Goodburns are leaving?" I asked, surprised.

"Well, that's what I heard. My husband's niece knows one of the secretaries. Dr John's a lot older than Dr Rachel, retirement age, I should say, even though he still looks all right. But it takes its toll, doesn't it? Did you know he was married before? He's got a daughter, lives somewhere locally. A funny set-up, if you ask me, two doctors married to each other. Rather like film stars marrying film stars, I suppose –" No doubt she would have explained her train of thought at length, but I stopped her.

"Do I understand you to mean they're *both* leaving the practice?"

"Yes. Selling up and retiring to Portugal, so I heard. Mind you, she's been going right off lately, if you ask me. Same age as me, she is," she added, giving me a meaningful nudge. "What's that they say – 'physician heal thyself', or something? Well – do you know Mrs Fry from Lansdown Road? Apparently she prescribed her quite the wrong dosage of her blood-pressure pills and if it hadn't been for the chemist –"

After she'd gone, I went inside and made a note on my message pad, beneath the reminder to collect Keith's dry-cleaning, to call and see the Goodburns and find out if there was any truth in the rumour. Richard came downstairs while I was in the kitchen, still in his pyjamas, and he looked so awful I gave up the idea of gardening to make breakfast for him.

"What's up?" I asked.

"Carolyn won't speak to me."

116

"Why?"

He obviously didn't want to answer.

"It hasn't got anything to do with your little run-in with the police, has it?" I prompted.

"Don't be stupid! Why should it have? Every time I talk to you and Dad you just can't resist a snidey little comment about that, can you?"

"It wasn't meant to be snidey. Look, wouldn't it be a good idea if you broadened your circle of friends a bit, took out different girls occasionally? You're only twenty."

Richard gave me a disgusted look.

"Who do you think you are, Mum – Claire bloody Rayner? I'm going back to bed."

He pushed the scrambled eggs away, half-eaten. I couldn't remember love ever having put me off my food. I felt glad I wouldn't have to be his age again, and was just wondering whether to eat the eggs myself, when the 'phone rang. How sweet, Carolyn 'phoning to make up, I thought, answering it.

"Hello? Is that the Mrs Martin who works for the Herald?" The voice was female, rather shrill, anxious.

"Yes."

"This is Elaine Randall. I wonder if I could possibly see you this morning? It really is rather urgent."

My pulse raced. Elaine Randall, the probable murderer of Michael Stoddart. Did she know I knew?

"Er – is this about the merger?" As the words left my mouth I thought, oh God, supposing she thinks I said "murder"?

"No, it's not the merger, it's something quite different." Well, that was plain enough. "Shall I come over to you? Would half-an-hour be all right?"

I looked around at the state of the living-room.

"No, it's not really very convenient. Would you mind if I came to your house instead?"

She said she wouldn't, and gave me directions to her house. The gardening abandoned, I tidied up and peeled potatoes for lunch. There were movements upstairs; Keith had got the sock drawer jammed again. I put down the

117

potato-peeler and left to interview the murderer.

It was about half past ten when I arrived at the Randalls' house, and saw her peering anxiously out of the window from behind a World Wildlife poster. She opened the door before I got to it.

"Do come in. I'm so sorry to disturb your Sunday morning."

"That's all right."

She showed me into her living-room, which was actually more untidy than mine, but in a different way. Piles of books and papers teetered on chair arms, and the misty-green carpet was littered with sewing threads and paper clips. Evidence of industry, rather than indolence. I got out my notebook.

"Oh no – if you don't mind, I'd like what we say not to be written down."

I thought, the house is empty, husband and children out – she's going to confess to the affair.

"My husband wanted to be here, but he had to take the dog out," she said, confounding me. "He was a stray and I never got him properly trained, so someone has to take him out regularly or he annoys the neighbours." I presumed these latter remarks were references to the dog. I put my notebook away obediently.

Elaine Randall sat down next to a copy of the Sunday Times Book of Body Maintenance, and crossed her long legs.

"It's about – it's about Mr Stoddart," she said. I sat up straight. "I'm really hoping this won't have to go any further." She hesitated. "Well, I did something very silly. I was just so angry at what they can get away with in this country. I mean, it's our heritage, isn't it? Ours and our children's! There's always something being destroyed in the name of progress. You can say it's just a few fields and what does it matter, but it goes on all the time, this relentless chipping away –"

"I'm afraid I'm not with you."

"It's a full-time job, conserving what we've got, and nine times out of ten *they* win. So this time, when it was suggested, I jolly well thought, why not!" Her face reddened with emotion, and she pushed her glasses forcefully back into position.

"Could you explain?"

"Well, it was the thought of the bulldozers in Rampton's Hollow. I was walking the dog up there one day and making some notes when I met Mr Stoddart with his camera. He could see the beauty of the place, of course, and when I told him what they were planning to do – well! He was as upset as I was. I mean, who in their right mind wouldn't be? So he said surely there must be a way. He said what if some sort of rare animal or plant was found to live there? Well, I said, of course if that were the case, we might be able to get a conservation order –" She got up suddenly. "Would you like some coffee?"

"No, thank you. I've just had some. I'm not quite sure what your point is."

She sat down again. "Mr Stoddart said that Rampton's Hollow must be exactly the right habitat for some rare plant or animal. He asked – he asked if I knew of new wildlife colonies ever being deliberately created in these circumstances – seeded, so to speak. Well, of course, one does get to hear of these things –" She looked down at her hands clasped firmly on her knees. "Eventually I gave him a name, just a name, and that's all I know! Really, I didn't do any more than that. I know it was foolish but I honestly wasn't any more involved than that."

I blinked. "Are you telling me that those tree-frogs were planted in Rampton's Hollow to stop the new road going through?"

"All I know is that they weren't there before. Look, I know it was awfully dishonest but the developers and the planners have all the tricks up their sleeves – why shouldn't we win occasionally?"

A distant church bell chimed monotonously until the sound was obliterated by the roar of a powerful motor bike. Mrs Randall's face assumed a pained expression.

I said, "Look, I'm not sure why you're telling me this. Presumably you don't want to be quoted as a source?"

119

She looked horrified. "Oh dear God, no! I just wanted you to know how little I was actually involved. I mean, you seemed to think Sarah knew something about it and I can assure you she knows nothing. She happened to be at home the day Mr Stoddart called to collect the name and address, and as I said she seemed to like him – bit of a schoolgirl crush, I suppose. I mean –" She frowned in puzzlement. "You probably already know more about it than I do. The other reporter, the one you were with at the school, he said it would be best to tell the truth now and get things out into the open. My husband and I talked it over and agreed we should, and I felt I knew you so much better than the other gentleman. But I wonder – however did you get on to the story in the first place?"

"Ah. Yes. To be honest –" To be honest we didn't know anything about it until you just told me. To be honest Pete has suspected every member of your family, except – to date – your husband, of having sexual relations with Michael Stoddart, and that's what he was talking about. "To be honest, my colleague is handling this story himself, and I don't know all the details."

"I'm not trying to evade responsibility," explained Mrs Randall, earnestly. "If I were more deeply involved I'd jolly well admit it and be proud of it, but as you see I know almost nothing about it, and one hears such *dreadful* stories of people being hounded by the press. There has to be someone else in this, doesn't there? I mean, I don't know how involved poor Mr Stoddart was but he was only a teacher and these things cost a lot of money. So there's somebody much more involved than me who paid for it all. *That's* the person who's in the best position to give our side of things."

"And you've no idea who it is?"

"Somebody who jolly well cares about the environment and is prepared to put his money where his mouth is, I should think! I'd like to shake his hand, wouldn't you?" she asked, challengingly.

"Well – yes." I stood up. It was a bad move, because so did Mrs Randall, and she towered above me. "The other question, Mrs Randall, is – what was the name you gave to

Mike Stoddart, the name of the person who presumably decided Rampton's Hollow was a good site for tree-frogs, and arranged for the colony to be 'planted'?"

She gasped. "Well, I certainly won't tell you that!"

"Not under any circumstances? Not even if it means keeping your name out of things entirely?"

"Never! You can't prove a thing anyway. The tree-frog colony has been authenticated by experts and they start work on the new road next month. I don't know how you got on to this, but you're too late! Anyway, I'm quite prepared to go to prison if necessary – I would *never* compromise the conservation movement!" She spoke with all the brave defiance of a captain who would go down with anybody's ship.

I said, "I do appreciate your co-operation, Mrs Randall, and it's quite possible that you won't have to answer any more questions on this matter."

As I left, she told me again that she wasn't trying to evade responsibility, and that she hoped the Herald was enlightened enough to share her views on conservation. She contrived to look both relieved that she'd got it off her chest, and mortified that she might have betrayed the conservation movement. I was beginning to feel sorry for her in her moral dilemma, and would have said so, but she had to dash off to rescue a man who'd just been pulled through a hedge by a large dog.

When I got home I could scarcely contain my excitement, but Keith and Richard looked as though they'd had a row and Julie wouldn't have been interested. Besides, I remembered Keith's comment about my getting in too deep, so I just went dutifully into the kitchen and stuffed the chicken. Later, Richard and Keith must have made up their quarrel, because they called out to me that they were going to the pub for a pre-lunch drink. Immediately I dialled Pete's number. After what seemed an age the receiver was lifted and his voice said sleepily, "You must have a death wish, ringing me at this hour."

"Sorry. It's gone twelve, you know. Can I tell you about Elaine Randall?"

"All right. What?"

I told him. There was a long silence.

"Christ," he said. "Jesus, I don't know what to say."

"Nice to hear you feeling so religious on a Sunday morning."

"Oh, very funny! You must be really pleased – you've just screwed up my entire theory."

"Sorry. But this is better, isn't it? I mean, *who* stood to benefit financially from the road being re-routed?"

Silence. "I don't know. Pass."

"Eric De Broux! The road will go right past his hotel and he'll pick up the passing trade!"

"Oh, aren't you sharp this morning! And I suppose he killed Stoddart and hanged him from the Clocktower as a publicity stunt?" He was obviously jealous of my astuteness.

"Well, perhaps not exactly. But you must admit it's possible Mike Stoddart tried to blackmail him –"

"Yes, all right, but keep it down, will you – my head's hurting. God this could be big – Fraudulent Frogs halt 'A' Road. We could get this in the nationals even if De Broux isn't the murderer. A well-known figure involved in –" He emitted what sounded like the groan of someone in severe pain. "Look, I'll have to think this out when my head's cleared. I feel lousy."

"All right, I'll see you tomorrow then."

I started to hang up, but he said, "No, wait – I'm sorry I snapped at you, I thought you were Helen. She always extracts maximum nuisance value from her telephone calls. Listen, give me half an hour, then come over. I'll make you breakfast and we can talk about this De Broux thing."

"Idiot! I'm having lunch in half an hour!"

As I replaced the receiver I imagined him holding his head, groping in the bathroom cupboard for aspirin. I wondered if he wore pyjamas in bed, or . . . The potato-water frothed alarmingly at the top of the saucepan. I turned down the gas. If you lived alone, there really wasn't much worth getting up for on a Sunday morning. Keith and I had seen quite a few of our friends' marriages break up over the years, which was why we often congratulated ourselves on

122

our own having held together despite its imperfections. Divorce was always more traumatic than people imagined, especially when it meant losing touch with your children. Still, as Keith would have said, you should think of the price before indulging in the pleasure, not wait until you were boosting valium (or vodka) sales.

It was inevitable really, but I felt a little put out. Pete took the frog story out of my hands. He spent Tuesday in London following it up; although he didn't say it, he probably felt that trailing me along would have been an encumbrance. Anyway, that day there was an armed hold-up at a local supermarket, and in his absence I was assigned to cover it. I extracted a good eye-witness account from the lady on the check-out because she said I had a "nice, kind face", and it was on the way back, wreathed in self-congratulation, that I realised I had just passed the Goodburns' surgery. Memory of the note on my message pad at home prompted me to make an emergency stop. I reversed erratically into the small car park, most of whose spaces were helpfully marked "For doctors' cars only", and pulled up rather too close to a new black BMW. As I was locking up, Dr John Goodburn appeared from a side exit.

"I can't open my door," he remarked, testily, pointing at the Mini.

"Oh, I'm sorry, I'll move. But before I do –" This was an accidental, but surely quite clever, twist on the salesman's foot-in-the-door ploy. "Would you mind answering a few questions?"

He frowned. "I saw you up at the Clocktower, didn't I? You're from the Herald."

"Yes, that's right. We've heard a rumour that –"

He frowned. "Rumours are dangerous things. I don't know who started this one, but I can tell you that any comment I may have made to you at the Clocktower immediately after examining that young man's body was entirely speculative and without a proper –"

"No, no, it's not about the murder." He was obviously rather touchy on the subject of his inability to spot the difference between death by hanging and overdosing on heroin. "It's about the possibility of your leaving this practice."

He frowned again. "I don't see that that's any of your business."

"No, not mine personally, but your patients –"

The word "patients" obviously angered him.

"Look, are you going to move this car? I'm late for an important appointment!" He took a step towards me as though he were contemplating snatching the keys from my hand. He was tall, with the slight stoop of age, and his healthily-tanned face carried wrinkles that were more like frown lines than laughter lines. Perhaps he suffered intermittent back pain, I thought, remembering the slight limp I had noticed at the Clocktower, and this accounted for his bad temper. I moved the car.

When he'd gone, driving his BMW with the same confident purposefulness that accompanied his stride, I decided not to give up. I went into the waiting-room, which was deserted except for a large well-worn teddy bear and several dusty cactus plants. The receptionist was not at her post, but I could hear voices coming from somewhere. The bell on the counter said "ring for attention", but was unblemished, as though no one had ever dared touch it. I certainly didn't. I amused myself reading the "Aids" poster, and the "When not to ring your surgery" advice.

"Yes?" The receptionist maintained her position about six feet from the counter, looking like a goalkeeper prepared to dive in any direction to stave off an attack.

"I wonder if I might see Dr Rachel Goodburn."

"Have you an appointment?"

"No, I'm afraid not. Actually, I'm not a patient." I knew this would have a calming effect. "I'm from the Herald. I'd just like a couple of minutes."

"I'll see."

She disappeared for long enough to have filled in two Inland Revenue forms, and I was on the point of leaving when she returned to announce that the doctor could spare me a moment.

Dr Rachel sat at her desk surrounded by patients' files and a variegated ivy plant that had got out of control. She was in her late forties, her dark hair shot through with grey, but beneath the white coat she had the slender figure of a young woman.

"What can I do for you?" she asked, glancing up without smiling.

"Well, I've heard a rumour that you and your husband may be giving up the practice here and I wondered if there was any truth in it?"

She sighed and leaned back in her chair.

"I can't imagine how you heard that. Nothing is finalised. John and I have merely been reviewing our position."

"I see. I can tell you that you are, personally, extremely well-thought of in this town and would be sadly missed. And your husband, too, of course."

"Really. Well, any decision we make would have to be in our own best interests."

I decided to press a little further. "Of course, your husband is rather nearer to retirement age than you are. I suppose general practice takes its toll?"

Her eyes narrowed. "What are you implying?"

I had in fact been thinking of Dr John's back trouble, and his apparent difficulty in diagnosing causes of death, but I said, "Oh, just that you must both have a very full case load which would be exhausting at any age. A lot of your patients come from Edgeborough Avenue and the big council estate, and –" Her expression had changed. I couldn't read it. I'd intended to comment on the fact that people who are financially deprived often have more health problems, but I lost my gist and started again. "You must both be delighted by the prospect of the new drug abuse centre Leisching Pharmaceuticals has proposed?"

"Why? What are you getting at?"

What had I said? I frowned to cover my confusion. "Well, I just thought, you probably both have patients with addiction problems – surely you feel this would be a step in the right direction?"

"Now look!" She stood up. She was going rigid with

125

anger. "I've had just about enough of this! Every time someone dies in this town of anything remotely connected with drug addiction you people are round here, harassing my staff –"

"Why? Who's died? You're not referring to the Clocktower murder, are you? Have there been allegations that Dr John ought –"

"I swear I'll report you to the Press Council! I know what you're trying to do! This is harassment! Marjorie!" The receptionist's footsteps came pounding along the corridor. "Marjorie! This lady is leaving."

I said, "Look, I don't know what you think –"

Dr Goodburn said, "If you don't leave I'll call the police. And I would advise you most strongly against making any allegations you can't support." She was still standing, her fists clenched. Her face had gone very red and she seemed to be shaking. Marjorie gave me an uncompromising stare. I left.

When I got back to my desk I had a cup of coffee and a chocolate biscuit to calm my nerves. Within the space of a few hours I'd been congratulated on my sympathetic approach, *and* accused of harassment. There was something odd somewhere. Even if there were rumblings that Dr John ought to have recognised an overdose victim, it didn't explain Dr Rachel's defensive reaction. Dr John had been called to the scene merely to certify death, which he had done, and if he'd hazarded a wrong guess as to cause it couldn't be held against him. I had a hunch that was worth following up. I picked up the 'phone and dialled the number of the Goodburns' surgery.

"Appointments!"

"Oh hello, I'd like to make an appointment for my husband, Mr Michael Stoddart." My forefinger was ready to disconnect the call, but in my experience doctors' records were always weeks out of date.

"Which doctor is he registered with, please?"

"Oh, do you know, he didn't say. We haven't been married long – I just know it's one of the Goodburns."

126

There was a sigh, followed by a long silence.

"He's with Dr Rachel. I can give you Wednesday at ten, or –"

I disconnected the call. So he was one of her patients. She'd had two patients die of heroin overdoses in six months – but why the paranoia? She could scarcely consider herself in any way responsible for a patient being unfortunate enough to get himself murdered, by whatever means. She could have known, from his medical records, that he was an ex-addict, but doctors were not required to pass such information on, even to the education authorities in the case of a teacher. There wasn't a logical reason for this over-reaction, but there was a reason: stress, pressure of work, an over-bearing, humourless, husband – and all this compounded by the symptoms of the menopause. Thank you, Mrs Taylor. Thank you for reminding me of the tribulations ahead. Just as I thought I had drawn back from the abyss, life conspired to remind me where it was.

12

I was working on my shopping-list as an antidote to the day's traumas, when Pete rang from London.

"How are you getting on?" I asked.

"Not very well. Naturalists are like the medical profession, apparently. They stick together like bloody mussels."

"Funny you should say that."

"Why?"

"Oh never mind, I'll tell you when I see you."

"Ah. Yes, well, that's what I'm ringing about. How would you like a night out in town? I remembered this friend of mine who used to know Eric De Broux and I've arranged to have dinner with him."

"When?"

"Tonight."

"Oh." I sighed disconsolately.

"Is that a problem?"

"Well, yes. Keith goes out Monday nights, so if I went out tonight as well it would mean we'd hardly see each other."

"Forget it, then."

My brain had already started coming up with reasons why I should go – I hadn't had a night out in London since 1976 and the frog story was really mine anyway. "No. I'd like to come. How shall I meet you?"

Even before the receiver was back on its cradle I was working out ways of tackling Keith. It was all a question of approach really. I dialled the number and was put through to his office.

"Hello. Bad news, I'm afraid. I've got to go up to London this evening."

"Whatever for?" He sounded more surprised than angry.

"To interview someone. I can't get out of it, I'm afraid. There are so many people away on holiday." I hadn't intended to lie; I was just following a newly-discovered instinct for getting my own way. It seemed to be working, so I felt guilty. "Sorry. There's some of that nice lasagne in the freezer and Julie can make you a salad –"

That evening I dressed quite deliberately to look sexy, because I wanted to make an impression on myself. I chose very high heels and a tight-fitting black skirt, silky-feel blouse and tights. As I surveyed myself in the mirror I ran a hand down slowly over my hip and thigh, and liked the flow of the curve. For a few hours, Cinderella was going to imagine herself to be having a ball.

I was just about to leave, and thanking God that Keith was late, when Richard came home and saw me with the car keys in my hand.

"Oh Mum, you can't take the car! Don't you remember, you promised I could have it tonight. I'm taking Carolyn to see Cosmic Dandruff in Hudderston and I've got to have it."

"What's Cosmic Dandruff?"

"A band, Mum! Come on, you promised – Carolyn and I are only just on speaking terms again and if I have to ask her to take her car –"

"O.K., but only if you take me to the station, and right now! By the way, this band, has anyone ever recommended a good shampoo?"

"Oh, ha, ha! Yes, everybody!"

He drove me to the station and kissed me goodbye. As I got out of the car I gave him my most earnest, motherly look.

"Richard, you will be careful, won't you. You know what goes on at these pop concerts as well as I do. For God's sake, after what happened the other week –" He looked infuriated. "And make sure your Dad gets his dinner, and you too!"

The pub where I had arranged to meet Pete was in Bayswater. It was vast, all mirrors, dark oak panelling and a

129

ceiling dyed chestnut-brown by a century or more of nicotine smoke. I'd had a worrying time finding it, not being very good with the A-Z, and for a stomach-turning moment thought I wouldn't be able to find Pete either amongst the blur of alien faces. So much for my stolen evening out. Then I saw him, standing at the bar wearing his best leather jacket – the one without the rip in the sleeve – and, surprisingly, a tie, though this had been wrenched untidily loose at the neck. He looked depressed, but he smiled when he saw me.

"How's my favourite junior reporter?" he asked, handing me a gin and tonic. "You're late, and the ice has melted. Listen, I've had it up to here with these bloody frogs. I spoke to one or two people I can trust, and they all agree it's a great story, but before we go any further with it we need to get hold of someone who'll look at the colony and declare it fraudulent. Well, this may come as a shock to you, but you can count the number of tree-frog experts in this country on the fingers of one hand, and –" He closed his fingers into a tight fist. "That's exactly what they're like."

"So – what are you going to do?"

"Well, I'm not giving up. Not yet. I've got the name of a French expert, and the French, as you know, are always keen to drop the British in the shit. We'll see. Can I tell you you look lovely tonight?"

I smiled and glanced at my watch. "If you like. Where's your friend?"

"John? Oh, he'll be along. He's a freelance food writer. That means he'll eat anything for anybody, and write whatever seems to offer him the best advantage. He used to know Eric De Broux and I thought he could give us some inside info on the man. John's not the most scintillating conversationist I've ever met, but he's an expert on all-night drinking clubs. By the way, what were you going to tell me on the 'phone this afternoon when I mentioned mussels? Not another bloody wildlife story, is it?"

"Not mussels! Doctors! I went to see Dr Rachel Goodburn this morning and she almost had me thrown out. Threatened me with the Press Council and everything."

"Ah. Well, if you mentioned you worked for the Herald I

130

imagine she probably would. Don't you remember that story I worked on a few months ago, about the kid who died of a heroin overdose? A young girl, it was, and she was five months pregnant. She hadn't even been referred to a social worker. She was registered as a patient of the wonderful, caring Dr Rachel, but the wonderful, caring Dr Rachel swore blind she'd never examined her. I just didn't believe her, that's all."

"I always rather liked Dr Rachel. I think she's probably under a lot of stress at the moment."

Pete laughed. "Maybe, but that's not why she jumped down your throat. I almost camped out in her surgery for a while. 'Local Doctor's negligence leads to death of teenager and unborn baby' – it would have made a good story, but I couldn't get anywhere with it. I even took the receptionist out and wined and dined her and made vague promises about our future together."

"Not Marjorie?"

"Christ, no! June, the almost-pretty one with the lisp."

"Well, that would explain it then. Using your charms to elicit information, no wonder!"

"My charms weren't very effective." He ran his eyes slowly over me, resting momentarily on my legs in the black-tinted tights. "I've no doubt yours would be though, given the right circumstances. And talking of charms, here comes John. He's an unscrupulous bastard, so don't let him know what we're on to."

For some reason I'd expected a food writer to be small-boned, effeminate-looking, and perhaps slightly overweight, but definitely distinguished. John Blanchard was quite the reverse. He was over six foot and built like a rugger player's nightmare. He probably was overweight, but it was spread over such a large area you might not notice, and his clothing gave the haphazard appearance of having been selected at random from other people's dryers in a run-down laun-derette. He gave Pete a hearty punch on the shoulder by way of greeting, and treated me to a bone-crunching handshake.

"So, how've you been?" he asked, swallowing half a pint of real ale without blinking. "How long's it been – ten years?

131

You were in the Gulf last I heard. And how's the very lovely Helen?"

"We were divorced five years ago."

"Oh dear, that's a bugger. 'Course, you know Andrea and I were divorced. Women! Who knows what goes on in their heads? They ought to come supplied with a handbook!"

"That's not quite true of Helen. She's about as transparent as a sheet of glass and a bloody sight more dangerous to handle."

I gave a sigh of disgust.

"Sorry, Chris," said John. "Men's talk."

After another drink we went to a Greek restaurant in a back street which John said he had only recently "put on the map". It was decked out with fishing-nets, exotic shells and postcards of quaint-looking villages without any vowels in their names, and every table flickered with candle light. Although it was crowded, at the sight of John an army of waiters appeared with menus and order pads, and a vase of carnations was placed on the table. John brushed the menus away and gave a long and detailed order, ending with the instruction ". . . and hold the food until we've finished the first bottle." My head was already spinning after three gins in the pub. Pete announced he didn't much care for retsina, John said it improved your virility no end, and after a few tentative sips I remarked that it might well put Rentokil out of business. John laughed with unnecessary vigour at this, and tried to peer down the front of my blouse.

"Just so there's no misunderstanding," he said, "you and Pete, are you – ?"

"No!" I said quickly.

"Unfortunately no," said Pete. "Chris has achieved the near impossible – a happy marriage – haven't you, darling?"

I was saved the embarrassment of answering by the arrival of a large platter of stuffed vine-leaves. John immediately heaped his plate with them. He seemed to swallow them without chewing. Pete refilled my glass for the fourth time, and said:

"John, does my memory serve me correctly – weren't you a friend of the eminent Mr Eric De Broux?"

"Yes, that's right. I knew him in the days before he made his mark with Partridge De Broux and Duckling Peppercorn De Broux, and all that."

It was about this time that I felt something brush against my right thigh. John was sitting opposite me, with Pete to his right. I could see Pete's hands. I could see John's, too, but his legs were quite long enough to reach me without effort. I didn't say anything.

"Opened up a place in your neck of the woods, hasn't he?" added John.

"Yes," said Pete. "Bloody great hotel."

"I haven't been there myself," said John. "But from what I hear he's bitten off more than he can chew. His places in Kensington and Knightsbridge are still going like the clappers but that hotel's going to turn out to be a white elephant. He should have stuck to restaurants. Matter of fact, the word is that he's overstretched himself, and if the situation doesn't turn round pretty smartly he could be in quite spectacular trouble."

"Reckless with money, is he?" suggested Pete.

"Oh no, I wouldn't say that. Quite the reverse. He comes from an old blue-blooded family, you know – descended from William the Conqueror's falconer or something. They cut him off without a penny when he went into catering – joined the working-classes, the way they saw it, I suppose. Very reactionary family. Interesting, though. I looked them up once. His great-great grandfather killed two men in a brawl over a card-game."

"It's in his genes then!" I exclaimed, meaning murder, and being carried away by the wine and the warmth of the atmosphere. This time it was Pete who nudged my leg.

"What?" said John. He squeezed my right knee between his thighs and I looked at him sharply.

"Private joke," said Pete.

"Dangerous things, private jokes with married women." John kept his eyes on mine, challenging me to complain about what was going on under the table. I gave him a half-smile and moved my leg away.

"So – what, does he gamble, womanise, what?" asked

Pete.

John shook his head. "He's a bit of a bore, if you want my opinion. Lives for food. Well, there's no harm in that provided you indulge in all the other pleasures as well, is there?" He speared the last vine-leaf roll on his plate and slowly offered it to me in an overtly suggestive way, his eyes never leaving my face. "Why is our Pete so interested in Eric De Broux?"

I smiled with studied innocence and accepted the food from his fork, glad as I leaned forward that I hadn't put on a low necked blouse. Pete cleared his throat noisily.

"Have some more wine, John." The wine gushed from the bottle over John's wrist and up his sleeve. "Sorry. We're always keen to know about local celebrities. Was he ever married, or aren't women his thing?"

"Yes, he was married. Strange choice, too – an older woman. She's dead now. I imagine it was her money he used to buy into this hotel. She came from a fairly aristocratic background too, just like him."

At this moment a sweating waiter appeared with a tray of rice and kebabs and John – who presumably had asbestos coated fingers – pulled off a sizzling chunk of meat and put it in his mouth. I looked away and caught Pete's eye. He smiled. It was a warm, conspiratorial smile. I smiled back.

"She was a doctor's wife," said John. "I'll remember her name in a minute. Eric wooed her away from her husband with champagne and dinners à deux cooked by his own fair hands. Love at first bite, I suppose. Ha, Ha!" We all laughed automatically. John spat something on to the side of his plate. "Bloody undercooked pork. I'm sending this back. Mae Goodburn, that was it!"

"Goodburn! Are you sure?" asked Pete.

John shouted to the waiter and winked at me. His leg was crawling up mine like a caterpillar on a stalk of grass, but I did my best to ignore it.

"Did you say Goodburn?" I prompted.

"That's right – Goodburn. Where are these buggers? I'm going to the kitchen. Don't eat that, I'll get it changed. Can't have you spending all night in the loo, can we?" he added to me, implying by his look that he would rather I spent all night doing something quite different.

When he'd gone, Pete said, "Well, well, so Eric De Broux was married to Dr Goodburn's first wife – it's a small world, isn't it?" He poured more wine into my glass.

"It's a small table as well," I said, trying not to giggle. "Your friend keeps touching my legs."

"What? Christ, you told me off for just mentioning your legs! Are you going to let him get away with it? I hope you're not going to ask me to hit him."

I leaned forward. I hadn't eaten so much yet that my waistband was tight, and I felt good about myself: why shouldn't I? I was eating dinner in a candle-lit restaurant with an attractive man.

"But I'm supposed to be nice to him, aren't I?" I asked in a low voice intended to hold a hint of mockery. "Isn't that why you invited me tonight, to tempt him with my charms?"

He looked shocked. "Christ, no. What made you think that?" I smiled to show that I was joking. He said seriously, "Chris, you do know why I asked you tonight, don't you? I thought we had developed an understanding, you and me."

I said primly, "I really don't know what you're talking about," but a blush of pleasure darkened my cheeks.

"Yes, you do –" He tried to read my expression, but I was still giving out contradictory signals. Finally, he grinned and said with a wink, "I'm talking about the fact that I desire you and intend to lure you into my bed tonight."

The words excited me. I said "Oh!" and we both moved forward. The candle flame started to lick hungrily at the tip of his tie, and instinctively I retrieved it and tucked it inside his shirt. My fingers caught in the small damp hairs on his chest. He looked at my mouth, and in a moment he was going to kiss me. I waited. Suddenly a black olive hit his nose, bounced off and struck me on the cheek. We ignored it. It was followed by another, less accurate.

"Break it up! You'll go blind, both of you, at your age," said John.

"Sod off," said Pete, tossing the olive angrily at John's face and – fortunately – missing.

135

The rest of the meal was eaten in an atmosphere of slight tension. John made bad jokes that Pete didn't laugh at, and I had to move my legs out of his way so many times I felt as if I'd spent the evening doing aerobics. Nobody mentioned Eric De Broux again and Pete kept refilling my glass and trying to catch my eye. Eventually John threw his napkin on to the table, smacked his lips and said, "Right, where to now?"

I looked at my watch and said nervously, "If we don't go now we'll miss the last train."

"It's no problem. We can stay overnight in a hotel," said Pete, looking at me intently.

John whistled. "Now there's a very optimistic suggestion which Chris has got too much sense to take you up on, old son!"

"She can make up her own mind without your help."

"I really must get back tonight," I said, desperately. Half a life spent opening cans of baked beans and pairing up socks had not equipped me for this situation.

Pete shrugged as though he didn't care one way or the other. "O.K. John, get the bill and we'll settle up."

John said, "Don't be stupid, there isn't a bill!"

Pete shrugged again and disappeared in the direction of the cloakroom. As soon as he was out of sight John seized my hand and thrust a card into it. "Give me your 'phone number. Come up to town next week and I'll give you a really good time."

"But –"

"Go on, you know you want to. I'm a man of the world, I've seen it all before. These bloody intense Italians are no good to you. Let a real man show you the ropes."

I gave him a weak smile and took the card and a pen. The 'phone number of Tipping's Aids Advice Centre came immediately to mind and I wrote it down and handed it back to him. I suppose it was a nasty thing to do, but take it from me, retsina affects the judgment. John accepted the card with an exaggerated wink and slipped it into his pocket. He removed a pink carnation from the vase and tucked it behind my right ear.

"Ah Pete," he said. "A flower for your lady."

Pete smiled coldly, selected a white carnation, and put it behind my left ear. I had to leave the restaurant with flower water dripping down both sides of my neck.

We both fell asleep on the train and wouldn't have got out at Tipping had a fellow passenger not fallen into my lap when the train stopped. It was twenty-five past midnight and the station was almost deserted. Pete offered to drive me home. He said he thought I'd had too much to drink. I said I hadn't got my car anyway and climbed into his. I fastened the seat belt and automatically gripped the edge of the seat as he turned on the ignition, but he drove slowly out of the car park and very slowly along the High Street. As we approached the roundabout he said, "Come back to my place for coffee." He slowed the car almost to walking speed.

"I can't," I said. "It's really late and I'm really tired."

He turned to glance at me. I stared straight ahead. We crawled round the roundabout, almost stopped, then made the circuit again. We were both wondering what I'd do if he took the road to his flat. Suddenly he accelerated sharply away in the direction of my house. He pulled up outside next door's conifers, out of sight of our darkened windows, and switched off the engine.

"Well?" he said.

"Well, what?"

He laughed softly. "Well, well. I was offering you more than just coffee back there, you know."

I giggled. "That's all right. I didn't fancy an After Eight mint either."

In the muted golden glow from the street-lamp I saw him smile wryly. He said, "I can't think why I'm letting you off so lightly," and leaned across me towards the door handle. His aftershave smelled sweet. He kissed me. He kissed me gently and tentatively at first, but there was a small explosion inside my head and my mouth opened eagerly. His tongue blended with mine.

"We'll go back to my place," he said, reaching for the ignition.

137

"No!" I opened the door and jumped out into the street. "Oh God, I've had too much wine!"

He groaned.

"No, darling," he called after me. "I got it just about right!"

The house was dark and quiet, and I went straight to the bathroom and washed my face in cold water, which is supposed to help, but didn't. When I brushed my hair the two carnations fell to the floor and I dropped them absent-mindedly into the toothmug, where I would have to face then, along with other things, in the morning. I tiptoed into our bedroom.

In the safety of my bed and with the scent of Pete's aftershave still in my nostrils, I wished fervently that I'd let him take me back to his flat in the first place. I imagined sitting in a softly-lit room with Dire Straits playing quietly in the background. I imagined Pete kissing me. I imagined that at first I'd say no – but no, this wouldn't do. I wouldn't just say no at first, I would say no to everything. I couldn't be unfaithful to Keith, not ever. It was unimaginable. But my pulses were still racing, and the taste and smell of my almost-lover wouldn't go away. So instead I sat on Pete's sofa and crossed my elegantly-curving legs, and he fixed me with a dark, smouldering look. Then he kissed me passionately and dragged me, protesting weakly, into his bedroom, where he wrenched off my blouse. My breasts, now mysteriously grown to approximately the size of those sweet, fragrant Charentais melons one sees on the market in summer, fell into his hands and he kissed them. I begged him to stop, but he ripped off the rest of my clothes and forced me on to the bed. So I closed my eyes and pulled in my stomach and he made love to me, brutally but beautifully, and . . . The fantasy overcame me at this point. I bit deeply into my pillow.

Keith gave a great snort and rolled on to my side of the bed. I closed my eyes and the room spun round and round in the darkness.

13

The pain started just above my right ear and surged across my forehead. I was so thirsty I almost choked. It took several seconds for me to register the fact that the Mini wasn't in the drive, and that it was ten to nine and I was stranded three miles from the office.

"Julie!" I called, breaking the pain barrier. "Where's Richard? Where's my car?"

"Didn't Dad tell you?" she asked, sucking marmalade off her toast.

"Dad didn't even wake me."

"Richard stayed with friends in Hudderston last night. He's going straight to work in your car."

"Oh, wonderful!"

I caught the bus. I'd never noticed before how bumpy the road was into Tipping town centre. Sexual harassment at work – there'd been a programme on Channel Four about it only last week. The correct procedure would be to complain straight away to Mr Heslop about Pete's behaviour. Taking me out, plying me with alcohol and thinking I'd be a push-over – he'd probably claim for our drinks on his expense sheet as well! Supposing he was working with a gay colleague, and the gay colleague tried the same trick on him – how would he like it? I went straight to Mr Heslop's office. He was sitting at his desk, chuckling over a pile of letters.

"Listen to this," he said, and assumed a high, rather cracked female voice. "'I am a widow and a pensioner, and for many years it has been my privilege to do the flowers in St Francis Church on Edgeborough Avenue. I was on my way home the other night with my bits and pieces in a brown paper bag –'" For some reason he found this highly amusing. (At least he was in a good mood.) "'– when a youth staggered against me, knocking the bag out of my hand. He kicked it across the pavement, and when I requested most civilly that he pick it up as I suffer from an arthritic hip, he proceeded to relieve himself against the wall!'" More laughter. "'Since this incident I have been unable to face going out at night for fear of being subjected to an even worse assault. The police did not take my complaint seriously. In my opinion the sooner the derelict buildings on Edgeborough Avenue are razed to the ground the sooner decent people – etc., etc.'" He shook his head, still chuckling. "Oh dear, oh dear – it's always the old dears least likely to be attacked who see a rapist round every corner isn't it? Silly old bat! Still, we're getting a lot of letters like that about the Edgeborough Avenue project – only a few so far who want to see the buildings preserved."

"Oh."

"You look a bit liverish this morning. Honey and cider vinegar with a dash of coarsely ground black pepper, that's what you need. I have it every morning, sets me up for the day. You should try it."

"I will. Thank you."

"Didn't you want to see me about something?"

"No. It doesn't matter."

Pete was sitting at his desk, writing.

"Hello," he said. "You look awful."

"I want to talk to you about last night," I said, with as much menace as I could muster.

"Yes." He put his pen down and looked at me. "Before you do, let me apologise. I behaved very badly and I'm sorry. Alcohol tends to loosen the brakes on one's desires."

"Yes. Well, perhaps you shouldn't drink so much," I said, feeling hot round the neck.

"Perhaps."

I turned to go.

"So – you think Eric De Broux murdered Stoddart because he was blackmailing him over the tree-frogs?"

I wasn't thinking of anything except the pain in my head. I said, "Well, he could have, couldn't he?"

"If Stoddart had been found with a meat-cleaver between his shoulders at the bottom of a lake I'd think it highly probable, but it doesn't really make a lot of sense for him to have killed him and hanged him from the Clocktower and left bits of evidence all over his own hotel, does it?"

"No, I suppose not. What are you doing about the frogs?"

"Trying to get hold of this guy in France."

"What about the possibility that De Broux married Dr John Goodburn's first wife?"

"I should forget about that. I don't see what it's got to do with anything."

"No, I suppose not. If Eric De Broux himself had been murdered then Dr Goodburn might have a good motive for doing it."

"Don't be silly. Running away with a man's wife is no motive for murder. I'd've paid someone to take Helen off my hands. Preferably an undertaker."

I didn't feel like laughing at anybody's jokes that morning. I said seriously, "I don't think you mean that at all."

His smile vanished.

"Go away and have an aspirin. I've got to start ringing half of bloody France."

The Mini was parked in the drive when I got home. Surprised, I went inside and called out to Richard, but he didn't answer. There was loud music emanating from his room, so I knocked several times on his door. Perhaps – horror of horrors – he was in there with Carolyn. Eventually I plucked up my courage and opened the door with violent rattling of the handle. He was lying on his bed, his pallor apparent through the darkness, staring at the ceiling.

"Are you all right?" I asked, alarmed.

"Yes."

"Haven't you been to work today?"

"No."

"Are you ill?"

His eyes left the ceiling and found me.

"I'm fine," he said, languidly.

"Well, you can't just take days off work when you feel like

141

it! God, I felt awful today but I went to work."

"Why?" he asked, in an edgy tone of voice.

"Well – ! Is it Carolyn? Have you two had another row?"

"No."

"You're not worth talking to!" I said angrily, and went downstairs to tackle the kitchen.

I thought about Richard as I washed up. What was the matter with him? He hadn't been the brightest child in his class but he'd always been "a trier" as Keith put it. It simply wasn't like him to give up work on a whim. Perhaps if I tried a friendlier approach I'd get somewhere with him. I made us both tea and took it up to his room. I sat on the edge of his bed and chatted about the Herald, and last night's meal, even going so far as to tell him what we'd learned about the tree-frog colony in Rampton's Hollow.

"So we think people may have gone there at the dead of night with frogs in boxes and planted the colony, just to get the by-pass re-routed!" I said, trying to make it sound interesting.

"Frogs in boxes!" exclaimed Richard suddenly. "Frogs in boxes!" And he began to laugh, softly at first, but gradually sounding more and more hysterical.

"Oh my God, Richard!" I said, suddenly alerted. "What have you taken?"

He went on laughing. "Taken? Why should I have taken anything?" he asked in a temporary lull. "Can't anyone be happy in this house without taking something? Dad's always bad tempered unless he's pissed, and when he's pissed he's – Oh God, frogs in boxes!"

I grabbed Richard by the arms and examined them. Well, no needle holes, anyway.

"You're being bloody stupid!" I shouted. "This won't do you any good! You'll lose your job if you go on like this!"

"Stuff the job! Who wants to be an accountant! Money stinks! Money and mortgages and twenty-one years of married bliss –"

I thought, well, we all felt like that in the "sixties" and look at us now. I said, "Your father will kill you if he sees you like this! You stay in your room – I'll say you're ill.

142

Don't you dare come out!"

I went out of the room and slammed the door with finality. Leaning on it, I thought how awful everything seemed. Here was I, just recovering from a monumental hangover, remonstrating with my son about drug taking. Suddenly I decided there was only one thing to do; I'd be an old-fashioned parent, I'd go and see the Reverend Harlow and discuss what our two children were up to. I felt a lot better once I'd reached this decision and I went back to the kitchen and made apple sauce to go with our pork chops.

The Reverend Harlow agreed to see me on my way home from work the following day. I was a little afraid of running into Carolyn, but the Vicarage was large and quiet and empty; if she was there, I didn't see her. He showed me into the drawing-room and opened the French doors on to a daisy-sprinkled lawn.

"I believe it's not too early for sherry, Mrs Martin," he suggested. "Or possibly a glass of wine? I have an excellent German white chilling in the refrigerator."

"That would be very nice, thank you."

Carolyn's pretty, determined face glared at me from photographs all over the room. Somehow I had never really liked her. Accepting the wine, I said:

"I wanted to have a little chat with you about Richard and Carolyn."

"Getting along splendidly, aren't they?"

"Well – yes. I'm afraid that's part of the problem. Richard is only twenty and he's still got a long way to go before he qualifies. I really would rather he didn't get too serious with anyone."

"Ah, well – but there isn't an awful lot one can do about these things, is there? Youngsters today are extremely headstrong. Since Carolyn's mother passed on I've found it best just to let things take their course."

I hesitated. "Well, of course, one doesn't want to interfere – but perhaps a little gentle influencing in the right direction. Richard is even talking about giving up his career."

"Oh dear. Oh yes, that would be a shame. Yes, I see.

143

Perhaps if I were to suggest that Carolyn takes a little holiday, visit her aunt in Rhodesia – sorry, it's Zimbabwe nowadays, isn't it? Lovely place. Do her good, I suppose, to see some of the world. Yes, Mrs Martin, I'd no idea. I will do all I can. Have some more wine?"

I thought that indeed he really did have no idea, and I accepted the wine thankfully.

"Yes, dear me," said the Reverend Harlow. "One never knows what to expect with these young people. In some ways early marriage is a good thing, of course. We mustn't ignore the facts of life, must we? Especially not now there is the ghastly spectre of Aids lurking before us – however there are other considerations –" He studied his wine speculatively, and said, "Any more news on that awful business at the Clocktower?"

"Not that I've heard, no."

"A most unfortunate young man. I met him just the once, briefly, at the Conference. All the tenancies were handled through an agent."

I blinked. "Sorry?"

"He lived in one of my properties. Oh, I suppose you wouldn't know. Not that it's any secret. I used to own a couple of houses in Edgeborough Avenue – sold them about a month ago, actually. Bit like Monopoly, isn't it?"

"Is it? I didn't know you were in the property business?"

"Oh, hardly that, Mrs Martin. Just a little dabble. There's nothing wrong with making money if you are gifted with the opportunity. I did rather well out of those two properties. Money can be put to extremely good use."

He had drained his glass, and seemed to be deciding whether to refill it. I said:

"Whatever made you buy property in Edgeborough Avenue of all places? Not a good bet, I'd've thought."

"No, and many would have agreed with you, I'm sure. Once an area starts to go down it's hard to save, though I did what I could for my bit of it. You wouldn't have heard any of my tenants complain of poor conditions, I do assure you. It was at the Church fête a couple of years ago. I mentioned to my old friend, Bruce Duncton, that I had a small legacy to

144

invest, and he suggested that Edgeborough Avenue was an area due for an upturn in fortunes."

I said, "You do know that they're thinking of knocking down a lot of the houses in Edgeborough Avenue and siting the Leisching Pharmaceuticals building there?"

He succumbed to temptation and refilled his glass. "Well, I'm sure the good Major and his colleagues on the Planning Committee will come to the most satisfactory decision on that one. One mustn't try to halt progress, Mrs Martin, just for the sake of it. In any case, I was approached by a property company about a month ago and I sold them both my properties at a more than handsome profit. So it's really out of my province now."

I suddenly remembered the paper I'd seen in Mike Stoddart's flat; it had mentioned the name Harlow and listed the numbers 17 to 31; it also included the name of a property company – Greyfield Properties.

"Was the company that bought your properties called Greyfield, by any chance?"

"Yes. Yes, that's right," nodded the Reverend, looking surprised. "Interested in property development, are you, Mrs Martin?"

"Well, not really. It's just that there's quite a row developing over Edgeborough Avenue. Would you happen to know if Greyfield bought up any other houses in Edgeborough Avenue at the same time as yours?"

"Well – I wouldn't know. A parishioner of mine, Mrs Parkes, used to own number twenty-nine. She bought it at about the time I did, also on good old Bruce's advice. We went to an auction together, Mrs Parkes and I, to pick up second-hand furniture. Quite a daunting task for an elderly widow, arranging builders and decorators and furniture, you know. She had some tenant trouble, too – most unfortunate. I've no idea if she still owns the property. As a matter of fact I'm glad you reminded me about Mrs Parkes. I haven't seen her in Church lately. Must pop over there."

I had almost forgotten about Richard. I said, "Well, thank you for your time. I'm glad we understand each other about Richard and Carolyn. We don't want them to make any

145

mistakes, do we?"

The following morning I arrived at work early. I consulted the file on the Leisching Development and confirmed that it was the numbers seventeen to thirty-one Edgeborough Avenue which were to be demolished (should planning permission be granted) to make way for the new office-block. I wasn't quite sure what this meant, but I was sure it meant something. As it was Friday there was a relaxed atmosphere in the office and I found Pete with his feet up on his desk, trying to translate a letter from a Parisian Institute using a pocket dictionary and a tourist phrase-book.

"Are you still after the frog expert?" I asked.

"Yes, but I wish you'd put it more tactfully. The last thing we want is an international incident. Do you know any French?"

"I can point at a menu."

"That's a big help! I think it says this guy's on holiday but we should contact his assistant in Bordeaux. Here." He handed me the letter. I looked at it but could only just about understand the date. I gave it back to him.

"Listen. I went to see the Reverend Harlow last night –"

"I absolutely refuse to believe you've done anything worth confessing, darling," he interrupted, mockingly.

"His daughter goes out with my son, if you must know. Anyway, it came up in the conversation that he owned two houses in Edgeborough Avenue, including the one Mike Stoddart lived in. He apparently bought them two years ago on the advice of Major Duncton and sold them about a month ago after being approached by a property company called Greyfield."

"So?" He was still reading the letter.

"Well, apparently Major Duncton advised both the Reverend Harlow and another lady to buy houses in Edgeborough Avenue. He said there were profits to be made. And the thing is, Mike Stoddart had a list in his flat of the people who owned numbers seventeen to thirty-one Edgeborough Avenue. So –"

"So what! If this is a roundabout way of accusing the

146

Reverend Harlow of Stoddart's murder, I don't buy it. I'm a born-again atheist, but honestly, darling, there are limits."

"No!" I slapped the sole of his foot in exasperation. "Not the Reverend Harlow! Not anybody specifically. I'm just saying it seems odd that the Chairman of the Planning Committee is going around advising people to buy property in a run-down area. Then, out of the blue, a big drugs company wants a site in Tipping, and suddenly Edgeborough Avenue is being considered. Not only that, but before it's made public Greyfield Properties comes along and makes a good offer –"

"But not half as good as it would have been after the announcement that Edgeborough Avenue might be redesignated for commercial use," said Pete, suddenly interested, taking his feet off the desk. "You're suggesting that Major Duncton is involved in a deal with Greyfield Properties. Matter of fact, I've got a notice here about an emergency planning meeting to discuss a change of use for the site. Somebody's really pushing this thing through."

"Do you think Mike Stoddart knew about it and was blackmailing the Major?"

He laughed. "I think that's a giant leap of the imagination! Just because he blackmailed one unfortunate old lady and possibly a restaurateur who'd fallen on difficult times, we mustn't assume he was blackmailing everybody. The whole thing's pretty tenuous as it is."

"Don't you think it's worth following up?" I was disappointed. I didn't like the Major.

"Oh yes. After I've sorted out the frogs. Bill would love it, you know – 'Edgeborough Avenue Property Scandal' or something. He's got a pile of letters this morning from a bunch of lunatics calling themselves the Friends of Tipping's Heritage. I told you – people in this town *love* this sort of thing. Their diaries must read: went home, mowed lawn, wrote letter of objection to planning committee, drank Horlicks, complained about next-door's dog barking, screwed wife – that's if it's Saturday, of course –"

"Yes," I blushed. "So what about the list I saw in Mike Stoddart's flat? If I could get the key from Lynn Cazalet,

147

what would be the legal position on going in to have another look?"

"Well, if she's in legal possession of a key, and she willingly hands it to you I don't think there'd be a problem. But they'll probably have re-let the flat by now. I'll ring my friend Taffy at the police-station and see if he knows."

"Thanks."

"All right. Now do me a favour – stop distracting me and let me concentrate on the few words of French I know so I can ring Bordeaux."

I gave a mock salute, then said, "One thing, Pete. How can you be a born-again atheist?"

He grinned. "That's easy. You just open your bedroom window every morning and shout 'I don't believe in you, you bastard'!"

I returned to my desk and rang Social Services. They left me on "hold" for about half an hour, but eventually gave me an extension number for Lynn Cazalet. They then cut me off. Two cups of coffee and a lot of time spent listening to an engaged tone later, I got through. She was out – on an emergency call, they said. It wasn't going to be my day. I decided to take an early lunch. Pete was still sitting at his desk, unbending paper clips with a vengeful expression on his face.

"The bastard's taking a long weekend," he said. "And it's a public holiday in France on Monday. They gave me another number to ring but it's always bloody engaged!" He slammed down his fist with tremendous force on the telephone, and it gave a feeble trill of protest.

"I know just how you feel," I said sympathetically, adding with a deeper honesty than intended, "I've had a lifetime of things not working out the way I wanted."

He looked at me thoughtfully and said, "And so you came to work here –"

By mid-afternoon it seemed that Lynn Cazalet had disappeared off the face of the earth. Pete's 'phone was making odd screeching noises and he said it wasn't working. He came back from the Star and sat on the edge of my desk.

"I just saw Taffy," he said. "Apparently the landlord of twenty-three Edgeborough Avenue is in no hurry to re-let the flat –"

"That would be Greyfield Properties! They'll be waiting for the Planning Committee decision."

"Yes, perhaps. Anyway, the police haven't been able to track down Stoddart's next of kin so all his things are still in the flat. It's all yours."

"No, it isn't. I can't get hold of the key."

"Can't you?"

"No."

I tossed my pen into the in-tray, sighed, and leaned back in my chair. The window was open, and the sky heavy with cloud, but it was a hot, breathless afternoon. I felt swollen with the heat.

Pete said, "It's not been a very fulfilling day for either of us, has it?"

I shook my head and smiled.

He said. "Maybe there's something we can do about it. I've got a skeleton key at home. We could let ourselves into Stoddart's flat."

"Oh! Wouldn't that be breaking and entering?"

"It's only breaking and entering if you break something to enter. We won't break anything."

"How can you be sure the key will fit?"

"I can't, until we try."

I thought of Keith and his comment on the syringe incident, that I was getting in too deep and shouldn't cross the police. Pete stood up and extended a hand to me.

"Come on," he said. "Do you really want to sit around here all afternoon when we could be living dangerously?"

"It's the living dangerously part that bothers me! I don't want my husband to have to come and bail me out of a cell."

"Oh, he won't, darling. Your husband won't know anything about it."

I stood up and collected my handbag from the desk drawer. I already had a rather uneasy feeling that things were not going to go as planned, but I dismissed it as a general edginess induced by the weather.

149

14

It was when we pulled up on the forecourt of Pete's flat that about a dozen alarm-bells went off simultaneously in my head. He parked neatly in front of a rose-bush that looked exactly like the ones in my garden, festooned with bindweed and the sad dead heads of spent blooms, and switched off the engine.

"I haven't seen this key since 1974 so we'd better have a drink while I look for it. Come on."

"It's all right. I'll wait here, I don't mind."

He hesitated. "Well, *I* mind. I need a drink and I can't have one with you sitting out here. Besides, the neighbours will think you think I'm Jack the Ripper if you don't come in with me." He got out, slammed the door, locked it, and walked round and opened my door. "Come on."

I got out and followed him inside and up the bleak staircase. The voice in my head was uttering confused warnings. You can't handle this, it said, back out now or face dire consequences later. Back out of what? I queried – looking for the key, breaking into Mike Stoddart's flat? You're not suggesting, are you, that I shouldn't go into this man's flat with him? How absurd! I'm a mature married woman, and he's – well, not a rapist. We are neither of us interested in anything but the story.

Pete unlocked the door and stood aside, smiling politely and apologising for the mess. His living-room was unmistakably a man's room – no ornaments or houseplants and only three photographs in silver frames. They were of his children at different ages, and a plain piece of card obscured half of one (presumably covering his ex-wife's face). The room contained a table with a typewriter on it and a lot of papers, hi-fi equipment, a television and a shelf loaded with bottles and glasses. Pete made straight for the bottles.

"What would you like to drink? I've got vodka or vodka, Smirnoff or genuine Russian, and some tonic. I don't have guests very often."

"Smirnoff, please. A very small one with lots of tonic." The steep stairs had left me breathless; I hadn't realised I was so unfit.

He poured a large measure of vodka into a small glass and handed it to me with a bottle of lukewarm tonic. There wasn't room in the glass for much of the tonic, but I filled it to the brim and took a sip. I don't know whether it was the effect of the almost neat spirit on the back of my throat, or a stray carbon dioxide bubble bursting in my nostril, but I was suddenly overcome by a violent fit of sneezing.

"Oh Christ, you're allergic to me!" he exclaimed. He gave me a wad of tissues to sneeze into and stood with an arm round me. "Don't die, don't die! I don't want to have to explain your dead body to the neighbours."

"You're very concerned about your neighbours," I managed between sneezes. His arm on my shoulder was warm but not comforting.

"Actually, I don't give a shit about them. But I do care about you. Are you all right now? Have another sip. Do you feel a bit less tense?"

"What makes you say that? I'm not tense."

"Yes, you are, you're very tense. It's because of me, isn't it?"

"Yes. All right, I suppose it is."

I walked over to the table, put my drink on it and blew my nose. I wished he'd stop looking at me. My eye fell on a page marked "Chapter Eleven".

"Is this a new book you're writing?"

"Yes." He sat down on the sofa.

"I read the first one you gave me. I liked most of it."

He winced. "I rather wished I hadn't given you that. This one is much more fun. I've got to the bit where they're making passionate love in this car balanced on the edge of a precipice. One sudden movement, and –" He snapped his fingers. I gulped my drink. I felt as though I were pretty

151

close to a precipice, too. "Of course, making passionate love is nice anywhere. It doesn't have to be on a cliff edge. Sit down."

The sofa was dark green and new. It went well with the soft green carpet and curtains. I sat down. The vodka was going to my knees.

"Look, I really think –" I began.

"Don't think."

With a sudden movement he leaned over and kissed me, and this time I responded immediately to the remembered taste of his mouth. He was delicious, better than anything I could think of, but it was a taste I mustn't allow myself to develop.

"I can't do this," I said, wrenching free.

"Yes, you can. It's like whistling, you just sort of put your lips together, and –"

"Oh, don't joke. I'm serious!"

"So am I. Very, very serious." He held my face and kissed me gently on the forehead, then he moved his hands down slowly over me, caressing my breasts, my stomach, my thighs. My nerve endings anticipated each touch.

"Don't!" I gripped his wrists.

He sighed and sank back on the sofa, deftly twisting out of my grasp. He caught my hands and kissed them in turn.

"Just stop thinking for a minute," he suggested softly. "See how it feels."

"Look, we'll both regret this," I said desperately. "I thought we were friends. Don't let's spoil it."

"Of course we're friends, that's what makes it so irresistible. That's why I won't touch you or do anything unless you want it. But I know what I want. I want to make love to you. I want to kiss your ears, your neck, your breasts – the rounded part of your tummy, where it –"

"Oh stop!"

His eyes were closed, the long dark lashes lying on his cheeks. I put my hand on his chest to distance myself from him, but I could feel his heart beating fast beneath my palm and it vibrated through the veins of my hand, along my arm and into my body. I moved forward. I kissed the soft skin of

152

his closed eyelid. He said "Christ!" in a tone of slight surprise, and we found each other's mouths and fell into the
cushions. I'd stop any second and get up and walk out. He
struggled with my bra strap, and then my right breast fell
suddenly through my open shirt front and his fingers made
gentle circles round the nipple. I said, "Don't do that," and
he leaned over and took my nipple in his mouth instead, and
the ache low down in my stomach deepened. "Oh, please," I
began, as we rolled on to the floor.

"Shut up," he whispered. "Don't you know when to stop
talking? Don't talk or think about anything."

I felt him undoing his trouser belt.

"Oh no – don't!"

He pressed himself against me.

"I can't!" I said.

"You can, you can. Look at me. I love you. Say yes."

My body was saying yes. I said, "No."

He groaned painfully. "Oh Jesus!"

I stroked his face, thinking how beautiful he was. After all
these years of feeling nothing, the feeling was too strong to
be denied.

"Yes," I said. "*Now*, before I change my –"

Afterwards, I discovered we were lying under his writing-
table surrounded by screwed up typing paper and squashed
beer cans. The underside of the table wasn't stained dark
like the top, and the number 9337841 was stamped on it in
violet ink. I couldn't remember exactly how we'd got there.
Pete's face was resting on my shoulder, almost welded there
by perspiration. I looked at his dark curls, threaded through
with grey, and breathed in the scent of his skin. I had just
committed adultery, and I felt wonderful.

"Well," said Pete, taking a deep breath like a diver emerging from water. "You O.K.?" I nodded, and he smiled.
"Me too. Say something, then."

"I don't know what to say."

"Say you're not upset with me. Say it was nice."

"It was lovely, and I'm not upset with you."

A drop of perspiration fell from his head on to my cheek.

153

He blotted it with a finger.

"Think we can stay like this for ever?"

"No."

He sighed. "It's a pity you're such a realist. Kiss me."

We kissed.

A few minutes later he went to the kitchen and returned with a Mars bar and an apple, which we shared. He said there wasn't anything else to eat in the flat apart from stale peanuts left behind by the twins. We sat on the floor, leaning against one another, listening to Friday afternoon drift by outside. There seemed no need for conversation, and I certainly didn't feel like thinking. Suddenly I noticed that it was past four o'clock.

"God, we'd better hurry up and find this key," I said.

He laughed, and said, as I should have known he would, "I haven't got a bloody skeleton key. What do you think I am – a burglar?"

"Oh, Pete!"

"Look, darling, we were obviously made for each other. One of us had to do something about it. To hell with the Stoddart story and the damn frogs –"

"Made for each other!" I exclaimed scornfully. But when he moved to undo the last remaining button on my shirt I didn't resist. I lay back on the carpet and pulled his face down towards me.

Julie said, "Are you sure you're all right, Mum? You haven't seemed well all day."

It was Saturday night and I'd just dried up dinner plates and put them in the 'fridge. Yesterday afternoon kept playing in my head like a video tape. Julie took the plates out of the 'fridge and put them in the cupboard.

"Actually you *look* well," she said. "Nice pink cheeks and everything. It's just that you keep doing funny things."

"I'm fine, I'm fine," I said, hugging her. "And I love you more than anything in the world."

"Oh!"

This sort of declaration was not common in our household. Keith opened the door and waved the *Radio Times* at me.

"This is last week's!" he exclaimed. "I could be missing a good film!"

"You're not," said Julie. "It's all repeats and classical music tonight. I'm going to my room to listen to something decent." She gave me an odd look and left. I followed Keith to the living-room. I don't know why, but in that moment I hated him. I was the guilty party, yet for some irrational reason I blamed him for everything. We sat together, watching television – on screen two men in tweed jackets and trousers with turn-ups discussed their conception of God (Keith must have been asleep over the remote control unit because he usually couldn't abide a programme devoid of action). All these years, I thought, all these years you've made me feel dead and useless, ironing tea-towels to make you love me, washing your floors, making meals you didn't taste. You made me despise myself. You made me think I couldn't do anything except iron tea-towels and wash floors, and in the end I couldn't. I was dead from the neck up before I went to work for the Herald, and dead from the neck down until Pete touched me. Keith started to snore and the remote control unit slipped through his fingers. It fell on his foot and he woke up with a start.

"We might as well go up to bed," he said, yawning in disgust at the television.

"What's the hell's the matter with you?" he asked, from the darkness.

"I'm sorry, I just don't feel like it."

"I'll be very quick –" Somehow that made it worse.

"No! I've got indigestion!"

I twisted into a rigid curve, my back to him. I heard him swear softly and turn the other way.

15

On Monday morning Pete dropped a red rose on my desk. I recognised it as having come from the bush where he parked his car. When I picked it up an earwig fell out of it and scuttled across my desk into the paper-clip tray. I put the rose in some water, and hoped the earwig would not reappear.

I rang Lynn Cazalet first thing and said we were thinking of printing a few of Mike's photos in the paper (tactical untruths were becoming a habit) and could she possibly let me into his flat some time? She said that she had a very full caseload at the moment, what with staff holidays and a tummy-bug doing the rounds, but she'd leave the key in her office and I could collect it any time. She sounded very cheerful; perhaps she was happiest when over-worked.

Pete was not cheerful.

"I finally ran down the frog expert," he said angrily. "And he wants the most astronomical fee to come over and look at these damn frogs. There's no point even asking Heslop, so I told him to stuff it." He pulled a leaf off my rose and shredded it with his fingers.

"What about the nationals? You said they were interested."

"If we could break the story locally, they'd come up with the money."

"Oh."

"Right. So we're going up to the Clocktower to tackle De Broux. I've nicked Ernst's spare camera and you can put it round your neck."

"Whatever for? I don't know how to use it."

"Don't worry. I don't want you to use it. The mere sight of

a camera can be very intimidating."

We drove up to the Clocktower through a damp grey morning that seemed colder than August. I didn't actually feel like intimidating anyone; I kept glancing sideways at Pete and experiencing little twinges of remembered passion. He didn't look at me; he was concentrating his mind on being threatening.

There were quite a few cars in the hotel car park, and we soon discovered that a wedding reception was imminent. A woman with a large hat that billowed ostrich feathers like a nuclear explosion was arguing with Mr De Broux about the size of the baked salmon and the layout of the buffet. When she saw me she said, "Oh God, they've sent a *woman!*" to my intense puzzlement, and then told me to go outside and get into position for the pony and trap. Her manner was so imperious I almost obeyed, but Pete stopped me.

"This lady's not your photographer. We're Press, to see Mr De Broux."

"Well, can't it wait?" said Eric De Broux, testily. "I didn't send for you."

"Of course you didn't! We're responding to a report that the by-pass is to be re-routed back through Rampton's Hollow now that the tree-frog colony has been invalidated. Would you care to comment on that, please?"

Eric De Broux's mouth opened and closed soundlessly.

"When I ordered salmon," put in the woman with the hat, "I specifically and absolutely definitely –"

"If you wouldn't mind excusing me for a moment, Mrs Anderson," said De Broux unsmiling. "Mrs Jackson is the best person to speak to about this. Mrs Jackson! Would you be kind enough to assist Mrs Anderson. And would you two follow me, please."

He led us through Reception, down the steps and out on to the lawn. It was starting to rain, so this was not a welcoming manoeuvre.

"Well, Mr De Broux, as I said, we'd like your reaction to this latest development in the by-pass saga."

"What the hell are you talking about?"

"I'm talking about the fact that experts have been called in

157

to question the validity of the tree-frog colony, and –"

"Experts have already validated it! Where did you get this from?"

"Chris, a photo, I think, please," said Pete, and I raised the heavy camera obediently, hoping I'd got it the right way up.

"Put that bloody thing down! You're not getting anything from me. I've got no comment to make on anything. I say again – where did you get this story about the tree-frog colony being invalidated?"

Pete hesitated. "I can't reveal my source, Mr De Broux."

Eric De Broux frowned, then nodded slowly.

"Oh, I see. There's no enquiry, is there? You've come up here on some kind of fishing expedition. Not much news in August, is there, so pick on somebody a few people have heard of and try to start up a rumour! Let me tell you this, I'm a personal friend –"

"It's no fishing expedition, Mr De Broux. That tree-frog colony is a plant, as you know better than I."

There was silence. Pete, shorter than De Broux, waited with a slightly amused expression for an answer. A large drop of rain hit the taller man on the cheekbone and slid slowly down his chin. Suddenly he grabbed Pete by the lapels and felt inside his pockets. Pete's expression turned to one of long suffering as he let him do it.

"I know you bastards," said De Broux. "You're taping this." He looked at me. "I want to see inside your bag."

This was embarrassing because my bag always contains an assortment of very personal things such as a supply of soft toilet-paper, make-up stained tissues, and tampons for emergency use, but I showed him anyway.

"Satisfied, Mr De Broux?" asked Pete. "A lifetime in the public eye has taught you some things then. You've got to expect a bit of heat if you disregard conventional morality – like running off with other men's wives, for instance."

For a moment I thought De Broux was going to hit him, but he was far too controlled for that.

"I don't like you," he said. "I didn't like you when you first came up here, and if it wasn't for the presence of this

158

lady I'd be a lot more explicit. Go and pick over the dregs of someone else's rubbish tip. That's all you're fit for."

"Your rubbish tip will do nicely for now, thank you, Mr De Broux," said Pete, brightly. "And talking of rubbish tips, it's an odd coincidence, isn't it, that Mike Stoddart got himself disposed of on your premises?"

Again, De Broux was taken by surprise, but he covered it up quickly.

"What's floating through that sewer-like mind of yours now?"

"Was Mike Stoddart blackmailing you?"

"Blackmailing me? What the hell for?"

"For having arranged the setting up of the tree-frog colony."

Eric De Broux laughed. "Him? He couldn't arrange anything. He was an opportunist. Like you. Someone who wasn't fussy where he stuck his fingers. He's dead now, so it won't do you any good, but I can tell you that all he did was approach me with an idea, and give me a name. When I'd got my money's worth I paid him. And you can't prove a thing."

"Oh, but I'm doing quite well so far, aren't I? You'd be surprised how easy it is to put two and two together. Why don't you give me the name Stoddart gave you and then I'll leave you in peace. I might even be able to keep your name out of it."

De Broux put his hands on his hips and took a menacing step forward.

"You *will* leave me in peace and you *will* keep my name out of it. Now get off my property before I call the police." He turned his back on us and started towards the hotel. Pete called after him, loudly enough for the wedding-party, which was just assembling in the drive, to have heard.

"Why did you murder Michael Stoddart? Was it to keep him quiet?"

De Broux stopped and turned slowly. His face was full of contempt. "If I ever decide to murder anyone, you'll be the first in line."

The pony and trap arrived at that moment and a young

(male) photographer stepped forward to take a picture of the happy couple seated in it. When they rose to descend from the trap, I saw that the bride was at least seven months pregnant. Poor Mrs Anderson, no wonder she had wanted everything else to be just right. I'd only been three months gone on my wedding day, and my mother had vowed to kill me if I was sick.

When we got back to the car, Pete said, "Shit! I think we just lost the frog story. Shit!"

I huddled into my cardigan, feeling slightly shaken. "Did you believe him when he said Stoddart wasn't blackmailing him?"

"I don't know. He was very sure of himself. Now, that could be because he's disposed of the only person who was a danger to him, or it could be that he's telling the truth. Actually I don't think he's stupid enough to have let someone like Stoddart get something on him in the first place. Anyway –" He took a deep breath and shook his head. "Forget all that. Let's think about us. I can't wait for tonight."

"Why – what's happening tonight?"

"Your husband goes out on Mondays. It's your night off. It's our night together."

"Oh – oh, I don't know about that. I hadn't thought about it." I was thrown into a panic. "I mean, on Friday it was unpremeditated, but –"

"*Unpremeditated*?" He pretended to be hurt. "You've got murder on the brain. How can you talk about us like that?"

I smiled sadly and shook my head.

"I've never done anything like it before."

"Really? You were getting the hang of it nicely."

"Oh shut up! You know what I mean."

He sighed. "Yes, yes, I know what you mean. You mean you can't make up your mind if I'm worth it. Well, I think you are. I think you're worth any amount of suffering and expense." He looked at me sideways and grinned. "I went out and bought new sheets on Saturday because I thought you'd be shocked at how off-white mine are."

"Idiot! You can't expect me to have an affair with you

160

because of the state of your laundry!"

"No. Actually, I'm old-fashioned. I thought we might do it because we like each other."

He switched on the engine and threw the car backwards across the wet car park in a noisy circle. This move effectively ended the conversation.

The story we eventually wrote went like this: "A leading French expert on tree frogs, M. – , said today from his holiday home near Cahors in the Dordogne region of France (Pete: 'These boring, irrelevant details help to convince the reader you're telling the truth') that there was a strong possibility the tree-frog colony in Rampton's Hollow had been artificially created. (Pete: 'He may have said that: I couldn't understand a bloody word.') The Colony, which was allegedly discovered earlier this year and led to the new Tipping by-pass being re-routed over Clocktower Hill, consists of –" Here we inserted a piece culled from an earlier news item. Our concluding sentence was: "It seems likely that Department of Transport officials will want experts to take another look at the frogs in Rampton's Hollow, and there remains the possibility that the road will now take the course originally intended".

I looked at Pete. "It seems a pity, really. Those frogs must be nicely settled by now."

"Oh Christ, Chris! First rule of newspaper reporting – don't get involved. Anyway, it'll be a miracle if I can get this past Bill. I'll put it on his desk first thing in the morning. Sometimes he comes in with indigestion and he'll agree to anything just to get me out of his office."

I was sitting on Pete's bed, wearing a shirt that smelled of him, a watch, and my worn gold wedding-ring. We were eating cheese biscuits and drinking wine straight from the bottle. It was getting dark outside and Keith would be strolling towards the clubhouse.

Pete said, "You know, I've been doing some thinking about Mike Stoddart. I think we may have misjudged him. I don't think he was a blackmailer, pure and simple. He was

161

an outsider. He liked screwing people up. He didn't just do it for the money, he did it to get back at the bastards. He screwed up Mr and Mrs Jordan-Booth, who were rich and thoughtless, and Lynn Cazalet of Social Services, and the Department of Transport, and possibly Mr Tipping himself, the Chairman of the Planning Committee. Nice going. I've been targetting people like that for years and not getting half as far with it."

"You make it sound as if it was a sort of crusade. You sound as if you admire him."

"Not really. I don't admire anyone – unless they've got good legs and a nice smile, of course."

"Sexist!"

"There, you see, you are a feminist at heart. If someone told me I had good legs and a nice smile I wouldn't object."

"You have got a nice smile. Anyway, we're not getting very far with finding Mike Stoddart's murderer."

"No, that's true. All we know for sure is that it was someone he was blackmailing and that it was probably one of the Conference delegates."

"He was supposed to have an appointment with someone. *And* it had to be someone who could get hold of heroin."

"Anybody can get hold of heroin if they really want it. We seem to be short of someone with a clear-cut motive."

"Yes, a motive – what if it was a case of mistaken identity? You never saw Mike Stoddart. He was tall and dark – from behind he could easily be mistaken for Eric De Broux. What if he went out in the hotel grounds to meet a lady friend, and Dr Goodburn, mad with jealousy over his first wife, mistook him for De Broux –"

"And injected him with a syringeful of heroin he had brought along for the purpose of despatching De Broux? An odd choice of weapon, if you're determined it was a crime of passion."

"Well, it would explain why Dr Rachel went for me that time – assuming he'd confessed to her."

"But I've *told* you what was the matter with Dr Rachel. You ever thought of giving all this up and writing crime thrillers? Don't keep looking at your watch." I hadn't noticed that I was. "Does he always get home at exactly the same time, your husband?"

"More or less."

"Have you got a good excuse ready for where you've been, just in case?"

"Yes." I shivered. I wasn't cold. Pete put his arm round me and kissed me.

"I hope you realise I'm very taken with you," he said, licking my ear. "In future, I'm going to look forward to Mondays –"

I must have been extremely agitated when I got home that night. I remember seeing the garage doors gaping open, dark and empty, and thinking that at least I wouldn't have to try out my story on Keith. I ran straight in and found Julie in the kitchen. We had coffee and chocolate biscuits and talked over Angie's boyfriend problems. What I didn't do was switch off the lights of my car. How Keith drove past it without noticing I've no idea, except that it was raining hard by that time and he just hurried in with a towel over his head. Anyway, in the morning I had a flat battery and had to appeal for next-door's help with jump leads.

It was after half past nine when I arrived in the Herald car park, and no sooner had I switched off the engine than large angry drops of rain began exploding on the windscreen. Within seconds it was raining so hard I couldn't see the end of the car bonnet and the clattering on the roof made me feel like a war correspondent under artillery fire. I decided to sit it out; "my car had a flat battery" is a perfectly acceptable excuse for being late, whereas "my child was sick", or "the washing-machine flooded" never would be. Suddenly there was a frantic knocking on the passenger door. I unlocked it and Pete slid inside, dripping water from nose, hair and ears.

"You're late!" he exclaimed, shaking his head like a dog.

"And you're wet! What did you come out for?"

"I've been watching for you from my window. I thought something had happened to you, because I've a strong suspicion, darling, that you're not terribly good at deceiving people."

163

"Oh, I'm not so bad," I said, with a pang of guilt. "It's nice to see you, anyway."

We thought no one could see us through the rain. We sat together waiting for it to stop, and then we started kissing and cuddling like teenagers and didn't notice that it had. Keith hadn't kissed me in a car since he collected me from the hospital after Julie's birth. Then, for the second time that day, the passenger door was wrenched open.

"If you two must do that," said Bill Heslop, coldly, "I wish you'd do it on your own time. I want you both in my office – now!"

Mr Heslop sat at his desk with the confident malice of a headmaster who has just apprehended the wretched child who set fire to his wastepaper-basket. I sat down as I was told, but Pete leaned against the doorpost with his arms folded, refusing to be intimidated.

"Now," said Mr Heslop. "What's all this silly nonsense about frogs?"

"It's all there, Bill," said Pete. "It's a true story. Those are the facts."

"This is *it*? This is all you have?" He picked up the paper and studied it dramatically, as though looking for something written in invisible ink. "I'm not printing this! You've got nothing!"

"Bill – this is the truth. Eric De Broux paid for those frogs to be planted there. We know that, though admittedly we haven't been able as yet to nail him down. When we do, we'll –"

"I'm not printing this if you can't prove it!"

"We *will* prove it when the Department of Transport holds an enquiry, which they'll have to, if –"

"This is irresponsible reporting, Pete, and you know it! This newspaper does not go in for that kind of journalism!" He tossed the paper contemptuously into a tray on his desk. Pete seized it.

"For Christ's sake, we *know* this is the truth! You think it's irresponsible? I think it's bloody restrained! De Broux admitted it to us – I haven't even mentioned his bloody name!"

"I *will not* print it if you can't prove it. And you *can't* prove it. *And* I don't want either of you upsetting De Broux again. The man's an advertiser, for God's sake!"

Pete went over to the window and punched a dictionary on the sill.

"It's a bloody good thing you weren't running this newspaper when America was discovered," he said, furiously. "You wouldn't have printed it until someone came back with a hamburger and a copy of the New York Times!"

Mr Heslop turned slowly to look at him.

"Don't carry this Latin temperament thing too far with me, Pete. If you want to resign, say so."

Pete swore under his breath and scowled out of the window.

"Well, well," said Mr Heslop, turning to me. "I used to wonder what was the big fascination with this Stoddart thing. Now I know. Well, well."

I could feel my face colouring from the neck upwards.

"I blame myself in a way," he went on. "I should have seen this coming." Pete shot him a sharp look, which he ignored. "Listen, Chris, why don't you take a week's holiday, spend some more time with your family?"

Pete looked from one to the other of us incredulously. He seemed about to speak, but I said, "I've already got my holiday booked. In October, for my second honeymoon –" If I could have pressed a button and died right there, I would have. I didn't look at Pete. He walked out of the room and slammed the door behind him.

I stood up. "Thank you, Mr Heslop, but I don't want to take any time off. I'm sorry I was late in this morning. I think I'd better go and catch up."

Pete's desk was empty. I looked out of the window and saw his car speed out through the car park exit to the accompaniment of outraged hooting. Later, I received a message to meet him in the Star at lunchtime.

When I arrived, he'd obviously been drinking for a while but seemed surprisingly calm.

"It's just the way it goes," he said. "So near and yet so far,

165

the story of my life. Cheers – have a double. Apparently De Broux rang Bill after we'd left yesterday and complained about harassment. Then he threatened to withdraw his advertising, and finally offered him a year's free membership of the Gourmet Club. Well, we all know the way to Bill's heart. I used to know one of the secretaries rather well, and she told me all about it. So – it's farewell to frogs time. You're not taking that holiday, are you?"

I shook my head. "I feel awful, though."

"Don't. He doesn't care what we do with our lives. I could kill him, you know. I'm going to give his name to the British Heart Foundation – get them to send him all their literature about rich diets and heart disease. That'll put him off his bloody gourmet dinners!"

I laughed.

"There is one thing, though, that you should know," said Pete. "I just came from the police station. They expect to make an arrest in the Michael Stoddart case – within the next twenty-four hours."

16

At approximately nine-thirty on Wednesday morning the
Herald received a 'phone call about the hold-up of a
Securicor van just outside Hudderston. A guard had been
shot and in the ensuing car chase two cars and a milk float
were overturned – "blood and milk all over the road," said
the informant, cheerfully. Pete went out to cover the story,
and I was left to await the end of the Stoddart murder case
and my return to a non-stop diet of W.I. meetings and
planning disputes. I'd been thinking a lot about my "mistaken identity" theory, and I liked it. It didn't explain the
missing negatives, but perhaps there weren't any missing
negatives. There were bound to be a lot of unexplained
loose ends until the murderer was unmasked and encouraged to confess all. However, the biggest problem with my
theory remained the doubt over whether or not our Dr
Goodburn and De Broux's Dr Goodburn were one and the
same. I decided to try and find out. Then, if Dr Goodburn
was arrested, I could still do a "your own reporter worked it
out first" story.

I looked up the Goodburns' home 'phone number. It was
ten o'clock, and they were bound to be out and their house
empty, apart from – with luck – a maid. I was sure they
would have some sort of domestic help; one doesn't undergo
years of training for a profession only to have to load one's
own dishwasher. I dialled the number. Eventually an elderly
female voice announced: "the Goodburn residence".

"Is that Mrs Goodburn?" I asked, knowing perfectly well
that it wasn't.

"No. I'm the housekeeper."

"Oh good morning. I'm calling from Western Amalga-
mated Assurance. I have in front of me an old policy in the

names of John Goodburn and *Mae* Goodburn, who, I believe, was Dr Goodburn's first wife. The policy seems to have been superseded by one in the name of *Rachel* Goodburn, but before I lose it in the archives I wonder if you could confirm that Mae Goodburn was the wife of the John Goodburn at your address? I don't want to find I've got my Goodburns mixed up."

"Well, I –" The voice quavered. "I haven't been with the doctor that long. I think you'd better ask him."

"I see." I was disappointed, but I'd half expected something like this. "Look, there's a minor child on this policy. Their daughter, I believe –"

"Tamsin?"

"Yes, that's right." I wriggled joyfully in my seat. "I wonder if you could give me her present address?"

"I'll get the book." There was a long silence. When she came back, she said, "I don't think I ought to give you this over the 'phone. You could be anyone. You might be double glazing, or Timeshare, or cavity wall insulation. I saw that Channel 4 programme about telephone sales frauds –"

I clenched my fist and banged it soundlessly on the desk.

"Yes, yes, I understand. Don't worry, I'll write to Dr Goodburn." I put the 'phone down. The 'phone book had nothing listed under T. Goodburn, but then Tamsin would almost certainly be married by now. Even at the very end, I was to be thwarted in my efforts to solve the Stoddart mystery. There was nothing for it but to give up.

I was decanting my mid-morning coffee from the saucer to the cup when my 'phone rang. There seemed to be no one at the other end of it.

"Hello? Anybody there?"

"I want to see you." The voice was muffled, young and unrecognisable.

"Who is this?"

"Ian."

I went through a list of Richard's friends, but still couldn't connect anyone with the voice.

"Twenty-five Edgeborough Avenue," said the voice. "I've

168

got something for you."

I remembered.

"What've you got?" I asked suspiciously, not keen to resume Ian's acquaintance.

"If you want to find out, come and see me. Now. Otherwise I don't give a toss." The pips started clamouring and then the 'phone went dead. I looked at my watch. I could go over to the squat, see Ian, sneak into Tesco's for some shopping, and still meet Pete in the Star at lunchtime as arranged. Just in case anything went wrong, though, I told the messenger on my way out that I was going to meet an informant at twenty-five Edgeborough Avenue, and that if anyone wanted me after that I'd be in the Star. Mentioning Tesco's would have spoiled the effect.

Twenty-five Edgeborough Avenue looked even less inviting than previously. Somebody had smashed a hole through the front door in the middle of the carefully painted polar bear's head, and the door now balanced on one hinge. I eased myself carefully past it, as it was a heavy front door, and through the dark damp gloom of the hall could make out the door marked "Ian keep out". That, too, was half open.

"Can I come in?" I called warily. The place was eerily quiet, as though something had just died there. I detected a noise, a breath, behind the door.

"Ian?"

The door opened slowly wider, and I suddenly knew that entering would be a mistake.

"Hello, Ian, I'm Chris from the Herald," I said brightly, taking a half step forward. In the grey light from the partly boarded up window I could make out Ian standing behind the door. He looked ill. He was wearing dark glasses, and beads of sweat glistened on his pale, unshaven face.

"You don't impress me," he said, not moving from the dark corner he crouched in. "You don't impress me a bit. You couldn't do sod all for anyone, could you?"

I stopped pretending to smile.

"What do you want?"

"I want a reporter. You're crap, you can't do anything for me."

169

"O.K. I don't have to take this," I said, crisply, turning to go, and quite impressed by my own assertiveness. "Go jump in a lake!" The sunlight from the street touched my face briefly, and then a hand caught the fabric of my blouse and pulled me back into the darkness. The door slammed. My eyes were looking at Ian's through the gloom. Slightly alarmed, I said, "Look, you rang me and I came. Tell me what it is you've got for me and I'll go. I've got other appointments."

"They're hassling me," said Ian.

"Who? Who's hassling you?"

He didn't answer. It was very quiet in the room. A lorry passed by and the window rattled slightly, but the sounds of the street seemed far away.

"The police. The police have been hassling me," said Ian.

"Well, write a letter to the Chief Constable." I meant to sound hard, but my voice was shaking. Ian didn't move. He had his hand on the door. I said, "Well, you said you'd got something for me, what is it? Do you want money first, is that it?" The bag over my shoulder contained thirty pounds in cash, plus credit cards. I suddenly thought, oh God, I'm putting ideas into his head. He gave a sigh that turned into a gulp, and shuddered convulsively.

"I want you to put it in your paper," he said.

"What?"

"That they're hassling me! You thick or what? Put it in your newspaper that I'm being hassled. That's what you want, isn't it? A shitty story. You see what they did to my door? They turned my place over. They can't do that." He gave another convulsive shudder, and drops of sweat splashed from beneath his lank, greasy hair. I felt moisture on my arm. I took a step backwards.

"You need a fix, don't you?" I said.

"Why? You got some stuff?"

"Of course I haven't. Look – you're a junkie and you're getting hassled. This can't be a new experience for you." I thought of Richard with horror. "Have you tried the National Council for Civil Liberties? I don't know –"

"I want them off my back!" shouted Ian, suddenly

170

jumping out of his corner and gripping me by the wrist. "You said you wanted something – I'll give you something! It's Clare you want to know about. I'll tell you about Clare."

"Clare? You mean the girl who died here?" I glanced around the room, with its broken furniture and jumble of filthy bedding. There seemed to be a lot of noise coming from the street. I tried to pull my arm away from Ian but his fingers were surprisingly strong.

"You've got it! I tell you where she got the stuff that killed her, you put my story in the paper, get the filth off my back. Deal?"

Ian had wildly overestimated not only the power of the press, but my power in particular. However, this did not seem the moment to say so.

"Deal," I said, weakly, trying again to release my hand.

There was a sudden crash in the hallway outside and almost simultaneously Ian reached out with his other hand and shot home a long bolt on the door.

"Police!" The door shook under the weight of pounding and rattling at the handle. "Open this bloody door!"

"I've got a woman in here!" screamed Ian. "Say something, bitch!" He twisted my wrist until something in my elbow clicked. I screamed. Ian let me go and stepped back from the door. "Get away! Get away or she's dead!" He reached into the pocket of his denim jacket and pulled out what looked like a silver fountain pen. He jerked the top off and it wasn't a pen; it was a knife with a four-inch blade tapered to a skewer like point. We both stared at it. The banging on the door had stopped.

"All right, son," came a self-confident voice from the street. "Let's not play games, shall we? You'll only make it worse for yourself in the long run. Come to the window and let's talk."

Ian wrenched me over to the window by the shoulder and forced me up against the sticky, cracked glass.

"See the bitch, do you? See the bitch?" He jabbed the knife into my adam's apple and I gagged on it, forcing the steel deeper into my throat. I waited for the warm rush of blood. For several seconds, everything went black.

171

". . . do anything silly." The voice floated into my consciousness, sounding less self-confident now. "Let's everybody keep calm. We'll talk about this."

Directly outside the house was a police car, its blue light turning relentlessly, and in the distance approaching sirens whipped up a frenzy of sound. As far as I could tell, I wasn't actually bleeding; at least my chest didn't feel wet, but then my whole body was numbed. A lot of people were gathering outside. Some were policemen, some women with shopping bags; through the grey smears on the glass and my panic they all looked unreal, like fading images on a badly tuned television screen.

A policeman with a flat hat and a loudhailer came forward.

"Ian! Ian Duggan! Come on son, let the lady go. There's no need for all this. You're putting yourself into a worse position. At the moment you're only wanted for questioning at the station. Let's clear this up, shall we?"

Ian laughed. He pulled me away from the window, only to force me up against it again hard enough to deal me a crushing blow to the nose. Suddenly I was seeing pictures of a little blonde-haired girl in a pink dress picking flowers, a little blonde girl in a red plastic mac on a climbing frame – Julie. *My* life should be flashing before my eyes but instead it was Julie's. Oh God, I thought, I'm cracking up, this is it, if I go into hysterics I'll never get out of here. I'll die in this dark place that smells of urine just like Clare did. We could hear noises inside the building, a splintering of rotten floorboards, terse muffled instructions. Ian shouted out of the window, "You won't get to me before I kill her! I'll do it now!"

The loudhailer response was immediate. "All right, son, O.K. I'm withdrawing my men from the house. Got it? We'll all calm down. Stand still and watch them come out."

There was further noise in the corridor. We saw four men leave by the front door. It went very quiet. There was only me and Ian in the world. His breath was coming in short painful rasps, and I wasn't breathing at all. A distant plane growled across the sky. I must be breathing or I'd be dead.

172

My elbow hurt where Ian had wrenched it and I tried to reach it with my other hand. Instantly Ian shifted the knife menacingly and muttered, "Stay still, bitch."

"Ian – Ian." At the second attempt I discovered that a whisper put only bearable pressure on the knife blade. "You were going to tell me about Clare." At that moment I didn't care about Clare, but it seemed like a mutual interest.

"What about Clare?"

"You were going to tell me where she got the stuff that killed her, you said. She was pregnant, wasn't she? She lived here with her boyfriend. And you were staying with them so you knew what was going on. Were you here the night it happened? Perhaps you tried to help her get a doctor. Did she feel ill and overdose by accident? Was it the fault of the pusher? Who –" I'd just about run out of the babble of questions I'd hoped would keep me alive when he interrupted contemptuously.

"Christ, you talk a lot of shit! You know nothing, do you, about being a junkie and being pregnant. You know nothing about anything. You're all the same, you do-gooding rich bitches, with your big cars and your fancy promises. Gives you a thrill, does it, taking risks, doing good for people. Long as *you* don't get your face rubbed in the shit, eh? Always a way out for you, isn't there? Well, not this time, there isn't!"

Ian was suddenly seized by a violent convulsion and hunched over in pain, releasing me. I ran through the semi-darkness towards where I hoped the door was and found instead another door, not bolted. Sobbing I grabbed the handle and wrenched and pushed, but not hard or fast enough. His fierce hands were on my neck again. I screamed. He laughed.

"Think you'll get away, do you? Don't make that noise! I broke into a flat in Holland Park once. There was this woman there with blue hair and a blue budgie. She screamed and so did the bloody budgie. I tied her up with a curtain cord. Then a got a kebab skewer from the kitchen. Know what I did? Know what I did?" I closed my eyes. Inside my head I said, don't tell me, don't tell me. "I'll tell you – I

173

skewered that budgie to the floor of its cage!" He laughed, but he'd gone very white. "You're not getting away from me again, any more than the bloody budgie. Put your hand on the wall."

I looked at my hands. I looked at his knife. I looked at his contorted face and clenched teeth. I knew exactly what he was going to do.

"Do it!" he screamed.

The left hand, I thought, at least I'll save the right one. Slowly I raised my left hand with the worn gold ring on the third finger and placed it on the flaky grey plaster of the wall.

Maybe my heart stopped at that moment, I don't know. Suddenly there was a tremendous explosion of noise and light in the room, and a blow to the back pitched me on to an evil-smelling mattress. I looked up in time to see Ian collapsing like a split sapling with dark blood bubbling from his mouth. The room was full of policemen. I was dragged out into the sunshine, over smashed doors, and people stared at me. A blur of strange faces, voices:

"Get her to the hospital –"

"You can see a lady doctor, if you want, love –"

"– take a statement later."

"What name shall –"

"Christ, who let the bloody Press through?"

Then, Pete's voice. "She's with me. I've come to collect her."

He looked at me and said, "Jesus Christ, what the hell have you been up to?" He was pale and shaken. His car was parked at an angle in the middle of the road and appeared to be splashed with milk.

"Get in, let's go," he said urgently, opening the passenger door, but I felt a heavy restraining hand on my shoulder.

"Oh, it's you, is it? I might have bloody known!" Inspector Franks loomed against the sun, looking menacing. "Well, I want you down at the station. You've just screwed up a perfectly routine operation."

"Not now," said Pete. "I'm taking her to the hospital."

"I'm O.K.!" I protested, leaning on the car for support.

"A couple of words for local radio?" said someone, thrusting forward a microphone.

"Sod off," said Pete.

Inspector Franks had disappeared into the crowd.

"Quick, let's get out of here," Pete said, pushing me into the car. Just as he was closing the door I saw Ernst approaching, grim-faced. He prodded Pete in the chest and glared at me.

"You two keep your hands off my bloody equipment," he said, and snapped off half a dozen pictures of my pale, dirty face and dishevelled hair. He had absolutely no sensitivity. Pete swore at him and jumped into the car. He switched on the engine and revved noisily, scattering onlookers in all directions. We accelerated away with a squeal of tyres.

"Are you all right?" he asked, driving erratically.

"Yes. That Ian is a lunatic! Oh God!" I took several deep breaths. I wished he wouldn't drive so fast.

"Are you sure you're all right?"

"Yes. I'd be better if you'd slow down. Thank you."

He drove into a cul-de-sac and stopped abruptly.

"I love you, Christine, and you're a bloody idiot," he said, suddenly and passionately. "I feel like hitting you."

"It wasn't my fault!"

"I still feel like hitting you. Christ!" He banged his forehead deliberately against the steering wheel, then sighed. "O.K. No more violence. You're white as a sheet."

We were parked outside a builders' merchants. Two men with shaven heads and tattoos were staring at us.

I said, "I'm afraid I feel a bit sick."

"Christ," said Pete. "Let's take you home. You need brandy and bed." He re-started the car. I looked at him in alarm. "Don't be silly, I didn't mean that," he said. "I do have some finer feelings. We'll talk all this out tomorrow."

When we arrived at my house, Keith's car was in the drive.

"Oh shit," said Pete, with feeling. "Bill must have rung him."

I could see Keith in the living room on the 'phone.

"You'd better go," I said.

"No," said Pete.

Keith saw us and put down the 'phone. Pete came round and helped me out of the car. He started walking up the drive with his arm round me.

"Here we are, safely delivered!" he said to Keith.

"Well, no bloody thanks to you lot!" shouted Keith.

"Come on, it could be worse – how would you have felt if they'd sent her to the Falklands?"

"They didn't send you to the Falklands, did they!"

There was silence. Pete's arm, on my shoulder, went rigid.

"I was in the Gulf at the time, working on an English language newspaper," he said, evenly. "Now there's trouble in the Gulf, and I'm here. That's the way it goes."

"Yes, you would say that, wouldn't you? You people, you thrive on the suffering and misery of others!"

Pete laughed without humour. "Yes. Well, I've had this conversation so many times –" The completing phrase "and with better men than you" hung on the air between us, fortunately unuttered.

I said, "I really don't feel very well."

"Course you don't, darling," said Pete. "Go and have a brandy and sleep on it. Write it all up in the morning. We love you." He kissed me lightly on the mouth and smiled disarmingly at Keith. "You should take care of her. She's really something."

As he drove away, Keith took me into the house, glowering, and poured me a large brandy. Then I had to tell him what had happened. I toned it down a bit – well, a lot – and this made him more angry than reassured. Why did he have to get called away from important meetings because of my escapades? Other wives had perfectly respectable things happen to them, like car accidents or appendices perforating – why did I have to get into such sordid and inexplicable situations? I sat and listened to the silence left behind by Pete's car engine. Keith had tossed his jacket and tie across the sofa arm and I would have to pick them up and press them. I came closer to panic then than at any other time that day. I buried my face in a cushion and stifled a scream.

17

At about midday on Thursday, in plenty of time for Friday's edition of the Herald, it was announced that Ian Duggan had been charged with the murder of Michael Stoddart and had made a full confession.

"But it's ridiculous!" I said to Pete. "What possible motive could he have had?"

"Motive? What do you mean *motive*, for Christ's sake? Psychopaths like that don't need motives, especially not when they're full of drugs. I've seen perfectly normal people do some pretty weird things after drinking too much home-made beer, let alone taking heroin."

"Well – yes. The old lady who lived next door to him did say they had an argument and he admitted it himself. Yesterday he said he had something to tell me about Clare and about her heroin supplier, and then he kept on about do-gooding rich bitches – it was almost as though he were confusing me with someone else."

"There you are, you see. Deranged. It's ironic, really. Someone like Stoddart who makes a career out of making enemies goes and gets bumped off by a common or garden lunatic. Just see what a lucky escape you had." He hesitated. "Was – did – Your husband didn't seem very sympathetic about it."

I looked away. I didn't want to discuss Keith with him. "I told you. He doesn't approve of my working for the Herald. I didn't dare tell him just how awful it really was yesterday."

"I see. Not exactly a close and caring relationship then, is it?"

I turned to go.

"Chris – get on to your social worker friend some time. I'd like to have a look at that list of Edgeborough Avenue houses. It might be worth looking into, and if Stoddart did some homework on it we might as well have the benefit of it."

To say I had a bad weekend would be putting it mildly. In the first place, I kept waking at five every morning with a start and looking at my left hand to see if there was a knife in it. On Sunday, in the half-light, I thought I saw a large spider sitting there on top of the grey blue vein which protrudes just a little beneath my second finger. I screamed and woke Keith. I had steeled myself for a horrific injury and some part of me was cheated that it had not materialised. Keith cuddled me, but couldn't resist remarking for the fourth time that lady reporters shouldn't be sent to interview criminals, especially when there were loud-mouthed jerks like Pete (he didn't use the word jerk) who were just made for the job. He had come home from work on Friday enraged by my appearance on the front page of the Herald, because apparently most of his colleagues found it necessary to ask him if I'd run down Lord Lucan or the Brinks Mat gang yet, and what was it like being married to a Mrs James Bond! To add to this, we received more than a dozen 'phone calls from local people, some of whom we vaguely knew, all anxious to confirm that I was the lady in the Edgeborough Avenue drama and to ask a few not very discreet questions about the experience. I began to have some sympathy for the view that the tabloid press only caters for the prurient curiosity of ordinary people. Anyway, late on Saturday evening I'd just about had enough and when an elderly female voice enquired "Are you the lady on the front page of the Herald –" I snapped "yes, and if you'd care to send me a stamped addressed envelope, I'll let you have a signed photo with details of my bra size and the brand of cornflakes I eat!" I instantly regretted this, in case the caller turned out to be someone I knew, but Julie, who was listening, said "Brilliant!"

I called in at Lynn Cazalet's office early on Monday morning, and she was actually there. She'd done something different to her hair and wasn't wearing glasses; also she'd painted her fingernails red. She looked at me strangely, and I realised that she didn't recognise me either, with the perm and re-vamped make-up. I wondered guiltily if we both had new men in our lives.

"You said you'd lend me the key to Mike Stoddart's flat," I reminded her.

"Oh, yes." She smiled, opened a drawer and pulled out a stack of files, cartons of paper clips, and an enormous box of Belgian chocolates with a red ribbon and a scrawled message on the lid. Her eyes registered a warm glow at the sight of this. She produced the key and handed it to me.

"They're all coming down, those houses," she said.

"That's not really definite."

She shrugged. "All I know is, there's a lot of people needing to be re-housed. Some very difficult cases, too. Oh!" She looked at me in sudden surprise. "I don't often read the Herald, but weren't you – ?"

I managed to smile. "Yes. Best forgotten about, actually."

"Really? Haven't you been recommended to seek counselling?"

Inwardly I groaned. The last thing I needed was to have to talk to someone else about the events of the previous Wednesday.

"I'm fine, honestly. And you – are you all right – over things now?"

She took her breath in sharply and let it out again. "To be honest, it's a period of my life I'm not particularly keen to remember. Still, we all do things we're not proud of, don't we?"

"Yes, I'm afraid so."

"And of course," she went on, "now they've caught the murderer the whole thing's over with. It's odd, isn't it, but somehow the very name of Edgeborough Avenue seems to be synonymous with death and misery. Perhaps it'll be as well when it's wiped off the map."

"There are quite a few people who agree with you." I thought of the dark, filthy room where Ian Duggan had lived and where a girl called Clare had died. It can't have been a good place to await the birth of your baby. "Tell me," I said,

179

"if a girl gets pregnant, and she's also a heroin addict, would there be any particular problems?"

She looked understandably surprised by the question. I could have mentioned Clare by name, but it seemed likely that Pete had already harassed Social Services on the subject.

"It's just that I've got a friend with a daughter in this predicament. My friend is extremely worried."

Lynn shook her head. "Well, so she should be. Her daughter probably won't carry the baby full term, and when it's born it'll be addicted. Is the girl a registered addict?"

"I don't know."

"You see this is part of the problem. These girls desperately need medical help, but they won't seek it because they're afraid their babies will be taken into care. And I have to say that they frequently are. It's a critical time, pregnancy. And what with Aids and everything – if we could only get them not to share needles. There's always the risk of tainted heroin, too, and miscarriage –" She shook her head again.

"Yes. I see. Not a happy picture." Her 'phone rang. "Well, I won't take up any more of your time. Thanks for this. I'll return it."

Lynn lifted the 'phone with her hand over the mouthpiece. "No," she said, very definitely. "Don't bother."

The door and windows of Ian Duggan's late residence were covered with brand new boards, glinting with nails, but already someone had spray painted obscenities across them. We parked outside Mike Stoddart's flat, had a quick look round to make sure the area was devoid of police, then let ourselves in to the flat. It smelt of mould and musty bed linen. His wardrobe and chest had been emptied, and the contents packed into cardboard boxes. The bed had been stripped to the extent that the mattress was patterned with diagonal cuts, spilling wadding on to the floor. An unwashed shirt, thrown carelessly over the pile of blankets, was mute testimony to the fact that this had once been someone's home.

"Eerie, isn't it?" remarked Pete. "All that's left of a man's life."

He tipped out the contents of the wastepaper-basket: empty Kodak film boxes, Polo mint wrappers, a broken pencil.

"Fast film," he said, holding up one of the film boxes. "For night photography without a flash, in case you didn't know."

I was afraid that at any moment we'd be discovered in our search and Keith would be called away from work yet again, this time to bail me out of the police-station. I helped Pete check quickly through the contents of the cardboard boxes; one contained clothes, another, books, papers and photographs. Pete examined these with swift expertise and shook his head.

"The only interesting thing about the contents of this box is what's missing – negatives. There are literally hundreds of photos and not a single negative. I know it doesn't seem to matter any more, but it is odd." He picked up an empty wrapper marked "Reynolds and Dobbs, photographic suppliers". "This reminds me. I haven't sent off my holiday snaps yet."

"I don't think I've taken my Christmas ones out of the camera yet, either. You know – you don't think Mike Stoddart might have had a film in for processing?"

"That's a thought! Yes, that is a thought. If someone went through here and took his negatives and the film from his camera, would they think of checking with the processors? And if not –"

"I could call in when I'm shopping. It's next to the dry-cleaners."

"You're so practical! Will you do me a favour and put my film in at the same time? It's in the car."

We went next to the kitchen. The drawers had been removed from the kitchen dresser and stacked on the floor, their contents crowded on to a small table. The pad which had contained the list of numbers and names was next to the drawers, but the top sheet had been removed. I held it up to the light, trying to make something out of the faint impressions that remained on the paper.

181

"What possible reason could the police have for taking away the list?" I asked.

"I can't imagine," said Pete. "Unless they guessed what we guessed. Or – more likely – somebody wrote down a racing-tip on the top sheet and took it away with them. It's a bloody nuisance. I'll have to start from scratch looking up who owns what in this street. Still, it'll take my mind off you." He gave me a chaste kiss on the lips.

There was little else to see in the flat. The police had searched it thoroughly for drugs, lifting floorboards, dismantling the toilet cistern, and removing the front of the gas fire.

"I wonder if they found anything," I said.

"I don't know, but I had a call from Taffy this morning. He wants to meet me in Hudderston this lunchtime. I like the sound of that – it means he doesn't want to be seen with me, so he must have something interesting to tell me." He crossed to the front window and looked out. "Well, Stoddart had a good view of his friendly neighbourhood psychopath," he remarked, looking across at the boarded up windows of the squat. "Most murder victims turn out to have been killed by people they knew well – comforting thought, isn't it?"

On the way out I noticed the door of Edie Clough's flat half-open. A pale face peered at us.

"I'm not going," she said. "It's no good to me, electric heating and that. I got all the hot water I want."

"Hello, Edie," I said resignedly.

"There's so many of you," she went on. "Council and Social and all that. I won't go. This is my home."

"How's Gladstone?"

"Gone! I think they poisoned him." She started to cry. "They want to stop me. They think it's not important, what I do. I made parachutes, you know, hundreds of them. Men's lives depended on me! I did my bit! This is my *home*! Can't you do nothing?" Her hand reached out, snake like, and fastened on to my arm.

"I'm from the Herald, Edie. I'll make a note of your protest." I didn't particularly like strangers holding me, but I shook her off gently.

182

As we got into the car I took a long look at the boarded up door of Number Twenty-Five, once resplendent with its arctic scene.

"Pete, when you followed up the Clare story, did you talk to Ian?"

"No. He wasn't there. I couldn't even get hold of the boyfriend. He'd called the ambulance – too late, of course – and then panicked and 'phoned his parents. They came down in a Mercedes and took him off to their big house in the country. I couldn't get to him at all. I think they sent him away for a cure. Why?"

"Would you mind very much if I tried to see him? Just curiosity, really."

"No, of course I wouldn't mind. But it's a dead story, darling, people like that forget very quickly."

Pete dropped me off in the High Street and I collected Keith's dry-cleaning and called at Reynolds and Dobbs. Sadly, my brilliant idea came to nothing; there were no uncollected photographs in the name of Stoddart. Still, I handed in Pete's film and bought new films for my camera, ready for our once-so-looked-forward-to second honeymoon. I was still analysing my reactions to this forthcoming event when I reached Tesco's. On her way out, walking straight out with a wire basket of groceries, was Rachel Goodburn. Nobody stopped her or looked at her. She marched out to her black BMW parked on a double yellow line, dropped the basket on the back seat and sped to an emergency stop at a red traffic light. Heavens, I thought, what you can get away with if you have the right air of authority! Then, more soberly, I remembered my interview with her and Mrs Taylor's remarks about her "going right off" lately, and I felt guilty. The poor woman was clearly at a difficult point in her life, and being harassed by people like Pete and me could in itself have contributed to this appalling lapse. I was glad to see that no one had followed her.

Pete did not return to his desk that afternoon, nor did he 'phone to confirm our evening assignation. I went home feeling rather uneasy. Richard and Julie were in the kitchen, having a row. It seemed to be about who should clear the mountain of washing up in the sink so one of them could prepare a snack. They stopped when they saw me.

"Mum'll do it," said Richard, with Keith's old beguiling smile.

"Mum won't!" I said angrily. "Sort it out between you. We all work in this house now." (Julie had just started a summer job in a refreshment kiosk.)

"You'll be sorry when I'm gone," muttered Richard, with a wink at Julie.

"What's that supposed to mean?"

"Why don't you tell her?" said Julie. "She probably wants to let your room out anyway. Or can I have it – we could knock down the wall and make a nice big –"

"What are you two on about?"

"Richard's going to Africa!"

Richard had suddenly dived into the washing-up.

"What's this about Africa?"

He ran water noisily into the sink. "Well, Mum, it seems like such a good opportunity. I'm only *thinking* about it. Carolyn's been invited out to Zimbabwe, and we're thinking of buying an old van, doing a sort of tour –"

"But Richard, your career!"

"It'll wait! I can come back to it. You and Dad are always saying how you wished you'd done more things when you were young. I'm only thinking about it."

I glanced at my watch and pushed Richard away from the washing up.

"You're mad. You're not thinking about it at all. You're just thinking what you want to think." My plans for Richard and Carolyn seemed to be backfiring on me badly. I attacked last night's shepherd's pie dish with determined savagery. "I don't know what your father will say!"

"Will you tell him tonight when he gets in?" asked Julie, a glint in her eye.

I looked at my watch again. "Well, perhaps not tonight. He goes out on Mondays."

"You going out as well?" she asked.

184

"Well, yes, I might. If no one's going to be in I thought I might as well call and see Judith." Judith was an old school friend and my "alibi".

Julie stared at me accusingly, hands on hips.

"You and Dad are always out these days. When one goes out, so does the other. It's like Bleak House around here. Which one of you is having the affair, I should like to know?"

I caught my breath. "Don't be so silly! That's that Heather talking! What nonsense!"

The two of them exchanged amused glances. This was the old pattern, one getting the other into trouble, then the two uniting and defending themselves by a divisive attack on Keith and me. I shouldn't take Julie's remark to heart. She couldn't possibly be serious. I blushed into the washing-up bowl and finished the dishes while my children waited politely.

I rang Pete's doorbell for a long time, but no one answered. His car was not in its place. I sat in the Mini and stared at the net-curtained windows of the downstairs flat. Perhaps Pete had gone to the off-licence. Why were men so unpredictable? No, that was a pointless question; Keith was always predictable, and Richard would have been were it not for the dreadful Carolyn. I should have explained things more strongly to the Reverend Harlow. Richard would leave home, Julie would go away to college, and I'd be left with Keith. I wanted to bang my head on the steering-wheel. One of the net curtains twitched slightly, and I glimpsed a grey face watching me. How many other ladies had sat where I was sitting now, waiting for Pete to honour them with his presence? He said he loved me, but that could mean anything or nothing. He said I made him feel as if he was nineteen again, and if his novel about the adventures of the nineteen-year-old Nick was anything to go by, that must have been intended as a compliment.

For perhaps ten minutes, my thoughts see-sawed back and forth over my various problems.

My friend Judith had once had an affair with a dentist. She

was in her late twenties at the time – the right age for such things, while one's children are chocolate-mouthed and leaky, and one's husband has suddenly developed a passion for hang-gliding or almost anything that will get him out of the house and parental responsibilities. I provided her with alibis when required. The affair ended when the dentist got back together with his wife and Judith, sadder but wiser, decided to have a third baby. Her husband never found out, and she confided that the whole thing had been absolutely and totally worth it. But what would happen to Keith and me after Pete? We certainly wouldn't have another baby.

I looked at my watch. He's not coming, I thought, he doesn't want me any more. "How could he do this?" I moaned aloud, not sure which hurt worse, being rejected, or being without him.

Reversing has never been something I do well, and I was concentra‥ng so hard on finding the gap in the forecourt wall that it wasn't until the last moment that I saw the dark green shape of Pete's car behind me. Overwhelmed by relief I jumped briefly on the accelerator instead of the brake. Pete, who must have lightning reactions, swerved violently and there was an explosion of breaking glass followed by the sound of a myriad falling fragments. I had somehow stopped and stalled the engine. Pete got out, looking startled, and went to inspect the damage.

"Bloody hell, Christine," he said. "What were you trying to do? You're supposed to run into your lover's arms not his bloody car!"

"I'm so sorry – I don't know how it happened. I'll pay for the damage," I said, climbing weakly to my feet.

"Don't be insulting! It's only a headlamp anyway. Hello, Mrs MacDonald!" he called out loudly to a movement behind the net curtains. "She wants to see if I'm going to hit you. Let's give the old bat something to think about." He seized me and bent me backwards over the bonnet of the Mini, kissing me passionately and melodramatically.

"That'll teach her to mind my car with her shopping trolley," he muttered.

"You're very cheerful, considering," I said. "Have you

186

been drinking?"

"Yes, of course I have. All afternoon in a Chinese restaurant in Hudderston. But that's not the reason. Come on,
let's clear this mess up and I'll tell you all about it."

Impulsively I put my arms round him and hugged him
tightly. He couldn't have known the reason for the gesture,
but he hugged me back.

His flat was untidy with the untidiness of a person who
lives alone and never bothers to put anything away, and it
didn't look as though the Hoover had been used since my
last visit. He'd brought home two bottles of wine and a
carrier bag of Chinese food.

"It should still be hot," he said, handing me a fork. "I
went through two red lights to get here. It's all for you. I
don't think I'll ever be able to look a prawn in the balls
again."

I love prawn balls and I was suddenly hungry, so I picked
up the fork. Pete drank a glass of Alka Seltzer and then
reached for the vodka.

"You eat, darling," he said. "I'll talk. Let me tell you first
about Taffy. I've known him ever since I came to Tipping.
He's a good old-fashioned policeman – joined the force to
catch criminals and keep old ladies on scooters off the
motorway. There aren't too many of his kind about nowadays, believe me."

"Well, Inspector Franks certainly isn't one of them."

"No, right. I'm coming to that. It's the Ian Duggan confession that has upset Taffy. Apparently he made it about as
voluntarily as a pig goes to the slaughterhouse. Not that
anyone expects a criminal to be responsive to tea and sympathy, but Taffy reckons this is a real stitch-up. Apparently
the Inspector had been spitting blood over the Stoddart
murder. He wanted a quick result."

"I suppose it was an embarrassment to him, having been
so close to the scene of the crime when it happened."

"Probably. Anyway he hit on Duggan as being a likely
suspect right from the start, because he's got previous con-
victions for theft and assault and he's heavily into drugs.
They pulled him in for questioning a few times and turned

his place over looking for illegal substances, you know the kind of thing."

"That's what Duggan was complaining about. He wanted us to run a story on police harassment."

"Well, finally they decided to pull him in and get a statement out of him. They tailed him around for a couple of days so he wouldn't have access to his usual sources of drugs, then when they were sure he was desperate for a fix, they pounced. And that's when you unfortunately got in the way." Pete reached for his jacket, which was slung over the back of the chair, and produced his notebook. "Taffy repeated to me some of the statement. Listen. It was a sunny evening and Duggan had had a fix. He went out in the street and sat on the bonnet of Mike Stoddart's Cortina. Stoddart came out and told him to piss off. They had quite a row about it – to which there was a witness, apparently – and then Stoddart went off to the Clocktower Hotel. Duggan thought things over for a while, then decided to follow Stoddart up to the Clocktower. He walked and hitched his way there, and by the time he arrived it was dark. He hung around in the grounds waiting for Stoddart to come out. Eventually he did come out and Duggan accosted him. He says Stoddart laughed at him and called him names, there was a struggle, and Duggan got angry and jabbed him with a syringeful of heroin."

"What – he took heroin with him as a murder weapon?"

"No. According to the statement he had the stuff on him for his own use – one syringeful would have been enough for two or three fixes – fatal, of course, if administered all in one go. What he's saying is that he did it while he was out of his mind – it seemed like a good idea at the time." He shrugged. "It makes sense of a sort, and of course it would clear police books of the murder. But they need evidence to support a confession and this is where we get to the interesting bit. Duggan says in his statement that he carried the body up the fire escape and hanged it with the tow-rope – he's not sure where he got the tow-rope from – and then he took Stoddart's flat and car keys, went back to the car and stole the camera. All right, so far, so good. He was about to go

188

when he decided he was hungry. So he entered the hotel through an unlocked kitchen door and helped himself to cheese. That was when he deposited the syringe in the Stilton. Then he wandered round a bit, got scared, and dumped the camera and flat keys in a wastepaper basket –"

I stopped a forkful of beanshoots on its way to my mouth.

"But that can't possibly be true because the camera and keys weren't found until –"

"Exactly. But wait, there's more. He says in the statement he drove off in Stoddart's car, changed his mind, abandoned the car in Rampton's Hollow and walked the rest of the way home. The police have no witnesses to any of this, of course, *but* they have got a good set of Duggan's prints on the camera. And this is what particularly concerns Taffy. He believes that Duggan's prints got on the camera *while it was in the police-station.*" He leaned back in the chair, taking a large sip of his vodka.

I shook my head, uncomprehending.

"You mean the police framed him and got him to invent the whole confession? Why would he do that?"

"Oh, come on. He was desperate for a fix. They convinced him that if he confessed to killing Stoddart while temporarily unbalanced through drugs he'd get a light sentence, and then they worked on the confession, bit by bit. It was Inspector Franks himself who obtained this confession. By the end of it all Duggan would have signed anything to get himself a fix."

I remembered Richard's comment that he'd have said anything the police wanted, just to get out of the station.

"And you really believe that Inspector Franks would go so far as to falsify evidence?"

"I do, but it isn't what *I* believe, it's what Taffy is alleging. And we know ourselves that that camera can't have been put in the wastepaper-basket on the night of the murder. Taken together, these two facts call into question the whole confession. Don't look so shocked. You must know that if the police get someone for burglary they'll encourage him to admit to fifty-nine previous offences just to clear their books. Duggan is a dangerous menace, and it was a small

189

step on from normal practice for Inspector Franks to see to it that he was well and truly stitched up. But he reckoned without Taffy's conscience – and us, of course."

"Yes, well, I didn't like the Inspector much –"

Pete smiled. "He's got fancy friends, apparently, and he likes to keep in with them. A mugging or a burglary in the better parts of town would get high police priority, as compared to a similar offence in, say, Edgeborough Avenue."

"Yes, people with red box burglar alarms," I murmured, thinking of something Lynn Cazalet had once said. "The Inspector is a close friend of Major Duncton. They own a yacht."

"Really. Well, good old Taffy doesn't think much of his methods of policing Tipping." He gave a sudden, bright smile and kissed me on the forehead. "And the best thing, darling, is this. Look." He produced a pocket cassette recorder from his jacket and placed it on the table next to the chicken with crispy noodles. "I got it all on tape."

"Did Taffy know you were doing that? No, wait. I don't think I want to know that. It's your conscience."

He grinned and helped himself to crispy noodles. "Police harassment. A false confession. Tampering with evidence in a murder case. This is Sunday Times material! When it comes to trial, I may be able to sell it to their Insight team. Maybe we can even present them with the real murderer by then."

I looked at him. I'd come out tonight steeled – well, anxious – to commit adultery, and instead I was involved in police-corruption and deals with the Sunday Times.

"Here's to fame and fortune and to hell with frogs," said Pete, filling his empty vodka glass with wine. We touched glasses. He looked tired, but happy; in fact his face looked younger and softer than usual. I wondered if this was because of the story – or me. I put down my fork, leaned forward, and kissed him gently on the throat.

"Don't let's think of it now," I said. "I want to make it up to you for the car."

"Oh! Well." He held his car keys out to me. "In that case, here – go and drive the damn thing into a wall. That ought to

190

be worth a whole night with you."

When I left, Pete escorted me downstairs. He said, "Chris, I've got to see more of you."

"You've seen all there is to see of me."

"Silly! You know what I mean. I'm only sure I'm alive when I'm with you."

It was too dark to see his face.

"Me too," I said.

He took a deep breath and let it out slowly. "Go home now, if you're going."

"I'm really sorry about the car."

He laughed and said enigmatically, "And I'm really sorry about your husband."

On the way home, I thought, I'm forty, we're both forty, we know better than to imagine ourselves in love. This is awful, but it isn't catastrophic. I parked the Mini, switched off the lights and went into the house. I didn't once think about Mike Stoddart, Ian Duggan, or Taffy's story of police corruption.

18

"What do you know about Ellis Willard?" enquired Mr Heslop, rolling up his sleeves to inspect his suntan.

"Who?"

. "Ellis Willard. I thought you listed literature on your C.V. as one of your main interests."

Yes, I had, but that was when I still thought an interest in English literature would be an asset to a newspaper reporter.

"Ellis Willard was apparently Tipping's only published poet of any note," said Mr Heslop. "He lived at number thirty-one Edgeborough Avenue for a time, and this bunch calling themselves the 'Friends of Tipping's Heritage' have dug him up as a reason to preserve Edgeborough Avenue in its original form. They'll be after one of those blue plaques and a bloody tourist guide-book next. Anyway, find something out about him from the library, will you?"

"Yes, Mr Heslop."

"This dispute is building up nicely. We can keep it going right through August. They're holding a public meeting on the 23rd, by the way, in the old Church Hall, to display the plans."

"I hope it doesn't rain then. The last time I was there the roof leaked."

He sat on the corner of my desk, arms folded, looking at me.

"You know, you're normally so practical and sensible. You're too old to need fatherly advice, and of course I'm too young to give it to you, but really – you seem to have some sort of blind spot where our mutual friend is concerned."

I didn't answer.

Mr Heslop sighed. "Don't forget about Ellis Willard."

                    *   *   *   *   *

I spent a morning in the library looking up Ellis Willard. He
was a minor nineteenth-century poet who didn't make it into
the Oxford Dictionary of Quotations, and his chief claim to
fame seemed to lie in the fact that he once removed and
burned all his clothes on the doorstep of a lady love who'd
spurned him. He was also a hopeless opium addict, and it
seemed quite appropriate to me that a Drug Abuse Clinic
should be sited in the vicinity of his home. I said so in my
story. Mr Heslop looked at it and shook his head.

"No," he said. "Let's keep the issue clear cut. It's a case of
jobs and a clinic against architectural and cultural heritage."

"But don't you think there's a certain irony in –"

"Look, this is the Tipping Herald, not the bloody Guard-
ian! And I want some nice bits of poetry, too, about autumn
leaves and English woodsmoke in the nostrils. You know,
impressions of an English countryside the cretins round here
actually think exists!"

He'd got severe indigestion. I said, "Yes, Mr Heslop,"
and left him to it.

On Wednesday evening, Richard announced that he and
Carolyn had changed their minds about going to Africa.
They were going to withdraw all their savings and "do the
world".

"I blame you for this," said Keith, predictably. "Ever
since you started work on the Herald things have gone from
bad to worse. Look at the state of this place! No wonder the
boy wants to get away. This isn't a home any more, it's a
hostel – and a bloody poorly-run one at that!"

"The boy wants to get away because he'd like to see the
world and he's found someone who'll happily share his
sleeping-bag with him while he does it."

"My God! That's fine talk coming from you! What the hell
do you know about sharing sleeping-bags? You get your
kicks from playing around with phrases on bits of paper,
making up nice stories about boring people. Yes, and don't
remind me about sleeping-bags. We did share one once,
didn't we, and I've paid for it ever bloody since!"

"You've paid for it! What about me?"

"What about you? I've given you everything you've ever wanted! If it wasn't for me you wouldn't be able to afford to play at being a newspaper reporter. Even in the sixties not every girl who was stupid enough to get herself pregnant got married off at the point of a shotgun."

"Oh, that's not fair! Nobody forced you – you wanted to marry me! Just because we're going through a bad patch don't twist up the past!"

"A bad patch" was putting it mildly; ever since Pete and I became lovers I hadn't been able to bear Keith touching me, and he was getting increasingly resentful.

"Well, anyway," went on Keith, in a lower voice. "I want Richard to get off to a good start in life. He can piss about later if he wants to. He's got all the opportunities I never had and thousands of others would give their right arms for. Whose side are you on?"

"Really, I just want him to be happy –"

"Happy? That sounds like sixties crap to me! I don't even know what happy means – do you?"

The following morning, I asked Pete for the address of Clare's boyfriend's family.

"What do you want this for?" he asked. "It's a dead story."

"I don't know really. Ian Duggan seemed to think there was something in the Clare story we'd be interested in and I can't get to him any more. Her boyfriend is my only hope. Actually I've got a personal interest in errant youngsters at the moment."

"Your son?"

"Yes. He wants to go round the world with his girlfriend."

"Then let him go!" said Pete, with feeling. "Otherwise he'll end up just like us, wondering where it all went."

"It isn't as simple as that. Keith wants him to do his finals first and get his career under way."

"Well, he would, wouldn't he? That's just what I'd expect him to say."

"You don't know him –"

194

"I don't want to know him!" snapped Pete.

The Massinghams only had a two line address, so I knew they had to be rich – "Tillings", Roehatch. With the aid of a magnifying glass I found the village of Roehatch on the map, and set off from Tipping with a full tank of petrol and a packet of sandwiches. It took me over an hour of exceptionally nervous driving to get there. I hate narrow lanes bordered by cows and hedges and cornfields, and tractors that suddenly appear head-on out of nowhere, followed by convoys of Land Rovers and milk tankers.

"Tillings" had probably once been a small farmhouse with a couple of outbuildings, but now it was divorced from its agricultural origins by a gleaming green swathe of lawn complete with shimmering blue swimming-pool. The garage doors were open to reveal a black Mercedes and a red Porsche, and parked in the driveway was a dusty Land Rover. As I switched off my car engine I could hear dogs barking somewhere inside the house. I pressed the doorbell, which appeared not to respond but must have, because the barking reached a crescendo.

"Yes?" The door was opened by a tall woman with a billowing mane of flaming-red hair. She was in her mid-forties, wore very little make-up, and looked disturbingly fantastic in jeans and an old shirt that was probably her husband's. A quick glance told me that in the same outfit I would have looked like an escapee from the Siberian salt mines. Even more unsettling was the fact that I was sure I knew her from somewhere.

"Yes?" she repeated.

"Oh! I'm sorry. I'm looking for David Massingham."

It was as though a cloud passed over her brilliant smile.

"Well, I'm Jill Massingham, his mother, can I help?"

"Will he be back at all?"

"No, I'm afraid not," she said, tight-lipped.

"Oh. This is the last address I have for him. Perhaps you can tell me where I might find him now?"

She sighed. "You'd better come in. Does he owe you money? I really thought we'd seen the last of all that now."

She led me through into the kitchen. It was beautiful – low-beamed ceiling, Aga cooking-range, glass-fronted antique pine cabinets and a large china vase of assorted wild flowers on the table. I thought immediately of advertisements for fruit-cake, packet soups, vitamin-enriched bread – anything in fact where someone wanted to convince you of the wholesome naturalness of an unspeakably artificial product. Except, of course, that this kitchen was the genuine article, in a setting so quiet and rural you could hear the housemartins in the rafters preen the pesticide from their feathers.

"How much is it and who shall I make it out to?" she asked, reaching for her bag.

"No, Mrs Massingham, it's not money. I'll be honest with you." Well, as honest as seems convenient. "I'm with a newspaper and a short while ago I attended a Conference on Drugs and Alcohol Abuse. I'm now doing a follow-up feature where I'm trying to put together some actual case histories." I hesitated. She hadn't reacted. "I know this must be painful for you, but I gather David had a few problems with drugs, and I was rather hoping –"

She laughed suddenly. "A few problems! Oh excuse me, but that really is good! Here do have a coffee. Cigarette? No, of course not. Unfashionable habit." She lit up a long cigarette and poured out the coffee. "So what's your angle then? Are you looking for classic cases of poor little rich boys? Or broken homes and battered mums? Where do you think *I'll* fit? I'll tell you this – having children is a game for losers."

"Yes. Well – perhaps if you could tell me a little about David's early life." I sipped the hot coffee. I was even more sure I'd seen Jill Massingham somewhere before.

"David's early life. Well, quite simply, I loved him. He was the elder of my two boys and my favourite. Michael was the cleverer of the two, but David was the kind one. You can't help having favourites, can you? We gave them everything, you know, both of them. Don, my husband, is in advertising. He started up an agency in the sixties boom time, and we've just never looked back. I don't know what an unpaid bill looks like, can you imagine that?"

"No."

She laughed, and reached for an ash-tray. "Well, I'll tell you something. I've probably missed more of life than you have." She paused to let the remark sink in. It sank in, but I didn't believe it. "Well, anyway, both boys had exactly what they wanted – *fantastic* train sets, adventure holidays, every Action Man ever made – I've got an attic full of those wretched things! Waiting for the grandchildren." She took a long pull on her cigarette. "The grandchildren. Well, at least I shan't have to bear the guilt for how they turn out."

"Are you saying you gave the boys too much?"

She smiled pityingly. "You do like things simple, don't you? Have you got children?" I nodded. "And do you think it's worth it?"

I thought about it. "On most levels, yes."

She shrugged. "Well, you're lucky then. Oh, Michael's doing fine. He gets married next month, and I'm to be a granny at last." She flashed me the warm smile I knew I'd seen before.

"Congratulations. And David – when did things start to go wrong?"

"When he failed his 'A' levels. Oh, we said it didn't matter, and of course it didn't. We could have set him up in any business he fancied. We bought him a nice little Lancia to cheer him up and he drove the wretched thing into the side of a bus. In a bus station! Thank God the bus was empty at the time – witnesses said he did it deliberately." She sighed. "I don't know. What can you do? Then he went out by himself one day and got a job in a supermarket filling shelves. He wore old clothes and started speaking with a dreadful accent, but we didn't mind. He got involved with some girl or other, older than him, with a couple of kids by different fathers. God! That was awful. Don said she was a gold-digger and David left home. We didn't hear from him for months, and then we got a call from a Birmingham police station. This time it was drugs and he'd stolen a car." She sighed again. "This is so boring, isn't it?"

"No!"

"All right, I'll go on. We bought him another car and Don gave him a job at the agency. He didn't do any work, he spent all his time smoking pot and doing obscene drawings on the desk-top. Finally he sold the car, pocketed the money and disappeared." She stubbed out her cigarette, half-smoked, and gazed out at the golden glow of cornfields beyond her kitchen window.

"Er, is that all?" I prompted.

"No. No, it gets worse. We eventually got a call from David from a place called Tipping – well, you probably know it, it's only about an hour from here. He was living in a squat with a girl, and he wanted money. Don didn't want me to give them any. He said it would go straight into the drug dealer's pocket. I did, of course. What can you do – they'll only start stealing things. David was just rotting in this place, not doing anything with his life, and then one day he 'phoned and said the girl was pregnant." She made a sudden choking sound, and tears came into her eyes. "Oh, I'm sorry. David was so pleased, you see, so happy. I thought, thank God, he's happy at last and he's going to be a father. This will change everything." She lit another cigarette. "The girl was a junkie, too. Don doesn't know it to this day, but she'd had a baby before and it was taken into care. I told David he had to take her to a doctor but apparently she wouldn't go because she said they'd take the baby away again." Jill shook her head. "Well, there was some sort of crisis – premature bleeding, I think – and David managed to get her to see a doctor they could trust."

I leaned forward over the coffee cups. "You're sure about that – she definitely saw a doctor?"

"Yes, of course I'm sure. It was my first grandchild, and I 'phoned them every week, sent money. All for nothing, though. The silly girl overdosed herself.'

"Oh, that's dreadful."

"My first grandchild. Dead in a dirty basement in a dead junkie's tummy. There are no euphemisms for that."

I watched her silent, suddenly old face.

"Look," I said. "Could I possibly see David? Do you know where he is now?"

Jill Massingham turned her gaze slowly towards me.

"He's in Canada," she said. "Working on an Indian reservation, so I heard. He's changed." She shrugged. "He doesn't use drugs now, and he doesn't write to me, so I don't know where he turns for consolation. We all need consolation, don't we?" She gave a light, fluttery laugh. "So – what's your verdict on me then? What will you write about me in your nice, clean little piece for which you will no doubt be handsomely paid?"

I looked away. "I'm sorry. I don't know. All cases are different. You've been very kind." I wasn't sure what I'd learned, but I wanted to leave the beautiful kitchen and the beautiful woman. I thanked her for her help, finished my coffee, and she showed me to the front door. Another round of barking from the dogs commenced as I set foot on the driveway. Almost back at the Mini, I turned to look at her again.

"I hope you won't mind my saying this, but I'm sure I've seen you somewhere before."

She laughed. "Yes, a lot of people say that. I used to be Miss Marigold. That's where I met Don. Remember, in the sixties?" She went into a little dance routine in the doorway and it suddenly came to me like a flash from the past. "Miss Marigold", a liquid household-cleaner for all surfaces, and the dizzy redhead in the flower costume who danced your troubles away – I looked at Jill Massingham, and we both laughed; odd how such trivia stick in the mind.

I drove away from "Tillings", up a hill, and stopped on the edge of a field to eat my sandwiches. It was strange, I thought, that on walking into Jill Massingham's kitchen I should have been instantly reminded of a TV commercial. Could that be part of the puzzle? Jill and Don Massingham lived in an illusion of their own making, an illusion which David might not have been able to share. I thought of Richard. It wasn't my fault if he loved Carolyn, and if Carolyn was wild and reckless and irresponsible – was it? Can it be your fault if your children choose another person's illusion of reality? "Miss Marigold – the solution to all your household's problems" – well, not really.

"You were right," I said to Pete, on Friday morning. "David Massingham's mother is absolutely positive that Clare received medical attention for her pregnancy. I couldn't see David though. He's gone to Canada."

He sighed. "Yes. I know a cover-up when I see one. We'll just have to file it under 'F' for frogs and failure."

"She was quite an interesting person, though, Mrs Massingham. Made me think. And would it really have been such a good story, Dr Rachel's negligence, if that's what it was?"

"Not just negligence, darling – falsification of records. Doctors aren't supposed to do that. Our lives depend on them. Once they start bending the rules to suit themselves there's no telling where it can lead. Misuse of drugs, for instance."

"What – you mean doctors supplying drugs like heroin for profit? Do you think that's what Ian Duggan was getting at? 'Rich do-gooding bitches taking risks', he said. Perhaps Dr Rachel was the one supplying Clare with heroin!"

Pete shook his head. "Who knows? It doesn't matter. The girl's dead, Massingham's in Canada, and Duggan's likely to stay behind bars for quite a while. If Dr Rachel were building up a little nest-egg for herself supplying teenage junkies, then she's got away with it."

I sighed. It was becoming depressingly easy to think the worst of everyone.

"Listen," said Pete. "Edgeborough Avenue. I've been doing some checking. Over the last two or three years all the houses between seventeen and thirty-one have changed hands. Apart from two which were bought by Greyfield Properties, all the others were bought by people who wouldn't normally speculate in property. Your Reverend Harlow and a Mrs Parkes, a nice respectable widow who bought a house on the advice of Major Duncton – such a kind, helpful man, she said. There was also a retired solicitor called Scott, who now lives in Malta and whom I haven't been able to contact. They were all the sort of people who'd be happy to make a reasonable profit and not look too

200

deeply into things. They all sold out to Greyfield Properties over the last few months – just about the time one would suppose Leisching first made overtures to Tipping Council for a site. And now the only thing that stands between Tipping and the Leisching Pharmaceutical complex and Greyfield making a huge profit is Major Duncton's Planning Committee – and of course The Friends of Tipping's Heritage."

"I see. So it looks as if the Major picked out Edgeborough Avenue some years ago as a site for commercial development, despite the fact that it was zoned as residential, alerted Greyfield Properties to its potential, and then persuaded other people to buy houses there. We're assuming Greyfield give him some sort of pay-off, are we? But why didn't Greyfield buy all the houses in the first place?"

"Well, supposing you owned a crumbling old house in a run-down street and a property company showed an interest in it, what would you do? You'd up the price, especially if you knew they'd made an offer to your neighbours as well. But if a dithery old widow wanted to buy it at the asking-price, you'd sell the bloody thing and laugh all the way to the bank. Remember, at this stage it was still a gamble for Greyfield and the Major. When Leisching came on the scene they could afford to offer Harlow and the others quite a nice price. The only obstacle is getting through the change of use for the site, and when you look at what's on offer for Tipping – a drug abuse clinic and hundreds of jobs – it doesn't look like much of a problem – especially with Mr Tipping himself on your side."

"All right. So what now?"

Pete made a face. "It's quite simple. We have to prove a connection between the Major and Greyfield Properties."

"Ah." I must have looked blank.

"Yes, well, I was being sarcastic. Naturally it isn't simple at all. Greyfield Properties operate from an accommodation address with the sort of directors who make a career out of appearing on directorship lists. One of them is interesting, though. A Mr Mears. I think he lives near you." He showed me the address.

201

"Yes. I know Drayton Cottages," I said. "They're just two-up two-down terraced cottages, not really director material. Shall I call on him on my way home?"

"Yes. Good idea. Find out all you can, who he works with, any other companies he's got an interest in. Your nice, soft voice should work wonders on him, like it does on me. I'll be working on my car this evening, fixing the dents you put round the headlamp."

I was sitting on the corner of Pete's desk and Mr Heslop gave me a disapproving look.

"We're just talking about Edgeborough Avenue," I said, defensively.

"Really. Well, that's a happy coincidence. Not doing anything tomorrow afternoon, are you?"

"Well –" Oh dear, not Saturday work, I had planned a major shopping-expedition to refill the freezer.

"St Francis' Church Fête. The Tipping Heritage people are going to be there with a petition. See if you can get some quotes."

"It's being opened by Eric De Broux this year, isn't it?" said Pete.

"It is as a matter of fact," agreed Mr Heslop with an air of suspicion.

"Wear your Kermit outfit, Chris," said Pete.

I went back to my desk and sat down. I put Mr Mears' address in my handbag and worked out how I could fit St Francis' Church Fête in with the shopping. I thought about Edgeborough Avenue, and how nice it would be if Major Duncton turned out to be a crook and I had a hand in bringing him down, but I couldn't really put my mind to it. Something was bothering me, two ideas trying to connect together. Suddenly I jumped up and ran down the corridor to Pete's desk.

"Listen!" I shrieked. "I've got it!"

"Oh God, are you all right?"

"Yes! Listen – Dr Rachel killed Mike Stoddart! She did it because he knew she was visiting Clare and supplying her with drugs. He photographed her through the window or

202

something, and tried to blackmail her, and she knew he was an ex-heroin addict himself, and –"

"Pumped him full of heroin and hung him from the Clock-tower," finished Pete. He smiled. "Actually, it's not a bad theory. There are two things wrong with it. One, I doubt very much whether she'd have had the physical strength to carry a dead body up the fire escape, or even to hold Stoddart long enough to administer the injection. True, she could have used chloroform or something more sophisti-cated on him – and there is the possibility that her husband helped her. But then there's objection number two. If she killed him with a heroin overdose the sensible thing would have been to have left him where he lay with the syringe beside him. Then Inspector Franks would assume it was an accidental overdose by an addict resuming the habit, I'd do a story on government education cuts driving teachers to drugs, and that would be the end of it."

"Oh. Yes." I gave him a rueful smile. "Have you noticed how hot it's getting? I think the heat must be doing some-thing to my brain."

Drayton Cottages once commanded a view over woodlands to the rooftops of Tipping huddling in the valley, but in the sixties the woodland was cleared and two housing estates built in its place. One day no doubt the cottages would be "improved" by the addition of double glazing, stone fascias, and the like, but that afternoon their ruddy brick exteriors glowed in the oppressive heat of a threatened thunderstorm, and much-mended net curtains hung limply at open sash windows. There was neither bell nor knocker at number six, but I rattled the heavy letter flap. Tired feet plodded slowly down the steep staircase, and the door opened to reveal a plump woman in a blue overall.

"Good afternoon. Are you Mrs Mears?"

"No, love. She goes down the Centre Friday afternoons."

"Is Mr Mears here?"

"No. It's his day for the physio. What's it about, love?"

"Well, I'd really like to speak to him. What time will he be back?"

"Look, love, between you and me there's not really much point talking to him. He's gone a bit – you know. Well, they are both in their eighties. I'm the home help. I've been with them for years, lovely pair they are. What's it about, love?"

I sighed. Perhaps Pete had got hold of the wrong address.

"Don't worry. It was about his business interests, but I think there must be some mistake. I'm Christine Martin from the Herald. I'm afraid sometimes we get things a bit mixed up!"

"Oh! His business interests! You'll want his son-in-law then."

This sounded more promising. "Well, where can I find him?"

"At the station, I should think. Give him a ring, I would, he goes out quite a bit."

"What, the railway-station, you mean?"

"No, love, not the *railway* station, the *police* station. His son-in-law is the Inspector – Inspector Franks."

"Inspector Franks! Are you sure?"

"Yes, love, that's right. You can catch him at the station. Look, I've got to finish the upstairs and get home to do my lads' tea – I'll tell the Inspector you called."

As she closed the door I shouted after her, "Oh, please don't bother the Inspector!" but I wasn't sure if she heard.

19

Keith came home from work before I had a chance to ring Pete, and he had a headache. We sat in the kitchen, half watching a regional news programme, and I wondered whether I dare mention Inspector Franks' name in front of him. The last time I'd talked about the Stoddart case, and ventured the opinion that the police might have arrested the wrong man, it had led to an argument.

"This is turning into a bloody left-wing anti-police crusade!" Keith shouted. "You'll jump on any fashionable bandwagon, won't you? Why don't you just apply for a job on the Communist Weekly or whatever it is?"

I'd looked at him and wondered if he were ill. Men of his age sometimes had sudden strokes. He'd got up and stormed out of the room, and later he had muttered something about needing a drink and he went to the pub. Really, he just seemed to need to be out of the house – and away from me.

Keith retired to the living-room to watch Channel Four news and nurse his headache. I was left with the washing-up and Richard's shirts to iron. Pete's phone rang and rang. Finally, his voice, out of breath, exclaimed, "What?"

"It's the lady who smashed up your car."

"Oh, hello you."

"Ronald Mears – he's Inspector Franks' father-in-law. And he's senile, and the Inspector handles his business affairs."

There was silence. Pete gave a low whistle. "Inspector Franks. Jesus!"

"He and the Major must have planned the whole thing, letting the Edgeborough Avenue area run down and get a bad reputation for crime. Will they really make a lot of money?"

205

"Lots."

"Can we prove it?"

"We'll have a bloody good try."

I hesitated. "If there's a lot of money involved, and if Mike Stoddart knew about it, do you not think it at all possible that Inspector Franks killed him to shut him up?"

Pete laughed, whether at the idea or my reticence in putting it forward, I wasn't sure. After he'd thought for a bit, he said, "As a suspect, I like Inspector Franks better than Eric De Broux, Rachel Goodburn, or John Goodburn and your mistaken-identity theory! Let's suppose the Inspector kills him with heroin and hangs him from the Clocktower to make it look like there was some sort of bizarre drug-scene connection. No problem there. But why dispose of the camera, keys and syringe at the hotel? Why not hang on to them until he'd singled out Duggan as a suspect and then plant them in his flat? Also, what was the point of driving Stoddart's car down to Rampton's Hollow? He'd've had to walk back to the Clocktower to get his own car."

"Well, Major Duncton probably helped him. And anyway, he might have met and killed Stoddart in Rampton's Hollow."

"Yes, that's true. Perhaps we ought to interview a couple of those bloody frogs."

I laughed. "Oh well. Perhaps we'll never know."

He said, "Come and see me tonight. We'll talk it over."

"I can't. Really."

He sighed. "I want to see you. I was thinking about you before you rang."

"Only because you were filling in the dents I made."

"Only because I think of you most of the time anyway." There was a rumble of thunder. I heard it reverberate around the evening sky and crackle through the telephone receiver. "Jesus, it's hot. I'm taking off my shirt. Come over here and I'll take off yours too."

"You know I can't."

Keith walked into the kitchen and opened the 'fridge.

Pete said, "Any minute it'll start raining. Hard, cold drops

206

on our hot flesh. We'll leave the bedroom window open and make love in the rain. I'll kiss the raindrops off your nipples. I can taste it already. Are you listening, am I getting to you?"

"Where's the bottle opener?" asked Keith.

"I am getting to you, aren't I? Tell him to find his own sodding bottle opener and come and see me. I'm waiting for you and aching for you –"

"I'll have to go now!" I said, sharply. "See you Monday!" I put the 'phone down before he could say anything else. "The bottle opener's in the right-hand drawer, Keith, under the tea towels."

He found it. "Who were you 'phoning?"

"Oh – Mr Heslop about the St Francis' Church Fête tomorrow. Would you like to come?" I tried to fan the flush from my cheeks with a magazine.

"You know we're playing away tomorrow. You look really hot. Are you all right?"

"Yes, of course I am. You'd be hot if you'd stayed in the kitchen, washing-up!" I replied with unnecessary savagery.

Julie and I got to the Fête as it opened, and I used my Press card to queue-jump, to Julie's great delight. The sun was just sulking out from behind receding clouds, and limp, wet bunting hanging around the field steamed spectacularly in the sudden warmth. It was to be a day of sundresses and gum boots, dark glasses and sweaty plastic macs. Eric De Broux, looking quite odd in sky-blue track suit and trainers, gave a short opening speech expressing his pleasure at having been honoured with the task, etc., etc., and urging us all to enjoy ourselves and spend freely in the cause of various charities. He had donated several raffle prizes in the form of free dinners at his hotel, and looked forward to welcoming the lucky winners. Then he announced that the caged pet com- petition would be starting in half an hour, and left the platform to an accompaniment of polite, uninterested clap- ping. Julie and I made for the produce stall and bought a cake and some apricot jam for tea before the rush started. We found the stand run by the Friends of Tipping's

Heritage, and it was manned by none other than Elaine Randall. She looked a little nervous when she saw me.

"Are you going to sign our petition?" she asked.

"Yes, all right, why not?" I agreed. "How's it going?"

"Oh, really amazingly well. People are expressing so much interest in Ellis Willard's work." A line drawing of a young man with a sensual mouth was pinned to a placard, and surrounding it were pages of poetry obviously typed in a hurry and with liberal use of Tipp-Ex. No one was looking at them.

After a quick appraisal of the terrified hamsters in the caged pet competition, and an abortive attempt (thank God) to win a goldfish at hoopla, Julie wandered off to look for friends, and I returned to question the curious at the Tipping's Heritage stand. The sun had come out fully by now, and the queue for ice-cream had grown so long that some of the people standing in it were actually reading Ellis Willard's poems for want of something to do. I was able to elicit some printable reactions to the Edgeborough Avenue development, though no one was struck by the poetry. Suddenly someone ran a finger down my back and I turned round to face Pete.

"What on earth are you doing here?"

"I came to see you, what else?"

"But my daughter's here!"

"So? So are several hundred other people. Why shouldn't I just happen to be here too?"

"Well, I shouldn't have thought this was your kind of thing anyway."

"It isn't." He looked at the ice-cream queue and laughed. "Last time Helen and I came to one of these I spent the afternoon in the beer tent, Helen was two hours in the pony-ride queue, and the kids all got lost and had to be rescued from the St John's Ambulance tent!"

"Well, at least you're laughing about it."

"Only in retrospect, darling."

"Anyway, I haven't forgiven you yet for talking to me on the telephone like that last night. All you ever think about is sex."

"So do you. That's why we're so perfectly matched. That's why one day –"

"Hello!" Julie was standing there, looking from one to the other of us, her eyes bright and curious and seeing everything. Pete smiled.

"Now you must be Julie," he said. "Apart from the hair, you look just like your Mum. I hope you'll take that as the compliment it's meant to be."

"Oh! Well, I don't know if I do want to look like her –" She turned to me, questioningly.

"This is Pete, whom I work with," I said quickly. "We just happened to bump into one another."

"*My* Dad's not here," said Julie. "He doesn't like these things. Did your kids drag you along?"

"Er, no, I don't actually live with my kids."

"Oh, you're divorced, are you, and your wife's got custody? That's a shame!"

"Julie, don't be personal!"

"My kids are quite grown-up now," Pete said. "They don't really need me any more."

"No, but you still need them, don't you? If I ever have kids I won't want some other woman looking after them. They're still bits of you, aren't they?"

There was an uncomfortable silence. Pete laughed.

"Let's all go to the refreshment tent and I'll buy a beer for Chris and me and a pint of AB Negative for little Miss First-Cut-is-the-Deepest here."

We found the refreshment tent and Pete ordered half-a-pint of warm beer for each of us, Julie included. It seemed to me that the two of them were playing up to one another, she, trying to be witty, and funny, and forward, and he encouraging her and letting her outsmart him. She wasn't like my little Julie any more, she was an adult indulging in repartee with another adult. I wasn't sure if I liked it, but it got me out of an awkward situation.

Afterwards, I bought us all "lucky" fête programmes and Julie went off, slightly flushed, but happy to rejoin her friends. Pete took my hand but I pulled away angrily.

"Don't! She's not stupid!" I opened the programme and

209

read it. At the other end of the field, we had apparently just missed a display by Tamsin Delaney's Young Unicorn Drama Group. *Tamsin* Delaney! "Pete, look – *Tamsin*. That could be Dr Goodburn's daughter by his first wife."

"It could be a lot of people, darling."

"Let's go and find out."

"What the hell for? What does it matter? I keep telling you, in real life men rarely resort to murdering their wife's lovers. And certainly not more than ten years after the event. As a matter of fact," he added, his tone changing slightly. "If it's a crime of passion you want, I can think of a far stronger motive for the lover killing the husband."

I glanced at him uneasily. "Oh?"

"Well, it's not great, you know, sitting at home on a Saturday night knowing another man is drunkenly screwing the woman you're dreaming about!"

He clenched his teeth and walked off. I caught up with him, almost slipping on the mud.

"Pete, we don't," I said, catching his hand. "I couldn't –"

He didn't look at me. I don't think he believed me. Ahead of us, people were laughing and sliding about in puddles; I couldn't talk to the back of his head.

The Young Unicorns ranged in age from about twelve to fifteen and were uniformly scruffy in jeans and tee-shirts, like all serious artists. They were stowing away their equipment – an old chair, a trumpet, several large hats and a dustbin – in a small trailer attached to a battered Citroen. A tall, blonde woman in her early thirties was instructing them in well-modulated, carrying tones. She looked not in the least like Dr Goodburn.

"Excuse me. Are you Tamsin Delaney?" I asked.

"Yes, that's right."

"Can you spare me a minute? I'm from the Tipping Herald."

"Delighted to. Hang on a second. Take a break everyone! Back here by four o'clock sharp and anyone late catches the bus! Oh, wait! You didn't want a photo did you?" she asked me. I shook my head. "Toddle off then!"

Tamsin seated herself on the edge of the platform, shaking her head and running a hand through her long hair.

"To be honest these things are more trouble than they're worth, but it's good practice for the kids, playing to an unpredictable audience. Now, what can I do for you?"

"You'll have to forgive me. It's got nothing to do with your Young Unicorns – whose performance, incidentally, I enjoyed very much. I'm doing a little piece on the Goodburn surgery." No response. "You are Dr Goodburn's daughter, aren't you?"

"Yes."

"Well, the rumour is that they're moving away from the area, and –"

"Are they?" She looked surprised.

"Yes – didn't you know?"

"No! I'm afraid they don't confide in me. You've really come to the wrong person on this one, I'm afraid!" She laughed, as though at some private joke.

"Oh dear," I said, also laughing. "Not the wicked step-mother syndrome, is it?"

"Rachel, you mean? Heavens, no. Quite the reverse. She's –" She hesitated. "Just a minute. What paper did you say you were with?"

I told her.

"Well, I really think you ought to be talking to Rachel and my father about their plans. I can't tell you anything anyway." She smiled encouragingly. "Now, if you wanted some background info on the Young Unicorns, I'd be very glad to fill you in."

Pete took a long breath and leaned back (rather unwisely, I thought) against the support pole of the coconut shy. He closed his eyes.

"'The high spot of this year's fête was undoubtedly the very accomplished display given by the Young Unicorns' Drama Group, who showed what can be done with a minimum of resources and a maximum of talent.' How does that sound to you, darling?"

I said "Fine," and Tamsin said "Super," because we each thought the "darling" was addressed to us. Tamsin looked pleased.

211

Pete said, "The Goodburn Surgery story. Chris is putting together a nice factual piece on how long it's been going, that sort of thing, but it does help to have an inside view. Anyway, darling, it's up to you." He shrugged, smiled, and looked away, as though losing interest.

Tamsin thought for a moment. "Honestly, I can't tell you much. My parents were divorced about fifteen years ago. Mummy married again, and my father married Rachel about six years later. Actually, I wasn't close to my father at all – not even when he and Mummy were married. He was always too busy being a doctor. Anyway, he and Rachel set up the practice here about eight years ago, and it was Rachel who arranged what family contact there was. Just one of those things, really – my father and I never got to know one another properly."

"Would I be right in saying that Eric De Broux is your stepfather?" I asked.

"Yes," she said, and added with a laugh. "You would, actually, but I hope you won't be mentioning the fact in your article!"

"Oh – why's that?"

"Well, ever since Eric bought the Clocktower Hotel my father's had a sort of persecution complex. God knows why. He never forgave Eric for luring Mummy away, despite the dog's life he'd led her. He seemed to think Eric had followed him to torment him. Oh, God, you won't use this, will you?"

I managed to swallow a gasp of triumph.

"Heavens, no, we're not the News of the World!" I said, with a sickly smile. "Thank you for your time. It was very kind of you when you've got so much clearing up to do –"

Eric De Broux and the sky-blue track suit suddenly appeared between us.

"Are these people annoying you, Tamsin?" he asked, glaring at Pete.

"No?" replied Tamsin, on an interrogatory note, looking puzzled.

"Because if they are, don't hesitate to call for police assistance. I assure you, you have absolutely nothing to fear from this very poor excuse for a journalist."

Pete laughed. "If I visit your restaurant, Mr De Broux, any chance I'll get a nice dish of frogs' legs?"

"If you visit my restaurant, a fist down your throat is what you'll get!"

"Eric!" exclaimed Tamsin, horrified.

"It's all right, darling, don't worry about it," said Pete. "The lengths to which people will go to protect their financial interests never surprises me. Come on, Chris."

When we were out of earshot, I couldn't resist saying, "I told you so! And now we know we've got the right Dr Goodburn."

He said, with heavy sarcasm. "Yes, and isn't it a pity we've got the wrong murder victim?"

Having decided not to wait to see if our "lucky" programmes had won anything in the raffle, Julie and I sat in the queue to leave the car park behind dozens of others similarly lacking in optimism. Julie was cuddling a pink teddy bear Pete had won for her at hoopla (he said the beer had steadied his aim).

"Mum," she said, after a long period of unnatural quietness. "Who is Pete?"

"I told you. He works at the Herald."

She held the teddy-bear by its leg and tried to fan herself with it.

"You two are in love, aren't you?" she asked, in a deceptively matter of fact tone.

"What? Don't be silly!"

"You were looking at each other all soppy when you thought I wasn't around. I saw it!"

"Julie, for goodness' sake! Don't say things like that!" The car in front edged forward and I followed, getting too close.

"He's quite good-looking for his age. He's got nice eyes. I don't blame you." She stared hard at me, and I could sense a sudden change in mood. "Are you going to leave Dad?" she asked in a quiet, child's voice.

"Oh, of course not! Will you please stop this silly talk? This is all absolute nonsense!" I began to feel slightly sick and wished I could get away from Julie.

"Mum," said Julie, after a long pause. "When I said that

213

the other day, about wondering whether it was you, or Dad, having the affair, it was Dad I was thinking of, not you. Don't you think it's funny that he wears his expensive aftershave to cricket practice? You know, the one in the brown bottle."

"Look, I've got better things to do than to go around smelling your father when he goes out for an evening. And if you don't stop this sort of talk *at once* you can get out of my car and walk home! Really – not everyone subscribes to the kind of lifestyle your friend Heather does!"

In the circumstances that was a pretty bitchy thing to say.

When we got home I went up to the bathroom and gave a quick shake to the brown bottle of aftershave I'd given Keith for Christmas. It was almost empty.

20

"'Edgeborough Avenue'", said Mr Heslop. "'The Dispute that has Split the Town in Two' – what do you think of that for Friday's headline?"

"Well," I said, thoughtfully. "It hasn't really split the town in two, has it? I mean there are a few people who think it would be a good thing for Tipping to have the Leisching complex here, with hundreds of jobs and a drug abuse clinic, and a few people who are worried about losing some nice old houses, but most people don't seem very interested."

Mr Heslop looked irritated. "All right – 'Edgeborough Avenue – Most People Not Very Interested' – how many newspapers do you think a headline like that would sell?" He put a folder containing a number of letters on my desk. "Now I want a page of pros and a page of cons. Use these and what you got on Saturday. Throw in some more of the poetry and go down to the Unemployed Centre and get a few quotes from there to balance things up. Oh, and don't be smart and chat up unemployed poets, either, I don't want any more bloody irony. This issue's going to coincide with the Leisching meeting to display the plans, so let's really sock it to them." Pete walked past, blowing me a kiss and mouthing "see you later".

"What's he up to?" demanded Mr Heslop, suspiciously.

"I don't know exactly," I replied truthfully. "He doesn't tell me everything."

"Hm. Well, it had better not be another time-wasting exercise."

That afternoon I received a 'phone call from Keith to say that he was going out to dinner straight from work to celebrate a colleague's fortieth birthday, and not to wait up for him. This was astounding news, as it would mean his missing

215

cricket practice for the first time in living memory, and I couldn't resist pointing out that my fortieth birthday had passed without so much as a portion of chips being festively consumed. In fact we had quite a bitter argument about it over the telephone, my anger being fuelled by relief that I wouldn't have to face him before meeting Pete. Pete suggested that in the circumstances we should meet early and have a meal out, but I said no; it didn't seem worth the risk. Perhaps the idea of being caught with Pete in a restaurant by my next-door neighbour started off a chain reaction in my brain, because as I drove home from work to lie to the children about visiting Judith again, I began to feel uneasy. I accelerated round the bend towards home, eager to escape the censorious gaze of dozens of pairs of eyes I had begun to imagine were watching me. Parked in the driveway of our house was a dark-grey Peugeot estate car I'd never seen before. I felt instantly alarmed, as though this intruder had something to do with my earlier train of thought.

As I parked in the road outside the house a man emerged from the garage. He was short and balding, and wore an ill-fitting suit, the pockets of which bulged with pens and pieces of string. He looked at me over the top of his clipboard.

"Mrs Martin?"

"Yes."

"Won't be much longer. You've just about got room here, I'd say. That drain's a bit of a problem but we'll see what we can do."

"I'm sorry. I don't know what you're talking about."

He had three strands of grey hair crossing his bald patch, and he pushed them out of the way flamboyantly, as though dealing with a mane of unruly locks.

"Mrs Martin? Thirty-one Barrington Avenue?"

"Yes."

He winked. "Thought so, love, I don't make mistakes. The double garage. Not squared it with your husband yet, have you?"

I was baffled. "Look, who are you exactly?"

"Bill Pritchard, ma'am, Pritchard Brothers, Builders." He handed me a card. "Matching brick, of course, we'll do a

216

nice job, don't worry. I'm sure you've heard of us. We did the extension on Number forty-seven."

"Yes, I've heard of you and a double garage would be wonderful, but I haven't asked you for an estimate or anything, and I'm sure my husband hasn't. We applied for planning permission for a carport last year and were refused."

He leaned against his car and looked me up and down. I didn't like him. He had body odour. He sighed.

"All right, love, have it your way. I'm a man of the world and I've seen it all before. It's no business of mine how you get favours out of the military. All I know is I'm on a backscratcher job and I'll do as I'm told." He made a few more notes on the clipboard while I stared at him in bewilderment. We didn't know anyone in the army.

"All right then, love, all done," said Bill Pritchard. "We've got a slack period coming up in September, we can do it then. Tell you what, seeing as you've got friends in such high places, I could give you a nice discount on a granny flat on top of the new garage. Add an extra seven or eight thousand to the price of your house, even if you haven't got a granny. Want me to do you a quote?"

I shook my head, just wanting him to go.

"Fair enough, love, you think about it. See you in September!" He got into his car, then leaned out of the window to give me another, longer appraisal. I was perspiring a little and he looked like the kind of man who would go for sweaty women. "Give me a ring if you like," he said, with a wink. "The discount on the granny flat's negotiable."

I watched him go, open mouthed. There was a Mrs D. Martin of Barton Gardens over the other side of town. A few years ago I'd been repeatedly sent her mail order catalogue and quantities of thermal underwear until I threatened to write to a consumer affairs programme. Somehow or other, Mr Bill Pritchard must have got his addresses mixed up, though it puzzled me that someone so fond of thermal underwear could be involved in what he had suggested. Well, I'd led a sheltered life and there were probably a lot of strange fetishes I didn't know about.

217

When I arrived at Pete's flat, as always our first few moments together were tense. We exchanged chaste kisses, and he poured us both a drink. We sat a foot apart on the sofa and smiled at each other and my hand shook a little.

"How have you been getting on with Greyfield?" I asked.

"Not great, actually. How was your day?"

"Pretty boring. I, er, thought a bit about the Stoddart murder." He smiled, so I carried on. "We seem to have three imperfect suspects. Number One, Eric De Broux. Mike Stoddart could have blackmailed him over the frogs. He probably took photos of their being planted. So De Broux arranged to meet him at Rampton's Hollow and pay him off, killed him, and took the negatives from the flat and the film from the camera. So far so good?" Pete nodded. "But then he proceeded to leave bits of evidence, including the body, all over his own hotel, which doesn't seem to be logical."

"O.K. Suspect Number Two," prompted Pete, edging closer along the sofa.

"Suspect Number Two is Rachel Goodburn," I said. "Stoddart lived next-door to Clare and saw Rachel coming and going, probably at night. He took photos of her injecting Clare, or accepting money, or something. After Clare's death he blackmailed Rachel, and finally she arranged to meet him at Rampton's Hollow where she killed him." I laughed. "And then she had some sort of brainstorm and took the body up to the Clocktower –"

"Yes, all right." He sounded impatient.

"Suspect Number Three is Inspector Franks and/or Major Duncton. I'd really like it to be them." I thought for a moment. "Stoddart somehow put two and two together about the Edgeborough Avenue development. I don't know what photos he could have had, though – the Inspector and the Major meeting someone from Greyfield Properties?" Pete shrugged. "Well, anyway, one or both of them met and killed Stoddart and then the Inspector set about framing Ian Duggan. And didn't make a very good job of it."

"O.K." he said. "But let me remind you of something.

Apart from De Broux we can't be certain any of our suspects had the slightest motive. We *think* Rachel Goodburn was visiting Clare, but we don't know and we don't know that Stoddart knew. We *think* Stoddart may have known about the Edgeborough Avenue conspiracy, but apart from a few notes which have disappeared there's no evidence of it. He may have known almost nothing about it."

I sighed. "We need those photographs."

"Well, we haven't got them and we never will have. I'm just grateful you've given up your mistaken identity theory."

"I'm not sure I have – I mean, the whole thing is so illogical that –"

"All right, darling, now forget about it, will you?" He had run out of patience. "If we can get this Edgeborough Avenue conspiracy story together, and of course the Ian Duggan frame-up, we shall have done extremely well."

"What – well enough to get you a job on a better newspaper than the Herald!" I suggested, with a hint of sarcasm. I turned away. And you'll leave Tipping and live in London, I thought, and I'll never see you again.

He must have misread my thoughts.

"Oh dear – is your husband getting suspicious?" he asked.

"No. I don't think so."

"Well – good, because *I've* been thinking about more important things than murder. I'd like to take you away somewhere for a couple of days. To a decent hotel with room service and no dead bodies on the fire escape." He reached across the gulf of sofa and took my hand. "You won't have to wash a dish or a sock or do anything for two whole days. Except think about me, and us, and be my mistress."

The feeling of edginess was still upon me. I said dangerously, "I bet you weren't this kind to Helen."

"No. No, I wasn't kind to Helen at all."

I hadn't expected such honesty, and tried to make amends. "Well, it's sweet of you, but –"

"It isn't *sweet* of me, for Christ's sake! I want to keep you awake all night and see you looking pale and tired and scarcely able to walk in the morning!"

219

"You say some awful things," I said, blushing.

The image of the hotel room with its tangled bed and us together on it in the early morning light became too strong. He looked down at my jeans, taut across my hips and stomach, and unzipped me. We fell back on to the sofa.

I left Pete's later than usual that night, and the moment I'd pulled out of the forecourt and waved goodbye the spell was broken. I started to worry in case some dreadful disaster had overtaken Julie or Richard during my extended absence. Perhaps that's why I didn't immediately notice the dark-blue Fiesta which followed me closely as I turned first right, and then left, and entered the roundabout. I don't like night driving, and always drive slowly, no matter how anxious I am to reach my destination. It was when the Fiesta didn't overtake as I left the roundabout that I got the distinct but uncanny feeling I was being followed. I accelerated; so did the Fiesta. I braked; the Fiesta braked. Ahead was a cross-roads where I needed to turn left towards home. I was beginning to panic. I indicated left, slowed, moved over slightly, then at the last moment accelerated with a squeal of tyres into a fast turn right. Blood hammered in my ears, almost drowning out the outraged hooting of a van driver who'd had to brake hard to miss me. The Fiesta was stopped at the junction. I breathed a sigh of relief. I'd lost him. On reflection I could now see that the sensible thing would have been to have driven straight home into my own garage and called for Richard's assistance if necessary, but I'd come from Pete's flat and was blinded by guilty conscience.

I tried to visualise the road before me. It was empty, lit by ugly, orange street-lamps and hemmed in between high fences topped with barbed-wire. I was sure there was a right-turn somewhere which would take me off the industrial estate. I slowed down slightly and the van passed, hooted, and disappeared. Now the road was empty in both directions, an incandescent orange corridor through a blackened landscape. And then there it was again, the blue Fiesta, suddenly bulging into view in the mirror. "Oh God!" I moaned aloud. Now there was nowhere to go. I stamped down the accelerator but nothing seemed to happen; the Fiesta was closing on me as though I were standing still. I could make out the pallor of the driver's face above the glare of his headlamps. "Oh please, please!" I begged God and the car, gripping the steering wheel too tight and dancing over the white line. The Fiesta flashed its lights. My heart was pounding in panic. I swerved back into my lane as we rounded a bend and suddenly he was beside me, the noise of his engine merging with mine into a crescendo of sound. The hairs on the back of my neck rose. I glanced quickly at the Fiesta, my foot hard to the floor. The driver's hands, glowing brightly orange, began to make a left-turn of the wheel, unmistakably towards me. I reacted instantly, swerving to the left and hitting grass with a jarring bump. As I ploughed on to the verge, braking, I knew he'd got me. "Oh God!" I screamed, and came to a violent halt.

There was silence. Frantically I reached over, and locked the passenger door and my own door. The door of the Fiesta was opening and a man climbed out, slowly, relaxed. As he stepped into the beam of light from a street-lamp I recognised him: it was Inspector Franks. The hairs on the back of my neck were still erect. He put his face against the windscreen and tapped on the glass. He was so close I could make out large open pores on the end of his nose. He pressed his police identity card to the screen. "Open the door and stand away from the car," he said. "I want a word with you."

Trembling uncontrollably, I unlocked the door and got out. There didn't seem to be much choice.

"Well, well," said the Inspector. "You don't believe in making things easy for yourself, do you? A classic piece of menopausal driving if ever I saw one – waltzing all over the bloody road!"

"I thought – I thought –"

"Yes, I imagine you had quite a few things on your mind, the life you lead." He walked slowly round the Mini, his feet crunching in the gravel and debris at the side of the road. In the distance a guard-dog barked in a bored sort of way, as though it had given up hope of anything ever happening.

"This your car?" asked the Inspector. "Know the number,

do you?" He bent down behind the car and for a moment I couldn't see him. Then I heard the sound of a heavy blow and glass breaking. I ran to the back of the Mini and there stood the Inspector with a brick in his hand, shaking his head.

"It's an offence you know, Mrs Martin, driving at night with a rear lamp missing. I might have to write this up." He dropped the brick. I stared at him, rigid with horror. "Been drinking as well, have you? Oh, but no, I don't suppose you'd've had time, would you? Too busy with other things." He advanced on me, slowly and menacingly. As he approached he raised his arms and I steeled myself for a blow to the head. One hand found my left ear, the other settled on my right breast and squeezed it painfully. "Nice cosy working-relationship you have with your colleague, don't you? I clocked where your car's been all evening!" His breath smelled faintly of beer. He chuckled and pushed me back against the Mini. "Oh, don't worry, I'm a family man. Coming up to thirty years of marriage and never a thought in the wrong place. 'Cos I've got my priorities right, you see. Wife and family – that's what it's all about. Insuring for their future – and mine, of course. And that's why, you see, I don't like people like you poking their dirty noses where they shouldn't. Know what I'm talking about?" I still couldn't speak. "Well, do you?"

"Yes. I think so."

"Well! That's good. I can be very unpleasant. You ask that son of yours. I've already had to speak to him once about his little habits – I might have to do it again. You understanding me, are you?" He started to walk back to his car. "But on the other hand, I *can* be quite reasonable. You tell your very close friend I want to see you both tomorrow. Nine o'clock not too early for you, is it? Good. Nine o'clock at Rampton's Hollow, then – just the three of us." His smile was unpleasant. "I'm off home to the wife. Oh and see to it you get that light fixed, will you? If I see it again, I'll have to charge you."

He got into his car and drove away without a second glance at me.

I stood still, taking deep, calming breaths. The dog barked again, drowning out the receding drone of the Inspector's car, and then there was silence. When I was sure the Inspector was far away I got into the Mini and headed back to Pete's flat.

"Christ! What's happened?" he demanded, seeing my white face. "What's the bastard done to you?"

"No – not Keith." Pete had a drink in his hand and I took it and swallowed the neat vodka. Slowly I felt better. "Inspector Franks. He was waiting for me outside. He ran me off the road on the industrial estate –" I took another sip. "He smashed one of my rear lights and threatened all kinds of things."

"Christ! You're not hurt?"

"No. He wants to see us both tomorrow." I sat down. "At Rampton's Hollow."

There was silence as we both considered the implications of this.

"What do you think he wants to see us for?" I asked.

"Well, with luck to offer us a bribe to drop the Edgeborough Avenue story," said Pete, with a short laugh.

And without luck to kill us both, I thought. I laughed too. My own thought had been funnier.

"I don't think you ought to come," said Pete, quite calmly. He was used to being threatened.

"Of course I'm coming."

"You look awful. Are you sure you're all right?"

He put his arms round me and kissed the top of my head. I could still feel the Inspector's grip on my ear and my breast.

"Oh God!" I said suddenly. "The time! And the car! What am I going to tell Keith?"

Pete let go of me. He looked pale.

"I know! I'll say I had an accident on the way home from Judith's. That would make me late, wouldn't it? Yes – he'll be angry but he won't suspect."

Pete picked up his jacket and his car keys.

"Get up," he said.

"What?"

"You want to go home, so go home. I'll drive behind you.

Hurry, for Christ's sake." He looked furious. I didn't know what I had done. I got up unsteadily and made for the door. He barred my way, and I thought for the second time that evening that someone was going to hit me.

"Nothing matters to you, does it," he said, through clenched teeth. "Except preventing your husband from finding out that you and I can't keep our hands off one another. That and his bloody no-claims bonus!" He slammed the door of his flat and the noise echoed loudly down the stairwell. From the downstairs flat came a muffled shout of complaint.

It was shortly after midnight when I got home and Keith hadn't been in long. He was sitting up in bed drinking whisky and looking red-eyed from earlier over-indulgence. I told him about the car. He stared at me as though he hadn't heard, then muttered something about it being the last bloody straw. I started to undress (hoping I'd put my underwear on the right way round) but he snapped off the light and turned his back on me with the sort of finality with which one switches off a boring television programme.

I didn't sleep much that night, and when I awoke to dark clouds and heavy rain it felt as though the day ought not to have started. Keith took a double dose of Alka-Seltzer and spent a long time in the bathroom. I had coffee and aspirin and donned jeans and an anorak, ready for Rampton's Hollow. I considered secreting a kitchen knife in my handbag – as though I'd be able to use it. I could already see the headline: "Two reporters found dead in Rampton's Hollow – was it a suicide pact?" (Mr Heslop favoured long headlines). The report would mention our love affair and detail the manner of our death – I felt sick and couldn't finish the coffee.

When I met Pete, at the end of our road, he said, "I'm, er, sorry about last night. Bad moment." He spoke awkwardly, as though he wasn't used to apologising. I shrugged.

"Let me do the talking," he said. "We take whatever he offers, all right? He's no fool, so I haven't even bothered with the tape." I was glad I'd left the knife in the drawer.

"Follow me."

I got in my car and followed Pete out to Rampton's Hollow through a tunnel of dark, dripping greenery. Leaves, loosened early by heavy rain, flattened themselves with shocking suddenness on the windscreen, and one caught in the wiper blade and scraped, groaning, back and forth across the glass. We turned into the lane, bumped round a bend, and there was the dark-blue Fiesta parked in what was probably a courting spot, and where perhaps Mike Stoddart's car had been abandoned – perhaps where he had died. Pete pulled up behind the Fiesta, with me close behind. I sat in the Mini, waiting for someone to move. The groan of the leaf had changed to a high-pitched whine. Pete got out of his car and came back for me. We approached the Fiesta together slowly, and the Inspector opened the door, a smile on his face.

"Oh dear, oh dear, what a state. So sorry the two of you had to get your feet wet." With distaste he got out of the car. To Pete, he said. "Hold your arms out." Briskly he searched him, presumably for a tape recorder, then he turned to me. "Open your handbag." He rummaged untidily through the contents, then ran his hands lightly over my body. We were quite damp by the time we got into the car, and I felt cold.

"So what can we do for you?" asked Pete, smiling. "Were you planning on making a statement to the Press?"

The Inspector chuckled. "No, sunshine, you've got that wrong! That's not what we're here for at all." He leaned against the steering-wheel, quite practised at intimidation, watching us.

"Not exactly 'Journalist of the Year' material, are you, either of you? There's Mrs Mopp over there, with her unfortunate tendency for falling over sharp instruments and getting her broom handle up everyone's nose, and then there's you, sunshine." He pulled a sheet of paper from his pocket and proceeded to undo its many folds. "Our computer's got your name engraved on its heart! Quite a little treasure, aren't we? Peter Enzo Schiavo. Speeding – speeding – driving without due care and attention – one year's disqualification for driving while unfit owing to excessive alcohol –

dear, dear – speeding – want me to go on? I'd hate to have to pay your insurance premium on that thing." He re-folded the paper and replaced it in his pocket, with a self-satisfied smile. "You're not really a problem to me, either of you. You, sunshine, have only got to so much as breathe on a bollard and I can have your driving-licence away from you for good." He glanced at me with a contempt which implied that no further comment was necessary.

"Still, I don't like to leave loose ends. Do things the easy way, that's me. So I'm prepared to make a deal with you – stop poking around in the affairs of my family and friends and I'll arrange a few things to your advantage." He paused for the meaning of his words to sink in.

"Such as?" asked Pete.

"Well," began the Inspector. "Mrs Martin. My friends inform me you've had your heart set on a carport for that rather battered vehicle of yours. You know, I think we can do rather better than that. I've got contacts, you see, and I can arrange for you to have a nice new double garage – no invoice, of course. How's that?"

I took a sharp breath, which he seemed to mistake for a gasp of delight.

"And tell your husband not to sweat blood over the planning permission, all right? These things can be arranged." He turned to Pete. "And you, sunshine – well, you drive that heap of yours over to a dealer of my choice and you'll get a hundred per cent trade-in deal. Up to a certain limit, of course."

"I suppose a Porsche would be out of the question," remarked Pete, drily.

"You suppose right, sunshine. Never make the mistake of over-estimating your own value. That could be fatal."

There was a moment's silence. Pete and I exchanged an involuntary glance and the Inspector watched us. His expression was one of delighted malice. He looked at his watch.

"Well, I'm a busy man. I've got old ladies to protect and criminals to catch. Which way are we going to do this – the hard way or the easy way?"

Pete said, "If you know so much about me you'll know I always prefer the easy life."

"Yes, that was exactly my opinion," agreed the Inspector, contemptuously. "And what about the very lovely Mrs Martin?"

"It's – yes, I don't want any trouble," I said, truthfully.

"Very good!" The Inspector looked at his watch again.

"And when will we get all these goodies?" asked Pete.

"Oh, don't you worry, I keep my promises, but we're none of us in any hurry, are we? Let's say – when the foundation stone of the Leisching complex is laid, shall we? And in the meantime, I'd deem it a great favour if you'd soft-peddle this Ellis Willard nonsense. My friends and I have put a lot of time and effort into this venture – which is in the best interests of Tipping, as you well know – and we don't want to see it torpedoed by a bunch of muddle-headed do-gooding trendies!"

"Oh, I shouldn't worry," said Pete. "We're printing some of his poetry. That should provide a pretty good case against him."

The Inspector appeared not to understand this remark.

"You people make me sick," he said, scowling. "Exposing this and that – rabbiting on about the people's right to know. What the hell do you care? You're as bent as anyone else!"

"Yes," said Pete. "Well, you should know."

"Right, piss off, both of you," Inspector Franks said suddenly. "And remember. One wrong word in that paper of yours and your nuts will be in my cracker."

Pete opened the car door, letting in a gust of cold, damp air.

"As a matter of fact," he said, "I think you're being most generous. We didn't know what to expect, in the light of recent events."

Oh God, I thought, don't say it, if Inspector Franks thinks we think he killed Mike Stoddart and he did –

"What recent events?" asked the Inspector, irritably, switching on his engine.

"Well –" Pete looked at me and must have decided that discretion is the better part of valour. "I suppose Chris here has got in your way a few times –"

"Piss off!" repeated Inspector Franks.

When we arrived at the office my hands were shaking, so Pete brought two cups of coffee and seated himself on the edge of my desk.

"Shall I go out for a brandy?" he asked.

"Look, I'm not used to being offered bribes backed up by death threats! What are we going to do?"

"I don't know yet. Look, don't take this death threat thing too seriously. I told you before we haven't a shred of evidence that Inspector Franks is a murderer, and anyway, killing the two of us and making it look accidental wouldn't be easy. He was only trying to scare the shit out of us – especially you."

"He succeeded."

"Great! The thing is, you can't prove someone's threatened to kill you unless you've got a knife between the shoulder blades – in this case preferably one borrowed from the police-canteen – and as for the bribe, well, without –"

I let go of my coffee cup too soon, spilling it into the saucer. "There's something I didn't tell you," I said. "About the double garage. A man came round to my house yesterday to measure us up for one. I thought it was a mistake, but he kept giving me sort of nudge-nudge wink-wink looks and insisting he'd been sent round by someone – I think he meant Major Duncton."

Pete froze in the act of dismantling a paper clip.

"He actually said that?"

"No, but he said something about my having done favours for the military –"

"Christ! I think we've got the bastards. Do you remember his name?"

"I've got his card somewhere."

"Give it to me."

I went through the jumbled contents of my bag and found it. "I don't see why he'd admit he does under-the-counter jobs for Major Duncton. This is his livelihood! What can we possibly offer him? After all, it's just my word against his."

228

"Well, darling, it's a question of approach. I'll say I'm doing a story on Council corruption. I'll say I've been approached by a lady, a jilted and vengeful mistress, who is refusing to take a pay-off, and that it's all going to be on the front page of Friday's Herald –"

"Oh, thanks a lot!"

"Well, it's only what he thinks already, very probably." He blew me a kiss. "I'm going, before someone else gets to him. This – Pritchard – obviously wasn't supposed to get in touch with you just yet but they've got their wires crossed and shot themselves in the foot – if you'll excuse the mixed metaphor."

He turned to go.

"Pete," I said. "Tell me something. Didn't you for a moment consider accepting the new car?"

He laughed.

"Well, it may come as a surprise to you but a very long time ago I did believe that writing the truth would change the world, and just occasionally I am still smitten by this fallacy." He hesitated, then added. "Of course, if he'd offered me a Porsche, it might have been a different story. Look, don't worry – I promise you it will all be all right."

As he spoke, I knew with complete certainty that sooner rather than later, everything was going to come crashing down around my shoulders.

21

The sun had come out, fierce with all the brooding strength of August, and turned the spilt coffee in my saucer to a dark-brown glue. Pete hadn't returned from his visit to Bill Pritchard, and it was almost time to go home. The sense of impending doom I'd felt this morning had lifted. Pete was right – this was dull old Tipping, not Chicago or Los Angeles, and the only real threat to my life was what I was doing with it.

As usual these days I was reluctant to go home. My "work" life was so much more enjoyable than my "home" life, that I wanted to make it last as long as possible. I had run out of ideas for trying to improve things at home. Meals were taken in sullen silence – Richard and Keith ready to fly at one another's throats, Julie anxious about calories, and Keith and I maintaining an uneasy peace – so the provision of little treats like steak or sherry trifle was no longer helpful. As for the house, as Keith frequently pointed out, it was showing signs of prolonged neglect (grass between the patio tiles, paint peeling from the bathroom walls). That was it! Tonight I'd start a new campaign to restore the house – no, not restore it – revitalise it! It would have the same effect as buying a new outfit of clothes: we'd all feel better. I pulled a piece of paper from my notepad and had just begun to make a list for the DIY store when Pete came in. He dropped a cassette recorder and a thick brown envelope on my desk.

"Do you remember I once told you that if you helped me get a story in the nationals I'd give you whatever your heart desired?"

"Yes, I do remember you saying that."

"Well, speak and it's yours."

I laughed. "I'll have to think about it."

230

"Oh, you do disappoint me. I was under the impression I'd already offered it to you."

There was silence. I smiled. He didn't.

"Pritchard?" I asked.

"Yes. Want to hear it?"

He pressed the switch and the machine emitted a sound like darts thudding into a board. After a few seconds the addition of clinking glasses and someone shouting "*Go for a double five*" confirmed that the sound was darts thudding into a board.

Pete: "Have a double this time."

Pritchard: "All right. Cheers, mate." Pause. "What you got that thing for?" (Suspiciously)

Pete: "Save me making notes. Ever tried holding a glass and a pen and a sandwich at the same time? Cheers, darling, have one yourself."

Female voice: "Oh, ta, thanks."

Pritchard: "Lovely pair!" Laughter.

Pete: "Yes. Just like –"

Pete leaned forward quickly and pressed another button. "I'll fast forward it a bit."

Pete: ". . . a few Council contracts?"

Pritchard: "Been bloody hard to keep going the last couple of years. We take what we can get, mate. Time was any silly cow asked you to fix a dodgy chimney-stack you'd tell her to stuff it. Now you got to take what you can get."

Pete: "So any work you can get out of the Council is very welcome?"

Pritchard: "'S'right."

Pete: "Got a special arrangement with anybody at the Council, have you?"

Pritchard: "Well, you know how it is, mate. You make contacts over the years. You get to know who'll put in a good word for you at the right time, know what I mean?"

Pete: "Sure, why not? Only idiots play by the rules."

There was an interruption of loud male laughter followed by muffled thumps and the clatter of cutlery dropped from a great height. An unidentified voice shouted "Shit!"

Pritchard: "That was my sodding pickled onion!"

231

Pete: "I'll get you another one. Excuse me, darling, send down the pickled onion jar, will you? Thanks, darling."

Pritchard (grumpily): "It's all these bloody office staff coming in all of a sudden. This used to be a decent pub."

Pete: "The thing is, mate, I've got a statement here from a lady on the subject of nudge-nudge wink-wink at the Council. It's going to be a big story, this one. It's got everything – sex, scandal, slush money, bribery – you name it. I've got quite a few people implicated, just ordinary men trying to earn a decent living, and that's why I want to get round as many of them as I can – give them a chance to put their side of things."

Pritchard (from a distance, sounding uninterested): "Oh?"

Pete: "I'm afraid your name's on the list, mate."

Pritchard: "What? What the hell are you talking about?"

Pete: "A Mrs Martin. She used to – well, let's just say she was a close friend of Major Duncton – you'll have to buy the paper to find out more."

Dramatic pause filled by raucous background laughter (I covered my face with my hands).

Pete: "I gather you were instructed by Major Duncton to carry out some alteration work to her house in – what was it – Barrington Avenue. No invoice – but a promise of finer things to come from the Council?"

Pritchard uttered a string of expletives heard frequently on the Watergate tapes.

Pete: "Sorry, mate, just trying to give you a chance to put your side. The public can be very sympathetic to small businessmen going through hard times. It's the big boys they want to see pulled down. Here, same again, is it?"

Pritchard: "Shit!"

Pete: "Know how you feel, mate. We're on the same side, you and me. It's those bastards up there, always with their heads above the bloody water line – Over here, darling!"

At that point the tape was interrupted by the sound of people falling over and glasses breaking. Somebody shouted *"Bloody pickled onions all over the floor – I've got a bloody interview this afternoon – look at the ketchup down the front of my interview suit!"* in a voice bordering on hysteria, and a series of clicks indicated a break in recording. When it resumed, the background noise had diminished considerably.

Pete: "So you had an arrangement with Major Duncton whereby he'd look kindly on planning applications you were involved in, in return for the odd favour?"

Pritchard: "Yes."

Pete: "Did you ever do any work at his home?"

Pritchard: "Yes."

Pete: "And did you submit an invoice?"

Pritchard: "What for? The bugger wouldn't have paid it!"

Pete: "And you were instructed by Major Duncton to carry out building work for Mrs Martin of Thirty-One Barrington Avenue and not to submit an invoice, in return for the award of future Council contracts?"

Pritchard: "Yes! The stupid cow! Bloody women are never satisfied, are they? I offered to do a nice little job for her, over and above instructions – 'Course, I had the measure of her, one look and you can tell, can't you? I could tell you a thing or two about –"

Pete snapped the machine off hastily and pocketed it. I wondered what further aspersions had been cast upon my reputation, and decided it was probably better I didn't know.

"Well, that's it," he said. "Like it? I even got some photocopies of his ledgers. What more can a man ask? Come here – Heslop's not around, is he? I want to kiss you."

I stood up quickly and held him at arm's length. People were beginning to sneak out early, intent on mowing their lawns, and I knew there was already gossip about me and Pete.

"You're acting as if you're drunk," I said. He was wearing my favourite sweet-smelling aftershave.

"With happiness, darling. I've got everything I want at the moment – except one thing. No, two, if you count the Porsche."

I picked up the DIY list.

"Come for a celebration drink, Chris, please," Pete said. "It's only just gone five. You can still get home before H.R.H. arrives."

233

I looked at the list in my hand. It could wait for another day.

We took the story to Mr Heslop at midday on Thursday. He had just set out, on his desk, a tub of cottage cheese, a package of bean sprouts and a wedge of wholemeal bread that had obviously caused the bread knife a lot of pain. He didn't look pleased to see us.

"What's all this?" he asked, adding sarcastically. "Pub closed for refurbishment or something, is it?"

"It's the big story this paper's been waiting for, Bill," said Pete, handing it to him. Mr Heslop took it delicately between two fingers, holding it away from him.

"This wouldn't have anything to do with frogs, would it?" he asked suspiciously.

"Absolutely not," replied Pete. "But I can't swear that there isn't a potential advertiser of a used bike or rabbit-hutch mentioned in here."

Mr Heslop ignored the remark and put the file beside his slice of bread. "Go on, then, I'll look at it after lunch."

"I think you'd better look at it now. Save reaching for the indigestion tablets later," said Pete, winking at me. Mr Heslop sighed, defiantly and noisily munched a handful of bean sprouts, and began to read. Three strokes of the jaw later he stopped in mid-chew and made the mistake of trying to gasp and swallow at the same time. Pete slapped him on the back with slightly excessive force and I handed him his vitamin-enriched orange juice.

"Good God!" he exclaimed, when he'd recovered. "How much of this is true?"

"All of it!" we replied, in unison.

"Well, I hope you've got some –"

"A bloody file full. See for yourself!"

Mr Heslop carried on reading, shaking his head occasionally, and ignoring the lure of the beansprouts. When he'd finished, he said "Christ!" and picked up the file. "I don't think I want to know how you came by all this. How much has it cost us, for God's sake?"

"Quite a lot in terms of personal sacrifice, actually, apart

234

from the cost of car repairs, etc., but that'll come through on our expenses. This is the story of the year, Bill, and I can tell you we wouldn't have got it at all if it weren't for Chris."

"Oh, well, it wasn't really –" I began. I'd been going to point out that it had actually been the Stoddart murder story I'd wanted, but I simply smiled and took the compliment.

"Well," said Bill, giving me a nod of acknowledgement (he is not known for displays of enthusiasm). "So much for the front page! Looks like we've got some thinking to do – we'll move the disabled bed-push on to Page Four – the Reverend Harlow's piece can go altogether – God, there'll be fireworks tomorrow at the Church Hall meeting!"

"Leisching will probably pull out beforehand," said Pete.

"Pull out? You mean, not go ahead with the project at all?" I asked. It hadn't occurred to me, before, that reporting the story would change the course of events; I'd been happy enough to bring down Major Duncton and the Inspector, the Leisching development itself had always seemed like quite a good idea.

"Of course not," said Mr Heslop. "They won't want their name associated with something like this."

"Oh! But I thought it was supposed to be such a shot in the arm for Tipping! Eight hundred new jobs and all that –"

They both looked at me in surprise.

"It's a real shot in the arm for this paper," said Mr Heslop. "Raise our circulation quite a bit."

Well, for better or worse, this is part of the story that went in the Herald under the banner headline "Edgeborough Avenue – the Blot on this Town's Honour":

"Important questions are being asked today as to who exactly will profit from the proposed business development at Edgeborough Avenue. Herald reporters investigating this astonishing story have been threatened, offered financial inducements, and, in one case, subjected to actual personal violence in order to persuade them to abandon their search for the truth. This is what we have learned so far:

That a senior police-officer has a considerable financial stake in Greyfield Properties, the development company at the centre of the row. This same officer, according to a statement from a respected and long-serving member of the force, has been responsible for the Edgeborough Avenue area being consistently "underpoliced" – a fact which has led to a sharp rise in crime and corresponding drop in property values. Charges of assault against this officer are to be made by a Herald reporter.

"That a well known local Councillor, close friend and business associate of the above mentioned police-officer, advised local people to invest in houses in Edgeborough Avenue some years ago because 'this is an area with a future'. All these people have recently been approached by, and have sold their properties to, Greyfield Properties, at a modest profit – but if this area is now re-zoned to 'business use' at next week's emergency meeting of the Planning Committee – who will make the real profit?

"It was this same Councillor who approached the director of a local building firm and requested him to carry out work at the home of a Herald reporter on a 'no cost' basis, in an attempt to 'buy' the silence of this newspaper. The builder concerned further stated that over the past few years he carried out extensive building work to the Councillor's home without submitting an invoice, in order to ensure he was awarded Council contracts . . ."

I went home that evening feeling pretty good. There was still the problem of explaining things to Keith (how I'd come to be assaulted by a police officer without mentioning it to him, for instance) but, just lately, he had shown so little interest in me and my manifold failings that I didn't expect to have to provide chapter and verse. Besides, it was a warm summer evening and the sky promised one of those glorious sunsets into which people drift off happily. In other words, metaphorically speaking, I made the fatal mistake of walking along the road whistling, without knowing what was around the next corner.

Richard and Julie went out together for once to a Young Conservatives' Barbecue – not that they were Young Conservatives, or Young Anythings, but there was to be an open-air disco and drinks at reduced prices. Richard said if it

236

got boring they'd stand in a corner and sing 'The Red Flag', but I knew he only said it to worry me. Keith took four cans of lager and the Telegraph crossword out on to the patio, and I got out the step-ladder, paint, and brushes and went to tackle the bathroom. I stripped to my pants, put on an old shirt of Keith's, and covered my head with a scarf. As I climbed the ladder I caught sight of myself in the mirror. Had Pete been around I would not have been safe dressed like this – not even at the top of the ladder. My reflection smiled back sadly at me. I wished –

I'd painted a small corner of the ceiling when the bathroom door opened. Keith came in and looked at me.

"Hello, I'm just starting on the ceiling," I remarked, rather unnecessarily.

He gave an odd smile and crossed the room in the two steps that was all it took. He reached up and placed his hand on my thigh. I froze for an instant, then carried on with an even, flowing motion of the brush. As I leaned into the stroke I realised that from where he was standing Keith would be viewing me almost naked right up to the throat. I tried to pull the shirt close to my stomach with my free hand and wobbled dangerously on the ladder.

"Come down," said Keith, his fingers tightening on my thigh.

"Look, I want to finish this. I've only just started."

"Come down." He climbed on to the bottom rung of the ladder and reached up, one hand on my hip, the other seeking my breast.

"Oh God, you'll have us both off!" I shrieked.

"Then put that bloody brush down and get off!"

"But it'll go stiff if I –"

He snatched the brush from me and threw it into the basin, splattering white emulsion over the pink tiles and carpet he had once so lovingly laid.

"Come on, let's have some fun for a change," he said, undoing his trousers. "It's been bloody months! Get off that ladder or I'm coming up."

I was panicking. I didn't want him, I'd been thinking about Pete. I climbed down the ladder. There wasn't any

237

excuse – would he believe me if I said I had my period?

"That's better. Take that shirt off."

"Oh, not in here – the paint – there's no room!"

He opened the door and pulled me across the landing and into our bedroom. He didn't bother to close the door. He pushed me on to the bed and kissed me and wrenched at the shirt buttons. I thought, there's nothing I can do about it, I'll just have to put up with it – it won't be any worse than before. But of course it was; in the old days I'd been able to shut my mind to it and think of other things, now his every touch was a travesty of what Pete and I did together. Keith didn't smell right, his mouth tasted, and felt, quite different – I wanted to scream and push him away with a knee to the stomach. Suddenly he stopped and flung the shirt back over me.

"You're useless!" he shouted. "You're not worth bothering with!" He turned away and pulled up his underpants. I sat up, cuddling the shirt to me.

"I'm sorry – what have I done?"

"You haven't bloody done anything! You never do, do you? I don't know why I even bother – you just lie there like a slab. How do you think a man can put up with it year after year?" He was red-faced with anger and hurt pride. "Well, I'll tell you – I bloody well can't and I don't have to. Do you hear me? It's your own fault! I found someone a lot more obliging than you!"

We stared at each other. We thought over the words, trying to make sense of them, working out what they meant to us. Keith's expression changed from anger to shock. He wished he hadn't said it. Suddenly I felt sorry for him, I wanted to make him feel better.

"Yes," I said, "I understand. I know –"

"You understand? You understand, do you? Yes, that's bloody typical, isn't it? You just sit there like you've done all our married life, crushing me with your bloody understanding! You understand everything, don't you? In a minute you'll offer me a cup of tea, or a whisky and you'll bloody understand – but you don't, do you? All these years and you don't really understand a single thing about me!"

238

He was so angry he was practically screaming.

"You're probably right," I said. "About us never really understanding each other. I do know what you mean." At this, he looked as if he might burst a blood vessel, so I hurried on, without thinking. "But this time I really can understand. You see for the past few weeks I've been having an affair with Pete."

He stood rooted to the spot, staring at me. I was terrified: I couldn't tell what he was thinking. Finally he said, "What did he do – give you hormone injections?" and walked out of the room.

Later, we sat on the bed, drinking whisky (which I've never liked) and talking. He said he'd been seeing Barbara Morrish, a lady from his accounts department, on and off for years. I remembered her from annual dinner dances – she was tall and blonde with angular shoulders and a large mouth. He remarked vindictively that it was really since I'd started work at the Herald, and been out so much in the evenings without caring where he was, that the affair had become more serious. Well, of course, I should have known; no one could do as much cricket practice as Keith and not end up playing for England. He kept telling me how "nice" she was.

"And so how's *your* big romance?" he asked sarcastically. His eyes were bloodshot from the lager and the whisky.

I shook my head.

"Well – has he asked you to leave me and marry him or what?"

I shook my head again. "He did say he loved me."

Keith laughed. "Oh yes, I'll bet he did! He'd say anything to get you into his bed and keep you coming back there. God, you're naive! He must have thought it was his birthday when he set eyes on you. My God, that mouthy little bastard – I ought to go round there and punch him in the mouth –"

The children came in just after midnight, and we were still sitting on the bed, drinking, and I was crying a little. They were laughing and stumbling about on the stairs, but I didn't go to see them. When the house had gone quiet again Keith took my hand and held it on his knee.

"I think we've both been rather silly, don't you?" he said. "Is it too late to – you know – try again?"

"I don't know what went wrong. I don't even know when it went wrong!" I said desperately.

"I'll stop seeing Barbara. She gets on my nerves sometimes anyway. There's the kids –" I looked at him. His shirt was undone and his beard was beginning to grow out of a white, tired face. He looked helpless. It wasn't his fault: it was mine; I should have made more effort.

"We'll feel better after the holiday," said Keith. "We could move, if you like. I was working it out last week. I could afford an extra ten thousand on the mortgage, and we could get somewhere out in the country. You always said you wanted a big garden."

I gazed at my knees. Pete had liked my knees. I had liked all of Pete. I suppose I'd loved him, but Keith was my husband. It was with Keith that I'd had children, built my home and planned for all the real things of life, like retirement, death, cold weather, next season's vegetable plot. Keith was real life, Pete just a diversion from it.

"I'll hand in my notice tomorrow," I said, "and of course I'll stop seeing Pete."

22

I don't think either of us slept much that night. In the morning Keith kissed my cheek as I lay in bed, pretending to doze. He came back into the bedroom to say goodbye before he went to work, and I opened an eye and looked at his face. When he'd gone I pulled the sheet over me and tried to remember what it had felt like when I was twenty with Richard's little feet inside me, and Keith had kissed me and gone to work and left me to play at being housewife. I couldn't remember.

I didn't go to work that morning. I 'phoned to say I was ill, and I'd come in after lunch. I sat on the patio and wrote out my notice. The 'phone rang several times, and I knew it was Pete, but I didn't answer it. After I'd watched the one o'clock news and washed up everything in sight, there was nothing for it but to go out and face the day. I checked methodically and uncharacteristically through my handbag to make sure I'd got everything, and came across the receipt for Pete's holiday photos. The pain started all over again. I drove into town beneath gloomy skies that threatened rain, and called in at Reynolds and Dobbs. The photos were ready, in a large yellow and black wallet that didn't want to be forced into my handbag.

As I parked outside the office the first heavy drops of rain began to fall. My desk was littered with files and notes and I sat down quietly and went through them. Mr Heslop's door was shut, and I knew that if I walked along the corridor I'd be bound to run into Pete, so I decided to delay handing in my notice, Then, suddenly, just when I'd managed to concentrate my mind on a badly-written letter from a lady about the number of cats missing from her estate, he was there beside me.

241

"Hello," said Pete. "You all right? Where've you been? I phoned three times."

"I'm all right." I picked up my 'phone. Anything to make him go away.

"You're not. What's happened?" He took the 'phone from me and replaced it firmly.

I swallowed hard. "I didn't feel well. Last night we had a hell of a row about things and I told Keith about you and me."

"Oh." He was taken aback. "You might have told me. I'm a rare blood group and I need to inform the hospital." He lifted the 'phone with a nervous laugh that died on his lips when he saw my expression.

"Yes, it's just funny to you, isn't it? Like everything else," I snapped. I'd had enough, and jokes were the last straw. "Well, don't worry about it – it's got nothing to do with you."

"Nothing to do with me?"

"No. Nothing. It hasn't got anything to do with you. We've talked it all through and we're going to work things out in our own way." He looked shocked and uncomprehending. I held up my hands in a defensive, barrier-forming gesture. "I'm sorry."

"You're sorry," he said. "Sorry, like 'Sorry your dinner's cold'." His voice rose into a cruel imitation of mine. "'Sorry your shirt's not ironed – sorry I don't want to screw you any more'!"

The messenger, who was passing, stopped and stared at us, open-mouthed. Pete still had the 'phone in his hand. He threw it at me, hitting me on the arm.

"Do what you bloody like!" he shouted. "Do what you bloody like and I hope it chokes you!"

He turned sharply and bumped into Mr Heslop. The messenger slunk away, disappointed that the show was over.

"Keep your voices down," said Mr Heslop. "Why are you still here, anyway? There's an enormous crowd outside the Church Hall apparently."

Pete and I avoided looking at one another. Mr Heslop said, "Well, I'm sorry to interrupt your private affairs but if

242

you wouldn't mind, there might be something worth reporting out there that won't conveniently wait."

I glanced at Pete. I'd expected him to laugh when I told him, and say something like "Well, it was fun while it lasted". He didn't look amused.

He said without expression, "Are you coming, Chris?"

I picked up my handbag and followed him out to the car park. It was raining hard by now. I got into Pete's car. As we pulled out into the traffic, I said, "Pete –"

"Shut up!" he said, angrily. "Just shut up! If you haven't got anything to say that I want to hear, shut up!"

When we arrived at the Church Hall the rain had eased off a little, but the sight that greeted us was of firmly gripped umbrellas and hooded plastic macs jostling for position around the porch. Placards were being carried at odd, dejected angles, and those written in felt-tip marker pen now appeared to convey Chinese revolutionary messages. I spotted Elaine Randall, defiantly without umbrella, her glasses blobbed with rain, standing on the porch steps, shouting. Her placard read, "Heritage before Profit", and she was in animated discussion with a young man, also umbrella-less, whose placard read "Jobs before Pricks" (I think it was meant to be "Jobs before Bricks", but the bottom part of the "B" had run off). Pete stopped the car two inches from the back of a man waving a "Tipping's Heritage" banner, jumped out and pushed his way through the crowd, to shouts of "who do you think you are, obstructing the pavement – what about the disabled?" from a woman with one of those lethally-spiked shopping trolleys. I followed him.

"What's happening?" he demanded of Elaine Randall.

"Oh – Mr Schiavo!" she exclaimed warmly. "No one's turned up to let us in. They don't dare show their faces after that wonderful story you did in the Herald. Absolutely super job – congratulations!"

Pete didn't even smile. I tried to. Another woman with an old-fashioned string-mop had pushed her way to the front in our wake. She blew smoke in my face.

243

"I must get in there somehow," she said desperately. "It's Jane Fonda tonight!"

"Sorry? What?"

"Jane Fonda. You know, all them fat ladies in purple leotards jumping about. They'll play merry hell with me if the floor's wet. The roof leaks, you see. The Vicar –"

"It's a fix!" shouted a voice from the crowd. "Left wing press bias! They're all in it together – the BBC and the newspapers – privatise the lot of them, that's what I say. Give free market forces a chance!"

There were hoots of derisive laughter.

"What d'you mean, privatise the newspapers? They *are* bloody privatised and they're all bloody fascists – You ought to –"

The rest of this interchange was lost as the crowd scuffled out of the way of the two men in suits who had parked their black Ford Granada close behind Pete's car. One of them carried a sheet of paper and the other handed him drawing pins. They attached the paper to the door of the Church Hall.

"You from Leisching?" asked Pete.

One of the men nodded. He jerked his thumb at the sheet of paper. "Statements from the Press Office," he muttered, and shouldered his way back through the crowd. Ernst had arrived, and industriously snapped off shots of the departing Leisching men, with explanatory placards and umbrellas in the background. I read the notice on the door and made shorthand notes; it said: "This afternoon's Public Meeting has been cancelled. A statement will be issued by Leisching Pharmaceuticals Press Office at five o'clock today." Further down the street there was more excitement as a convoy of BBC Outside Broadcast vans arrived, and the crowd streamed away in their direction. People were hoping to get a close look at faces they recognised, be filmed (women removed their scarves and started playing with their hair), or better still, get picked for "local reaction" interviews. The BBC crew were keen to get the refreshments van operative.

Pete said, "It's over. You can ring Leischings yourself and get the statement. I've had enough. I'm off."

"Well, so there you are!" Inspector Franks mounted the porch steps, barring our departure. He looked more than usually rumpled, and his expression was murderous. "You're a marked man. I'm going to get you." He spoke to Pete, ignoring me, as always.

"Are you?" Pete returned the stare. He didn't look triumphant or angry, just curious and detached. "Do me a favour then, try it now, will you? Before I forget who the hell you are."

The Inspector gritted his teeth. This was almost more than he could stand. And then Pete laughed and moved to push past him. Inspector Franks raised his right arm and delivered a heavy blow to his face. It made a muffled crunching sound, and somebody shouted "Christ!" Pete crumpled into the Church Hall wall amid a noisy scattering of pebble dash. I screamed. Ernst's camera rasped into action.

"For God's sake, Jim!" exclaimed the Inspector's companion. "Have you gone mad?" He pulled him away, and Ernst's camera whirred again. Pete stood up, clutching his face. Ernst took a picture of the blood streaming through his fingers and down the back of his hand, then gave him an oil-stained handkerchief.

"You'd better have bloody well got that," Pete said to him. "It's the only worthwhile thing that's happened today."

"You bet," replied Ernst.

"Are you all right?" I asked, adding softly. "Please speak to me."

He didn't look at me.

"Here, ducks, you from the papers?" asked the woman with the cigarette and the mop. "You seen what's going on down there? Old girl with a cat looks like she's going to jump off a building." Numbly I followed the direction of her deeply nicotine-stained finger. A few hundred yards from the Church Hall was the disputed territory of Edgeborough Avenue. It bristled with signboards proclaiming "Greyfield Developments". Standing on the ledge of a first floor window at number twenty-seven, was a frail figure with long white hair. She appeared to be wearing a nightgown, and clutching a large ginger cat.

"It's Edie!" I said. Pete pressed the handkerchief to his nose and we began running down the street with Ernst. People saw us and followed, splashing through the puddles and trampling their slogans into the gutter.

Edie Clough was wearing her scarlet lipstick and her white hair blew about wildly in the sharpening breeze. She had been out on the ledge long enough to get her rose-printed cotton nightdress wet. It clung to her, revealing her skeletal contours. Two youths with tattooed arms and tight jeans stared up at her, their arms folded and expressions of amusement on their faces.

"Yeah, you stay there, gran!" one of them shouted. "Who's trying to stop you?"

"What's happened?" I asked.

"Daft old bat," said the youth. "Nothing to do with us. We was just passing by and she started shouting at us about her bloody cat stuck on a ledge. Now she's got the cat and she won't come down. Got nothing to do with us." He suddenly became aware of the number of people gathering behind us. "Come on, Kev, let's get out of here!"

"I know who you are!" called Edie, to their departing backs. "You're Special Branch. You can't fool me!"

"Edie!" I called. "They've gone now. Come on down."

"I tell you, I'm not shifting. If I come down they'll get me and torture me. It's 'cos of what I know. They want to get hold of my papers. It's 'cos of what I know about Gladstone and where he come from!"

Had I not been already acquainted with Edie, I might have been tempted to ask for an explanation.

"Edie, please come down and go home!" I shouted.

"I can't. They're all after me. They keep coming round to board up my windows. I don't mind about the electric but I got to have light. I lost my can-opener –"

At that moment a black BMW edged through the crowd and pulled up outside number twenty-seven. Rachel Goodburn got out. It had stopped raining now and everybody was drying out in the breeze, but Rachel's hair hung in dripping ringlets, as though she'd been caught in a downpour and hadn't bothered to shake off the water. She col-

246

lected her doctor's bag.

"Does this woman need help?" she asked quietly, and there was a murmur of assent from the crowd. She walked up the steps, hesitated for just a moment, then went in through the open front door. When her face appeared at the window Edie started, wavering away from the wall towards the edge. Close behind me, a woman shrieked. The fall would probably have done no more than break a few bones, but beneath the window was a fence of spiked iron railings. If Edie jumped, she would almost certainly impale herself on them. Seeing this, Ernst stepped forward and began focusing his lens on the spikes, walking this way and that to determine the best angle.

It was impossible to hear what Rachel was saying. She spoke quietly to Edie, nodding frequently, and putting out her hand to stroke the cat. As I watched, I thought of the house next door, the dark basement, the frightened, pregnant girl. I looked at the window, now boarded up, where Mike Stoddart could have stood and watched the comings and goings from the basement. Now Rachel was holding Edie's hand, doing what she was best at – "caring for the whole patient", as someone had said. The little voice in my head confirmed what I already knew: that Rachel had helped Clare, supplying her with clean needles and heroin so she could have, and keep, a healthy baby. I didn't need the voice in my head to tell me that Mike Stoddart, with his warped desire for revenge against the world, would not have missed an opportunity for blackmail. Intuition, I suppose, told me what reason could not make sense of.

Edie was wavering a few short feet from death. I remembered how, when I'd asked her if anyone visited the house the morning after the murder she'd mentioned "the lady-doctor", and I'd assumed Rachel's visit was to Mrs Norris. But now I knew that she'd been to Mike Stoddart's flat to collect the negatives.

Rachel and Edie smiled at one another, and Rachel was holding the ginger cat. She looked relieved. She was pleased to have saved a life. She must have been pleased when it looked like she could save Clare and the baby, devastated when it all went wrong. And Pete had hounded her, and Mike Stoddart had come along with photographs and threats. Killing him, when it came to it, must have seemed like a relief – morally justifiable. She thought her work more important than the life of a blackmailer – was it? I didn't know. If I'd been sure, maybe I'd have walked away and said nothing.

Edie slowly edged along the sill, holding Rachel's hand, and climbed awkwardly through the window, to muted applause from the crowd. Two uniformed policemen had arrived and strode up the steps of number twenty-seven. I followed them. Rachel started down the stairs with her arm round Edie. I stood outside the door of Mike Stoddart's flat, next to the two policemen, who took no notice of me. Obviously I still didn't look like a reporter, because if I had, they'd have thrown me out.

As Rachel descended the final stair she glanced over at Mike Stoddart's door. I stepped forward. I held up the distinctive yellow and black wallet containing the photographs of Pete's sons.

"You take a very good photograph, Dr Rachel," I said.

She let go of Edie.

"Oh my God," she said. "Where did you get those?"

"They were waiting to be collected at Reynolds and Dobbs," I replied truthfully.

"Oh – God!" she moaned, wiping at her face clumsily with her sleeve. "Oh, God – I didn't know! I thought I'd burned everything." The two policemen looked at one another in puzzlement. Pete and Ernst stood in the doorway behind me, darkening the hall, and Rachel slumped on to the bottom stair. She seemed to be crying. Edie suddenly dashed back into her flat and bolted the door noisily. Rachel looked up.

"I've been punished enough!" she exclaimed. "Every single day! You think you know everything – you find out someone's made a mistake, a well-intentioned mistake, and you can't let it alone, can you? If it wasn't for people like you, and people like *him* –" She pointed at Mike Stoddart's door. "None of this would have been necessary. Wherever

248

you look it's the same – cure the disease, to hell with the patient – write the story, write *off* the consequences!" She stared accusingly at Pete, who was still bleeding into the handkerchief.

"Well, all right," I said. "You gave Clare drugs and needles and you looked after her. You shouldn't have done it but you did. We can all understand the reason. But she still died. And then –"

Rachel looked at me, the sharpness of her gaze stopping me in mid-sentence. She said quietly, "I was so tired. If *you* make a mistake when you're tired it doesn't kill anybody. That boyfriend of hers rang me in the middle of the night – I'd only just got back from the hospital. I made up a syringe, enough for two or three doses, got in the car and drove over there with it. Looking back, I can remember she was shaking when I handed it to her – I should have stayed and administered it myself. I don't know why I didn't, except that I was tired. She overdosed herself. It could have happened – no matter who supplied her."

"You supplied illegal drugs," put in Pete. "You falsified records. You would have been, and should have been, struck off. Stoddart blackmailed you and you murdered him, one crime leading to another, as it always does."

"He kept coming back for more money! He had photos and he wouldn't give them to me. When I met him at Rampton's Hollow I gave him the opportunity – I offered him five thousand for the negatives, which was all I could lay my hands on without going to my husband. He just laughed. I don't think he wanted the money. He said he liked being able to push me around the way he'd been pushed around by doctors and social workers. I don't know what he was talking about, but I could see it was no use trying to reason with him."

"You killed him in Rampton's Hollow," I said. "Why didn't you just leave him there?"

She hesitated, twisting her hair with her fingers. Then she stood up and addressed one of the policemen.

"I'm not saying any more. I want a solicitor."

"It was your husband, wasn't it? Your husband helped

249

you commit murder!" snapped Pete.

"No! No! He didn't know anything about it – *I* killed him, I told you – I didn't tell John anything about it because I didn't want to involve him. It was all a terrible mistake!" She covered her face again. "Oh God, what have I done to John?"

"She's covering up for her husband," said Pete.

"No," Rachel said. "I'm not covering up for John. All he did was to move the body. It was this silly feud with Eric De Broux. He didn't know what he was doing. John and I left the cocktail evening early because he couldn't bear being there. We went home and he had a few whiskies. I told him I had to check on a patient and I went to meet Stoddart. After I'd gone, John drank too much, he decided he'd go and – I don't know – punch Eric on the nose. On his way to the Clocktower he slowed right down on that sharp bend before Rampton's Hollow – had to almost stop, I think. I'd left Stoddart's car with its lights on, and John could see the body lying on the track. Naturally, he got out to take a look. He was going to do all the right things. He went back to his car and started to 'phone for the police, but then the idea came to him, the idea of humiliating Eric De Broux. He switched off the lights on Stoddart's car. He thought of just taking the syringe and leaving it on the reception desk or something, but by then he'd already tampered with evidence and touched things, so he thought, why not? Why not go the whole way? He put the body in his car and drove up to the Clocktower. Hanging Stoddart from the fire escape seemed absolutely brilliant to him at the time. What could be more spectacular? But I *swear* he had nothing to do with the murder. I didn't tell him the truth for some time."

"And the next day he put the syringe in the cheese to further embarrass De Broux?" I suggested.

"Yes."

"And you went to Stoddart's flat and collected all his negatives and the camera, and destroyed all the photos?"

"Yes. But I didn't think of –" She looked at the wallet in my hand.

"And the camera and the keys?"

"I took them with me to the Conference on the Thursday and put them in the wastepaper basket. It just seemed the – neatest sort of thing to do." She looked at me appealingly. "We were going to give up medicine altogether. I found I couldn't get over what I'd done. It made everything else seem degraded. When that boy was arrested I nearly gave myself up, but John said – John said he was just another nothing who deserved to be put away before he harmed someone. I just don't know, I just don't know –"

The two policemen moved forward and caught Rachel by the arms as she toppled unsteadily. I felt a surge of pity and guilt. Ernst backed down the steps, taking pictures of Rachel being led away by a baffled police escort.

Pete and I stood alone in the hallway of Mike Stoddart's house. His nose had stopped bleeding, but it was swollen and his face and shirt were smeared with blood. He didn't say anything for a moment. Perhaps he didn't know what to say to me. Then he took my right hand and shook it formally.

"You did great," he said. "You always do."

I wanted to say that I was sorry, that I hadn't been fair to him, that I should have considered his feelings.

"Are those mine?" he asked, indicating the photos. I nodded. He took them. "Thanks. Thank you, Chris. For everything. Have a nice weekend." He walked quickly down the steps and away up the street towards his car. I said "Goodbye," but he probably didn't hear.

Suddenly, Ernst reappeared. To my astonishment, he put his arms round me and hugged me.

"Great!" he exclaimed. "Fantastic! All those great shots! What a really wonderful day this has been!"

It was the only time he ever spoke to me, and he managed to say precisely the wrong thing.

We had eaten dinner in an appalling, total silence, and were watching a dreadful sitcom about a couple on the verge of divorce on holiday in Spain. It was so dreadful and so apt, that we were actually watching it. Julie and Richard had gone out together after dinner, whispering. I think Julie had

251

put two and two together and conveyed the result to Richard. They both knew when it was best not to be around, in any case. A huge roar of laughter erupted from the television, the credits rolled, and I had to think about·real life again. *My* real life.

In five weeks' time I'd be going on a second honeymoon with a man I no longer loved, and sometimes had to try quite hard to like. Why was I doing this? Ought I not to embark boldly on a new life – as a single career woman, perhaps, earning my own money, my children's respect, and making other people clean their fingermarks off light switches? The alternative, which I had acceded to so readily last night, was to re-dedicate myself to Keith and the house; to find a part-time job in an office and spend my time typing other people's words on to pieces of paper and despatching those pieces of paper to different parts of the world where other, equally bored people would type out answers. Last night this had seemed a welcome return to normality – why was I feeling so negative about it now?

Keith suddenly cleared his throat and spoke.

"Did you hand your notice in?"

"Yes." Mr Heslop had refused to accept it, putting the unopened envelope in his drawer and telling me to think about it over the weekend, but I didn't mention this.

Keith said, "I wish you'd remembered the Martini," and poured himself a whisky instead. "We'll bring back our full allowance of spirits this year. Pity you won't get all your holiday pay, but still at least you'll be off for a week before we go." He swallowed half the whisky. "Be a good idea if we can get all the decorating finished before you look for another job, if we're going to sell the house. It can make quite a difference, you know, being in good decorative order."

He picked up a copy of the Herald, open at the "Houses for Sale" section, then threw it aside angrily, remembering.

"I hope you told your boyfriend to start looking elsewhere for his fun?"

"Yes."

I thought, I haven't asked you if you've told Barbara to

look elsewhere for her fun.

"I don't know what you saw in him," he went on. "I really can't see it. I'd've thought you had more taste."

I thought, I haven't asked you what you saw in Barbara; I haven't told you I thought you had more taste. I said, "He made me laugh."

"What – false noses in the bedroom, was it?" asked Keith, without a trace of humour.

The 'phone rang. We both ignored it for a while, then Keith got up and answered it. He looked at me, and I heard him say, "You've got a nerve!" He dropped the receiver next to the 'phone as though it was something disgusting to handle. "It's for you. Your *ex*-lover," he said, and sat down again to watch television. I walked round to the telephone and picked it up.

"Hello. How are you?" I asked, not knowing what to say.

"Me? Oh, I'm all right. And how are you? Oh, you're all right too, aren't you? Nicely tucked up with your husband discussing your second honeymoon. Yes, of course you are, silly of me to ask!" His voice sounded strange and hard. "Still, I thought I'd let you know that my nose isn't broken and my teeth are all solid, but you don't really want to know that – do you?"

I turned my back on Keith. "That's not true."

There was a long silence. He sighed, and when he spoke again, the edge had gone from his voice.

"Is he still there with you?"

"Yes."

"Well, will you tell him in that nice soft voice of yours to sod off for a few minutes?"

I half-covered the mouthpiece. "Keith – would you mind – just for a minute?" Keith got up and walked out, slamming the door hard.

"He's gone."

Pete said, "Just listen. I've been thinking about you for hours. You're the best thing that's happened to me in about five hundred years and I can't simply walk away from you. You owe me something. You owe me an explanation at least."

253

"I know. I'm sorry. I just don't know what to say. Keith wants us to get our marriage back together and we couldn't if I went on seeing you. I handed in my notice today."

"Oh Christ!"

There was a pause. I listened to him breathing.

"But *why*, for Christ's sake?" he said. "Why are you doing this? Because of twenty years and marriage vows and the family heirlooms your bloody mother-in-law gave you? What about us? What about the next twenty years?"

"Well, I don't know. You never said –"

"I never said. Well, what could I say? You never talked about your husband or your marriage or what you felt. You were always worried about getting home and not creasing your clothes. How was I to know what I meant to you? Just a pleasant diversion from the washing up, was I?" I winced. "I still don't bloody know."

I said, "Well –" and couldn't go on.

"Look," he said, and paused to swallow something, probably vodka. "I'll spell it out. I love you. I live and breathe for you and I don't give a shit about anything, or anyone, else. I'd cut off my ears for you, though I'm rather hoping you won't ask me to."

I said slowly, "I love you too, Pete."

"Marry me, then."

"Are you serious?"

"Oh Jesus!" Something rattled along the telephone line, ice in a glass, perhaps. "Look, I've got 'A' levels, I can't be that bad at expressing myself, so it must be you. It's a simple question. Do you want to stay with him, or do you want to marry me?"

"Well –" I sat down. Keith's face, young and handsome, stared at me from our wedding photo. "What about my children?"

"Your children are old enough to understand. I only wish mine had been."

"Do I have to make up my mind right away?"

He hesitated. "I think if you can't, it's because you're going to tell me no."

I stared out of the window at the lawn. It needed mowing.

254

I didn't really mind mowing lawns or ironing shirts. My friend Judith had now become an ardent feminist, and if I were to ask her advice she'd give me her little speech about men being part of life's excess baggage and urge me to tell both Keith and Pete to go jump in a lake. Then she'd go home and secretly polish her husband's shoes. If I lived alone things would still need mowing and ironing, only there wouldn't be anyone else to look at them.

"Look," said Pete. "If it helps I could take our washing to the launderette. Only I would appreciate your advice on what to put with what. Those new sheets I bought have developed mysterious purple streaks –"

"Don't be silly," I said. "Of course I'll do all your washing for you."

Afterwards, I did wonder if this was rather a rash promise.